DEDICATION

In loving memory of Richard Landon.

Bursting with life and full of enthusiasm;

your memory warms my heart.

And for Kevin Lloyd and Jason Tong,

who included a lonely young man

and made him feel on top of the world.

Underwood

Devon De'Ath

Copyright © 2021 Devon De'Ath

All rights reserved.

ISBN-13: 979-8-50699-364-3

This is a work of fiction. Names, characters, businesses, places, events, locales and incidents are either the products of the author's imagination or used in a fictitious manner. Any resemblance to actual persons, living or dead, or actual events is purely coincidental.

CONTENTS

1	Stirring Relativity	7
2	Motherly Instincts	28
3	Dreams and Visions	50
4	Girl in the Water	72
5	Startling Compositions	92
6	Fuel to the Fire	115
7	Primary Purgatory	136
8	Destructive Developments	158
9	Conspirators	179
10	Burning Questions	198
11	A Hunger for Wealth	221
12	Retribution Conducted	239
13	The Conduit	260
14	Carrick's Lament	282
15	For Whom Belle Tolls	300
16	The Last Rites	321
17	Home	342

1
Stirring Relativity

"Why did they abandon this village? It's right next to Oakdene." Laura Barnes clambered over the dew saturated foundations of an ancient stone building. She raised a slender hand to shield her eyes from fierce shafts of sunlight stabbing down through a dense, broad leaf forest canopy.

"Mum said people got sick here, long ago." Anton Webb's curly dark blond bangs sometimes caused casual observers to mistake him for a girl. Slight of build with an empty expression, he could be the life and soul of any childish gathering, or withdrawn and aloof. This latter state had more to do with a troubled home life, which Anton concealed and avoided discussing. "It affected the entire country."

"How long is long ago?" Jane Perkins slipped on some moss while attempting to catch up with her fellow nine-year-old companions.

"Over three and a half centuries." Anton halted and studied their surroundings.

Grass, bracken and weeds choked the low, crumbling stone remnants of a long-forgotten village. It lay swallowed by surrounding woodlands, stretching down from a steep hillside behind. The most complete structure to remain was an ancient church, whose squat, ivy-clad tower only became visible once you entered a modest clearing. Its chancel lay open to the firmament, as though someone had rolled back a sliding roof on a nice day to let sunshine in, but forgotten to close it. Branches, heavy-laden with foliage from pressing trees, poked through the empty, arched windows and tumbling masonry. Dirt and grass formed the aisle now. Occasional passing animals attended its spectral services, with a choir of nesting birds chirping ad-hoc hymns of praise.

Laura and Jane reached Anton's side. Laura shifted round. "Where's Belle?"

"She was right behind me a moment ago." Jane waved a hand towards the undergrowth, gaze transfixed on the gutted house of worship.

"I'm going to explore the church. Come on." Anton pressed forward between low, leaning headstones like man-made stalagmites. They lined either side of a former path to the main door. Now it resembled everything else in the verdant lushness of a quiet, summertime Devon wood.

Jane followed, still sweating from a combination of her earlier exertions, a lack of fitness and borderline obesity. "I can't wait for the holidays. Only a few weeks, then we'll explore all we want."

Laura hesitated, her face lined with mild concern over their missing companion's whereabouts. She watched her other friends pass between those lopsided stone sentries to enter the silent heart of the ecclesiastical ruin. "Wait for me," she called, then hurried after.

A vigorous stone's throw distant, the missing girl froze amidst the outline of a former cottage.

One of Belinda Fairchild's teachers once described her in a school report as *'whimsical, and lacking any firm connection to reality.'* Her parents dismissed this assessment out of hand and treasured their daughter's thoughtful - if flighty - personality. A mop of fine golden hair hung in a constant mess about face and shoulders like a web of tangled silk. Brown, soulful eyes, deep and faraway as her imaginary worlds, pierced Belinda's surroundings with pinpricks of reflected light. Her father, Jake, liked to comment that she would turn many heads, a few years hence. Her mother, Karen, added that she'd be too distant and distracted to notice.

Belinda's sight blurred. The boughs above her appeared to sway. Only when she fell backwards to the woodland floor, jarring her coccyx, did the child realise it was she who had swayed and not the trees. Startled, yet still addled by a strange intoxication muffling sight and sound, Belinda tried rubbing her eyes. The mulch-laden ground beneath seemed to vibrate. All about, indistinct voices whispered in an overlapping cacophony. She pulled her hands away from her face and jolted. Semi-translucent luminous walls appeared above the worn foundations; a spiritual echo of ancient history. A woman wept somewhere outside. Belinda recoiled as she registered two children, a boy and girl her own age, curled up on straw mattresses nearby. Swollen, egg-sized lymph nodes around groin, underarms and neck were coated in black spots that had spread to speckle every inch of skin. A pungent puddle of blood-streaked liquid faeces seeped from beneath their motionless torsos. The afflicted girl faced away, but the boy stared at Belinda with lifeless eyes. His tongue lolled from a mouth opened at the moment he gave up the ghost. Hungry blowflies buzzed in lazy circuits about his crown, taking turns to taste excretions from pustules bursting clear of the tragic lad's skull. A rhythmic creaking tore Belinda's gaze away from that sickening sight to look straight up. Above, an adult male swung in a scratchy noose of knotted hemp. It suspended his dangling body from faint roof trusses through which Belinda could still make out blue sky in her own century. The man's eyelids fluttered open, allowing his gaze to fix upon her. Forlorn aquamarine eyes narrowed. His upper lip curled back in a snarl. Air wheezed from his throttled throat to form a croaking declaration in a single word. "Vengeance."

Belinda clasped her head and screamed.

"There's something in here." Anton peeped through a crack in the base of an unadorned stone altar. "I'm sure the sunlight caught a metallic object." He pressed his face flush against the fissure. Passing clouds allowed a fresh wash of warmth and illumination through the open church roof. "There." Anton tugged at the crumbling stone and broke a chunk free, wide enough to insert his hand through the opening.

"You're not supposed to do that. This is a church." Jane glanced around, as though expecting a responsible adult to appear and scold them.

"Not anymore," Anton grunted, his arm disappearing up to the shoulder. "Look at the state of it."

"But isn't that grave robbing?" Jane's voice wobbled.

Anton grimaced, moving his hand around by feel to locate the item he'd spied. "This is an altar, not a tomb, Jane. Or it was an altar, once." His face brightened at cold metal against his fingers. He clamped his fist around the object. "I've got it."

"What?" Laura asked. "What have you got?" She squatted beside him.

Anton pulled back, one arm coated in masonry dust. A dull, brass foot-long cross emerged in his hand from the blackness. Dirty and grime encrusted, the devotional symbol of faith still shimmered in a fresh shaft of light penetrating the house of worship as Anton raised it high. "Look what I've found."

"You can't take it, Anton. That's stealing." Jane's chin wobbled to match her voice now.

"No it isn't. We're treasure hunters." Anton wiped

smuts clear of his trophy with the bottom of his navy blue t-shirt.

"Jane's right; you should put it back." Laura cast a lazy, sidelong glance through the altar's base for signs of any other treasures.

An ear-splitting female child's scream cut through the woodland.

Laura whirled. "That's Belle."

Jane clamped a hand over her mouth and squeaked. "Oh no. What's happened?"

Laura ran for the doorway arch with her friends close at heel. Anton still gripped the brass cross in a determined hand as they wove through the haphazard, neglected grave markers towards ongoing shrieks of distress.

Laura batted low-hanging branches aside. Thirty yards ahead, Belinda sat amid ruined foundations yelling at the sky. Both hands clasped against her face obscured peripheral vision and masked Laura's hurried approach to calm her.

"Easy." Laura fought for control as Belinda lurched at her touch. Memories of trying to save her now departed baby brother from an epileptic fit stung her heart. "Belle, it's me. It's Laura."

Belinda's final wail faltered like water from a hose with the tap turned off. She stared at Laura, unblinking and unsure of where she was.

Jane caught her breath. "You gave us such a fright. We thought someone had attacked you."

Belinda glanced around the empty ruin, now devoid of vaporous walls and roof. She licked dry lips, voice hoarse. "What happened?"

Anton folded his arms with the cross tucked into the crook of one. "That's what we'd like to know."

Laura still crouched at her side, both hands massaging Belinda's shoulders. "Why don't you tell us? What made you scream so?"

Belinda shook her groggy head. "I saw something. People from the past. It was so real."

Jane fidgeted. "Do you mean like ghosts?" Her frightened eyes scanned the bushes.

"I don't know. It felt like being in the village long ago, yet still here at the same time."

"It sounds like too much chocolate and fizzy drink to me," Anton snorted. He kicked the moss-encrusted foundations. "You're still in the 21st century, Belle."

Laura frowned at him. "Belle's mum doesn't feed her junk with additives. I've eaten at her house before."

"Rather you than me," Jane muttered under her breath with a sheepish expression.

Anton chuckled. "Yeah. If anything is enough to cause nightmares, it must be that grotty place your parents are renovating. I don't know how you live there."

Laura shook her head. "You're full of yourself today, Anton. That makes a change, I suppose. Last week we couldn't get a peep out of you."

Anton's sarcastic demeanour evaporated. He turned aside and walked away.

"What's that?" Belinda pointed at a glimmer of brass in his lowering hand.

"Plunder. I found it in the old church." Anton waved

the cross at her.

Belinda's arms trembled.

"Belle?" Laura rubbed her shoulders again. "Crumbs, you're ice cold."

Belinda's face turned crimson, cheeks puffing. She panted a plea in Anton's direction. "Put it back."

"That's what *we* told him," Laura replied.

"Not a chance." Anton swung the cross about and admired its subdued sheen.

Belinda broke free of Laura's grip and staggered to her feet. "Put it back where you found it, Anton." Her voice came stronger now.

Anton set his jaw. "What is it with you three, today? You're no fun."

Belinda collapsed against a tree trunk. "That cross should remain where you found it."

"Why?" Anton's voice grew terse. "No-one knew it was there, or they wouldn't have left it. Nobody will miss the cross. Why lose my prize?"

"I think you should listen to Belle." Laura reached the tree where Belinda had sought support.

Anton sneered. "I think you should boil your head." He read the fear in Belinda's eyes, then stalked forward, holding the cross out towards her. "Here. It won't bite, Belle. It's nothing more than a hunk of metal."

Belinda recoiled.

Anton grinned. "Look at her. She's reacting to it like a vampire." He waved the cross under Belinda's nose and made spooky noises. "Woo, Belle. Woo, the cross is coming to get you."

Laura pushed him away. "Stop it, Anton. Can't you see something has scared her?"

"Imagination and being alone in the woods. Nothing more." A mischievous glint shimmered in his pupils. With a fluid motion, he lunged and walloped the symbol against Belinda's left forearm.

Belinda jolted and shook. She dropped to the ground, eyes rolling back in her head.

"Oh my God, she's having a fit," Laura shrieked and sank down beside her. Fresh memories of her kid brother surged up again with sickening vigour.

Jane wrung her hands. "What do we do?"

Laura held Belinda still. "She's coming out of it. Oh, thank goodness." She panted and allowed her tensed arms to slacken.

Belinda closed, then re-opened her eyes, looking into Laura's face. "Did I fall again?"

Laura nodded. "When Anton touched you with that blasted cross."

Anton bit his lip and swirled one shoe in an uncomfortable semi-circle. "That was weird. Who recoils from crosses except monsters and demons?"

Jane stamped a foot. "Shut up, Anton. Belle isn't a monster."

Laura helped Belinda back onto her feet. "How do you feel?"

"Weird." Belinda fixed on Anton's prize again. "Please don't take it away. It's wrong; I know it is."

Anton rolled his eyes. "Stop being so dramatic. I've had enough of silly girls for one day. I'm going home and taking my treasure with me." He set off at a determined pace.

Belinda looked from side to side. Wisps of vapour rose from beneath the ground like an expulsion of swamp gas. Her voice gasped in a whining whisper; half wonder, half terror. "Do you see them?"

"See who?" Laura followed her gaze, detecting nothing but lush woodland and plants swaying in a gentle summer breeze amidst the ruins.

Jane crossed her legs as though staving off an urgent trip to the bathroom. "You're scaring me. What do you see, Belle?" she whimpered.

The ground trembled beneath Belinda's feet and those indistinct voices called again. Belinda took a breath. "They're rising."

Jane spun in a tizzy. "I want to go home, too. This place feels weird now."

Belinda noticed the confusion in Laura's eyes, oblivious to any sensations or noises from the earth. She swallowed hard. "Jane is right. We should leave this place alone."

Jane bobbed on the spot. "Thank goodness. I never want to explore Underwood again."

"Right, let's go." Laura picked her way through the undergrowth with Belinda and Jane at her side. "Are you coming back through the village with us, Belle?"

Belinda shook her head. "No point. I can cut south and cross the meadow home."

Laura studied her with matronly affection. "Are you sure you're all right?"

Belinda nodded. "I'm fine. Thanks for being such a good friend today."

"Okay. We'll see you at school tomorrow. Come on, Jane; Oakdene is this way."

Belinda watched the pair stride onto a downhill track leading to a no-through road on the village outskirts. She took a deep breath, still catching faint whispers in the wind, and then turned south.

Because of its semi-renovated state, Ravensbrook was a hard house to pin a precise age upon. The rambling granite structure pre-dated the village of Oakdene, three quarters of a mile distant. It was believed to have once been a farm. Some local historians assessed the property to originate from the same era as Underwood, the present village's abandoned predecessor. All Belinda Fairchild knew was it felt dark and creepy, compared to their former tiny home nearby. Both parents assured her Ravensbrook would be a dream house, once they conquered its considerable list of updates. Belinda wanted to believe them, even if she found such a transformation hard to picture. After her scare while exploring with friends, that all-pervasive uneasiness surrounding the home's old bones faded during her approach. She sauntered across an undulating meadow rippling with an ocean of daisies. Its peaceful ground rose again on the other side towards the dilapidated house.

"Did you have an enjoyable time with your friends?" Karen Fairchild poked her head into the long, flagstone hallway as Belinda shut the juddering front door with a bang.

Belinda shrugged. "It was okay."

Karen's face fell. "What's wrong?"

"Nothing, Mum."

Karen entered the hallway, wiping her hands on an old rag and stuffing it into a pocket of paint-splattered overalls. "Was Anton mean to you? I swear that boy blows hot and cold."

"He was all right." Belinda considered mentioning the cross, but wondered how much trouble she and her friends might land in. Silence seemed the better option, for now.

Jake Fairchild appeared at his wife's elbow, clutching a paint roller. "Where did you play?"

"We explored the ruins at Underwood."

Jake tutted. "I hope you didn't get too close to the old church tower. A tumbling chunk of masonry from that could be very dangerous."

Karen raised a sarcastic eyebrow, then nodded at the structure around them. "That advice might carry more weight if we weren't living in the same ramshackle building we're renovating, honey."

Jake smacked his lips together. "I hadn't thought of that."

Karen pulled out her rag and wiped paint from the tip of his nose. "You'd better clean up the mess while I get some dinner on. We can't have Belle going to bed hungry. Not with school tomorrow."

Jake snapped her a comic salute and disappeared back down the hallway.

Karen tilted her head to catch Belinda's sullen face. "Peel some spuds for me?"

"Yes, Mum."

"Good girl. You know where they are. I'll be through to join you in a minute."

Belinda stood before a Belfast sink, her hands removing skins from a pile of white potatoes with unconscious, deft precision and practised flair. She popped each into a pan filled with water on the wooden drainer beside her. Evening sun cast long shadows across the meadow beyond the kitchen window. They stretched in creeping, skeletal fingers towards the woods on the far side where she'd played with her friends.

"Now there's an industrious young lady," Karen called from the doorway. Her daughter lifted the pan between both hands, ready for transportation to the stove.

"Thanks Mu-" Belinda's eyes bulged. The pan slipped from her grasp and struck the stone floor with a clatter. Water sloshed out, followed by a couple of spuds making a bid for freedom.

"Belle?" Karen rushed into a crouch and retrieved the items.

"What happened?" Jake hurried into the room.

Belinda stared across her mother's bent-over shoulder. In one gloomy corner of the dark, rustic kitchen, a slim, shadowy figure watched her with soulful eyes. He turned in silence and vanished, as though fading into the plastered stonework.

Karen led her daughter to a battered oak table. "I'd say you've over-exerted yourself today. Too much of a good thing. You'd better sit quietly while I cook."

Jake pushed a hand through his tattered mop of teak hair. "Are you all right if I take a shower before dinner, love?"

Karen topped up the pan and set it on an enamel range. She called over her shoulder. "Go right ahead. You've ample time."

Jake's feet sounded on the creaking staircase while Karen continued her culinary chores.

Belinda sat still as a statue. Her mind conjured visions of spectres who'd seep from the walls if she even blinked. Once her father reappeared, the family settled down to a chatty meal in which its youngest member played little part.

* * *

Belinda paused on the lane that dipped and rose beside the meadow, then cast a tense frown back the way she'd walked. Ravensbrook leaned like some saggy, crocheted model of a house on the rise behind her. A soothing babble from the watercourse whence the property took its name, gurgled through a culvert underneath her feet. Its glittering silver ribbon snaked in gentle coils before flowing into the River Torridge.

Why does my head feel so fuzzy? It had been a sleepless night, haunted with dreams of sick, dying and hung villagers like those in her waking vision at Underwood. All night long she'd drifted off and then awoken as though prodded by icy fingers. Each time, the same indistinct voices swirled about her room, only to vanish again when that sad-faced young man she'd seen in the kitchen materialised before her. Belinda couldn't bring herself to look at him. She shut her eyes tight and disappeared beneath the covers. Yet the man's voice crept up next to her bed and whispered soothing words she couldn't recall in her ear. When she'd come to the next morning, her parents were already up and working to address structural and re-pointing issues on a downstairs dividing wall. Belinda couldn't even remember having breakfast with them or kissing each goodbye before the walk to school. *It must be a lack of sleep. I hope I have a better rest tonight.* A gnawing in her gut willed Belinda to turn; to run back to the house and kiss her mum and dad, even if for the second time. She sighed to herself. *I'll see them later. I'd best hurry along.* She pulled the shoulder strap of her school bag higher, then set off down the quiet country lane towards Oakdene.

"There are times I hate this job." PC Lucy Maitland pushed open the green railing gate at Oakdene Village Primary. Through wide windows ahead, sleepy children with full stomachs - fresh from lunchtime play - dosed through their afternoon lessons.

PC Eric Walker eyed his colleague and closed the gate behind them. "We caught a break being notified while the girl was still at school, Lucy." He muted the Airwave police radio clipped to his rigid stab vest.

Lucy clicked her tongue. "True enough. If she's no other family close by, the teaching staff can provide support. What a way to learn your mum and dad have bitten the big one. Let's hope the poor mite has a friend's house to stay at while we trace her next of kin."

Kelly Poole, the school PA, ran from a bright office doorway in a flood of tears. Inside, the two constables stood before the desk of Oakdene Primary's head, Helen Masters. Helen watched her tearful assistant dash into the staff toilets, face lined with worry. Outbreaks of head lice and chickenpox were the usual crises Helen managed in her professional sphere. With less than eight years until retirement, she'd banked on easing from a happily uneventful career into twilight years spent in the company of afternoon tea and fond educational memories. In the few minutes since these two officers from Devon and Cornwall Police arrived, that dream had forever been blown out of the water.

"Please excuse my colleague. She's a gentle soul with a good heart," Helen said.

Lucy Maitland glanced out the office door, towards the toilets. "It's nice that she cares for the kids. What can you tell us about the girl?"

Helen sat back in her chair. "Belinda? She's sweet. Quiet, most of the time. Dreamy but intelligent."

"We're trying to locate other family," Eric piped up.

Helen stood and opened the top drawer of a steel filing cabinet. "She has no grandparents; they've all passed on. Her mother was an only child, but Belinda has an aunt on her father's side." She rifled through a set of labelled dividers, then pulled out a brown cardboard file. "Here we go: *Amanda Fairchild*. I've a current address and landline contact number for her in Bristol that I can let you have. No mobile."

"Thank you." Eric retrieved his pocket notebook to take down the details.

Helen held up the information while he wrote. With the task complete, she put the folder away and sat at her desk again. "Have you any idea what happened?"

Lucy cleared her throat. "The postman stopped by Ravensbrook late morning with a package. Apparently he knows the Fairchilds are always at home, working on their property."

Helen removed an enormous pair of glasses from her nose and wiped the lenses on a cloth. "That's right. They'd both taken sabbaticals from work to improve the place. Mr and Mrs Fairchild felt it a priority with a young child living there."

"Indeed," Lucy answered. "So, after the postman received no response at the door, he peered in through downstairs windows, hoping to catch them engrossed in DIY. That's when he noticed their limbs protruding beneath a semi-collapsed interior wall."

Helen hung her head. "How awful. I assume he called for help?"

"Right away. Even smashed a window to make entry and see if he could save them. Sadly, it was too late. That old house has high ceilings. There's a lot of weight above head height in its walls. The couple must have died instantly when a serious assortment of rubble came down upon them."

Eric fidgeted with his hands. Lucy nudged him into action.

"There's something else which might complicate the girl's suffering," he began.

Helen looked up with a frown. "What's that?"

Eric stared into her face. "Obviously the post mortem isn't back yet. We've only just found them. However, a medical examiner at the scene suggested they'd been dead several hours. Long before the postman turned up."

Helen fiddled with the collar of her blouse. "What are you saying?"

"That Belinda *may* have been in the house during the incident. It's not for certain, but a speculative time of death indicates it occurred before she left this morning."

Helen blinked. "That can't be so. Belinda may be a dreamer, but she'd have called an ambulance or something. She wouldn't just wander off to school like nothing had happened."

Lucy pursed her lips. "Like PC Walker said: it's speculative. We're only notifying you, in case it has bearing on the girl's reaction once we tell her." She looked at Eric, then back to Helen. "We're making no judgements about Belinda. Sometimes when a youngster witnesses a difficult or devastating scene, they try to block it out. It must sound crazy, but it's a form of denial: '*If I walk away and carry on as normal, none of this will have happened.*' That type of idea. Self-preservation or mental maintenance of the desired status quo."

Helen sighed. "It doesn't sound crazy at all when you've spent your working life teaching five to eleven-year-olds. I don't imagine such behaviour is restricted to children, either."

"No, it isn't," Eric replied.

Helen rose out of her chair. "I won't ask Kelly to fetch Belinda from class. That wouldn't be fair. Plus, we should keep drama to a minimum, if possible." She moved out from behind her desk. "Please wait here a moment. I won't be long."

Three minutes later when Helen Masters shepherded Belinda Fairchild into her office, the child already wore a beetroot face with a sullen expression.

PC Lucy Maitland moved her attention from the child's pretty young brown eyes to tilt her head in curiosity at Helen. "Have you…?"

Helen shook her head. "No." She rubbed Belinda's right shoulder with a gentle, affectionate hand. "Belinda, these are two police officers. I'm afraid they've some sad news for you." She turned and closed her door into the corridor, catching sight of Kelly Poole wiping her nose on a sodden tissue outside. "Why don't we all sit down." Helen wheeled her chair around from behind the desk to stop beside a bank of low, comfortably padded seats.

Belinda stood solid as a dolmen ravaged by time and weather, yet resolute. She stared into the constables' faces, then spoke in a subdued, matter-of-fact tone. "Mummy and Daddy are dead, aren't they?"

Lucy, Eric, and Helen's mouths almost hit the floor in unison.

* * *

A light passing shower in the graveyard at All Saints Church, Oakdene, meant attendees at Jake and Karen Fairchild's funeral observed the committal beneath an array of mismatched umbrellas.

Belinda held tight to Helen Masters' hand, reaching out with the other towards twin open graves. When she strained to move again, Helen let her go. Belinda dashed forward, then halted with a heartbroken stare. Her tearful eyes seemed to penetrate the wooden boxes far below, like x-rays. A rich smell of disturbed, red Devon earth filled her nostrils.

Helen remained where she stood and daubed running mascara with one corner of a dainty handkerchief. A portly woman sporting a furrowed brow sidled up to her. She leaned close to keep subdued comments from being overheard.

"What about the child's next of kin?"

Helen tucked her handkerchief away. "The authorities have yet to receive a response from Mr Fairchild's sister. She's somewhere overseas. Her landlord didn't have any contact details."

The portly woman shook her head. "Irresponsible."

Helen gave a thoughtful hum. "I shouldn't be too hard on the woman. Who expects something like this to happen? She'll find out soon enough."

"Fancy missing your own brother's funeral."

Helen grew agitated. "It's hardly deliberate, Maud. I can't imagine the agony she'll suffer upon hearing the news. One small mercy: the Fairchilds were forward thinkers. They'd arranged and paid for their funerals in advance. Quite something, considering their age. It illustrates the point that no-one knows the hour, as they say."

"Is the girl staying with you?"

"No. The Barnes family. They've taken her in for now. She and young Laura are friends from the same class."

"Will the Aunt remove her from the village?"

"I hope not. But, that's for her to decide. She'll become Belinda's legal guardian, as I understand it from the family solicitor."

Maud drew back, muttering under her breath. "Such a waste. And all for the love of Ravensbrook. What a shabby, rundown old ruin."

Maud was a busybody. Helen kept any inner turmoil over the specific chain of terminal events to herself. Neither she nor the police could coax anything further out of Belinda about how the child knew her parents were dead. Was it assumption upon seeing those uniforms at her school, based on programmes she'd watched on TV? When she collected Belinda from class, she already appeared cognisant of events. Awkward suggestions presented by those officers beforehand troubled Helen. But the last thing Belinda needed was an intensive grilling. However the tragedy played out and wherever Belinda had been, she'd lost her parents. Life would never be the same again.

2
Motherly Instincts

"Did you take enough photographs? Will you send me some of the best shots once you get back to Blighty?" Sarah Verity pulled her silver Chevrolet Sonic into a short stay parking lot at Seattle-Tacoma International Airport.

Beside her, an attractive thirty-year-old woman smiled and spoke with a British accent to match the driver, albeit a tad more 'West Country' and lacking the developing American twang of her naturalised US citizen companion. "Of course."

When Amanda Fairchild gave someone her attention, it left them in little doubt. A pronounced, elegant jawline beneath a diamond head tilted a fraction to the right, while bright eyes, the indistinct shade of misty opals glittered with life and energy. A shallow, half open-mouthed smile echoed the positivity in that effervescent facial aspect, while side-parted hair, the hue of burnished oak dallied with her chest in natural curls. Of medium height and build,

Amanda's semi-groomed appearance suggested a conflict between her present, carefree, bohemian artist's lifestyle and a former career in business management that she'd endured for an interminable five years.

Sarah got out of the car. "I can't believe you lugged that honking great digital SLR with you. What's wrong with a phone? Their inbuilt cameras take excellent quality shots these days."

Amanda hauled a large suitcase from the rear seats. "I'm between contracts on mobiles. My previous one expired, and I fancied something new with a different provider. I pitched the old handset. Besides, I've enjoyed no monthly costs for a spell. I'll shop around and source a new one after I get home."

Sarah bit her lip. "Are you sure you're all right for money?"

Amanda noticed her reach instinctively for her handbag. "I'm fine. You've done enough, putting me up for a three week vacation and driving the pair of us all over the Pacific Northwest."

Sarah beamed. "Don't be silly. Anyway, I get lonely whenever Greg is away on long-haul flights."

"I'm glad I saw your handsome, airline pilot husband now and again. It's the first time since the wedding three years ago."

"I know." Sarah reached for the pull handle on Amanda's case while she collected her carry-on bag. "Wherever does the time disappear to? So, did you find a favourite inspirational spot over here?"

Amanda shut the passenger door. "Snoqualmie Falls.

That's a special place. I might have to paint it."

Sarah pressed her central locking plip. "How will that fit in with your usual portfolio of English landscapes and historic architecture?"

Amanda set off towards a set of sliding glass doors. "I wasn't thinking of it as a commercial project. Maybe I'll send the painting to you and Greg as a thank you for my mooched holiday."

"You weren't mooching. I've missed you since uni. Life this side of the pond is grand, and I love our home in Overlake. But, I yearn for the old days sometimes, you know?"

Amanda grinned. "I felt like that in my corporate job. These days life resembles 'the old days' more than I'd like."

"You're broke and living on noodles?"

Amanda shrugged. "But happy, like we were back then." She looked around, eyes straining to discover the right direction.

Sarah pointed straight ahead. "British Airways are on the South Satellite Concourse. Did you leave your car at Heathrow or with a parking company?"

"On my budget? Nah, I keep long car journeys to a minimum. My sweet old banger has seen better days. It's a train from Paddington back to Bristol for me. Besides, I'll be creamed from jet lag by the time I land. I can nab some extra kip on the Inter-City."

Her return flight to London proved so lacking in passengers, Amanda enjoyed an entire row of seats to relax in for ten hours. Back in England she only dosed now and again on the rail journey to Bristol Temple Meads Station.

Amanda's rented, two-bedroom ground-floor flat faced a courtyard backing onto a nondescript alley, a fifteen-minute walk from the station. Her landlord, Gerry, was easygoing about her using the second bedroom as an art studio. All the floors were stone, with only occasional rugs in certain rooms. Messing up carpets wasn't an issue. Due to its lack of view and sub-prime location in an iffy neighbourhood, Amanda rented the place at a manageable monthly rate. A surge of business - both gallery and on-line print orders - followed a successful art exhibition in the Temple Meads Quarter two months prior. Flush from the result, she'd splurged on an airline ticket for her getaway to visit Sarah in Washington State.

A shabby bruiser of a black cat with one fight-ravaged ear mewed at Amanda as she wheeled her suitcase along the uneven alley paving slabs towards home. She paused and shook her head. "Look at you, Teddy Tum. Have you been getting in scraps with that ginger Tom again?"

The cat flicked its tail, then scrabbled over a wooden fence and disappeared.

Amanda licked her lips and muttered to herself. "I must have hit a nerve with that question. Who owns him, anyway? I wonder what his actual name is?" She swapped shoulders with her carry-on bag strap, then wheeled the trailing suitcase to a semi-rotten wooden back gate leading into the courtyard behind her flat.

"At least the students upstairs haven't torched the joint while I was away." She secured the gate behind, then fished out a set of keys to her dedicated entrance door.

Amanda stepped over a pile of mail and dumped her bags in the living room. She threw open a sash window, allowing fresh air into the stale space, then filled the kettle for a cuppa. A red light winked from an answerphone further along the kitchen worktop. Amanda clocked its LED readout and whistled. "Thirty-five missed calls. Here's hoping there's some new business amongst all the shitbag scammers trying to steal my bank information." She pressed the play button, then dropped a herbal tea bag into a china mug while the kettle boiled. Four scams, three unsolicited sales calls and two wrong numbers later, a brusque, female voice crackled from the speaker. "This is a call for Amanda Fairchild from PC Lucy Maitland of Devon and Cornwall Police. I need you to contact me as soon as possible."

* * *

"I'm sorry to see you go, Amanda." Gerry Scutt stepped aside for a removal man to lug a heavy cardboard box past. He mopped his bald, middle-aged head with a stained handkerchief.

Amanda Fairchild stood in the second bedroom she'd used as an art studio, making sure the more fragile items were treated with care by her movers.

"Thanks, Gerry. You've been a decent landlord."

"Back to your roots then, is it?"

Amanda rested her bottom against a magnolia wall. "Close enough. Jake and his family lived in a village on the other side of the valley where we grew up." Amanda realised she was putting on a brave face, her tone matter-of-fact and businesslike. The news her brother and her sister-in-law had died was bad enough. To learn the funeral took place with breathtaking efficiency while she was enjoying her first holiday in ages, cut her to the quick. Then the bomb dropped that she was now legal guardian to Jake and Karen's nine-year-old daughter. Amanda was never one to shy away from responsibility, despite yearning for an uncomplicated life as a free spirit. This development diverted her intended course, with an added hand grenade of grief tossed into the mix.

Greg watched her facial muscles twitch while she ruminated on the upset her apple cart had endured; all in the space of several phone calls less than a week before. "And you're going to be a mother, too, you said?"

Amanda winced. "Not a mother in the strictest sense. I always told my big brother I'd look after my niece, if anything happened to him and his wife. You know how it is: nobody ever expects to do it. It's so like Jake to have everything formalised and legal. He was always the more organised out of us two kids."

Gerry scratched one cheek. "I don't want to sound heartless, but putting the child up for adoption is a poss-"

"No," Amanda cut him off. "I don't know young Belinda well, but I'll not see her endure that. Blood is thicker than water. After Jake and his wife bought the near derelict, draughty heap they were living in, my occasional Christmas visits ended. I didn't want to burden an already challenging domestic situation. I've not seen my niece since she was seven." Amanda rubbed her eyes. "God, that sounds awful when you think I just flew thousands of miles to stay with an old uni friend. Worse when you consider Jake only lived in Devon."

Gerry wandered nearer and inspected a patch of flaking wall plaster. "That's families for you. If you don't mind my asking: is there a big loan or mortgage on the renovation property?"

"No, thank goodness. They bought the place with a legacy from Karen's late parents. Owned it outright. The home still needs a shit-tonne of work doing and my bro wasn't flush. I'll have to fix up what I can, as and when funds become available. No rent, though. One positive."

"To pay a greasy slumlord?" Gerry winked.

Amanda chuckled, appreciative at his attempts to buoy her mood. "Would I say a thing like that about you, Gerry?"

"No, *you* wouldn't. Plenty of others have, though. Will you work from the house?"

"If I can find a suitable area. There's no shortage of rooms. But, the whole place looks a mess, from the pictures Jake sent me a while back. If I flicked acrylic off my paintbrush over the walls and floors, it might improve the building. Still, doing it up was Jake and Karen's dream. I intend to honour that, however long it takes."

Gerry prodded the flaky plaster with an index finger. "I'm sorry for what you've been through."

Amanda spotted an exposed flap on one of the waiting boxes. She lifted a roll of thick brown parcel tape, then tore off a strip to secure the oversight. "I can't change what happened, nor the fact they're already buried. All I can do is try to provide Belinda with a stable and supportive home life. We're both going through hell, but it must be far worse for her."

"Where is she now? What about your parents?"

"Mum and Dad are no longer with us. The family of a classmate are putting Belinda up. I've spoken with them on the phone. They're good people."

"What about your niece? Have you talked to her?"

"I've tried. She was pretty unresponsive. Mrs Barnes - that's the friend's mother - said she's been in a daze ever since the accident. Even her daughter can't get much sense out of Belinda."

"It'll take time." Gerry brushed his hands together in a faint puff of plaster dust. "You're a caring woman; you'll win her over."

Amanda extended her hand to him while movers hauled out the last boxes. "Thanks again, Gerry. Good luck with your new tenant, whoever they turn out to be."

Gerry squeezed her palm. "Fair winds, Amanda."

Amanda's battered, blue Toyota Avensis left the M5 at junction 27, heading west towards Tiverton. She followed A-roads in a route that would drop her onto the quieter, pretty rural lanes of the Torridge Valley with little fuss, encountering few traffic hot spots. All the while she monitored the removal van following close behind in her rear-view mirror.

Lush hills, ancient pubs and strong communities miles from the nearest motorway; these simple characteristics endeared Devon's Torridge Valley to holidaymakers, retirees and down-shifters alike. To Amanda, the villages lining the River Torridge represented childhood and adolescence, prior to spreading her wings and relocating to the contemporary bustle of Bristol. Set between a steep, wooded arm of the valley and level broad meander in the river's course, the sleepy village of Oakdene added a picturesque, artificial adornment to nature's splendour. Classic thatch and tiled cottages followed a winding road skirting the steeper topography and river bend. A granite church built in the latter half of the 17th century competed for height amidst flourishing broadleaved woodlands nearby. Its modest tower displayed a black and gold clock below the belfry. Few residents paid it much heed in a place where time mattered little. A garage, village shop, hall and primary school, plus a single pub - The Royalist - represented the rest of Oakdene's community facilities.

Everything within Amanda wanted to stop at All Saints Church and visit the graves. But such an emotional appointment would have to wait until she'd bid her movers farewell. Jake's solicitor in Great Torrington drove to Bristol with the paperwork and a set of keys three days earlier. Now she was the legal owner and guardian of one ancient former Devon farmhouse that had seen better days, plus its only surviving resident. She'd collect Belinda from the Barnes family later. This would be a difficult and tiring day.

The black windows of Ravensbrook stared at the approaching car and van like an empty-socketed skull. Sun painted the meadow beside the road, while a zephyr caressed its nodding daisies. As the Toyota crunched to a halt outside, Amanda noticed a boarded-up, ground-floor window. *That must be where the postman broke in to help Jake and Karen.* Amanda unfastened her seatbelt and decamped. There was no mistaking the familiar clean air that greeted her nostrils. *I've been away from the valley for too long.* She waved at the removal crew, then retrieved her new keys and opened a stiff, chunky, iron-studded front door. Amanda had no idea if abundant cobwebs clinging to various corners were a recent addition, or something the renovators didn't bother removing due to the home's current state. She drifted from the kitchen across to a large room towards the rear. Blue and white police tape formed an artificial perimeter around a partially collapsed internal wall. *PC Maitland said someone checked the remaining wall for safety, but left tape in situ as a precaution. I guess I know what my first two jobs are: a replacement window and sorting this mess.* Her eyes fell upon dusty bricks, cleared into two tidy heaps after the bodies were retrieved. Breath caught in Amanda's throat. *So this is where it happened. This is the spot Jake and Karen died.* She shuddered.

One of the removal men knocked on an internal door to get her attention. "All right if we unload, love?"

It was late afternoon by the time Amanda waved off the workmen and climbed back into her Toyota. She sat for a minute before inserting the ignition key. The house loomed oppressive, yet sad, as though in a state of perpetual mourning for its departed residents. Amanda peered up at a bedroom curtain shifting in the summer breeze penetrating an ill-fitting window. *I wonder if any past residents linger?* She shook the thought out of her mind, like clearing Ravensbrook's abundant cobwebs. The key clicked round in her hand, dashboard lights illuminated, and the ageing, trusty Japanese motor rumbled to life.

Amanda drove back into the village and parked outside All Saints for her first port of call. Given Oakdene's limited size, she left a stroll to the Barnes household until after paying her memorial respects. The car could remain in situ throughout both tasks. Amanda smiled at a friendly old couple walking their plodding West Highland White Terrier. They nodded with kind faces masking a curiosity that still twinkled in their eyes. Who was this new arrival in their peaceful idyll? Amanda pondered which was likely to go first: the sad, tired old dog or its loving, bent-backed owners. She opened the boot and reached in for a spray of flowers purchased in Bristol. *It's a poor substitute for missing the funeral, but I know Jake and Karen won't hold it against me. I doubt this will be my last visit to lay flowers here.* She opened the churchyard gate, her attention already drawn to two fresh mounds of earth, side by side nearby. The flowers sagged in her hands as she drew near enough to read temporary brass plaque placeholders:

'Jake Robert Fairchild : 1985 - 2019' and *'Karen Emily Fairchild (nee Trehane) 1986 - 2019.'*

Amanda stood at the foot between both mounds. "Hey, Big Brother. It's me." An empty exhalation wheezed from her nostrils. She raised her eyes to the clear blue firmament. Words failed her. In that moment, alone in the quiet churchyard, tears didn't. It wasn't the first time she'd cried since hearing the news. But witnessing that dirty pile of offending bricks firsthand in an empty house, and now standing before these metallic assertions of the simple but awful truth brought it all up like an undigested meal. She wiped her nose, squatted, and set down the spray. Trembling hands reached out to touch each earthen bulge. Her voice became a sniffing whisper. "Don't worry. I'll take good care of Belinda. Whatever I have to do, she'll get the best start in life I can give her. That much I promise you."

Amanda dried her eyes, rose, and walked back towards the lane. She cast one last glance behind at the gate, speaking to herself. "Time to make good on that vow."

'The Old Bothy' was a classic thatch and whitewashed cob house, curving around the corner of a no-through road at the western side of the village. The thoroughfare in question rose at an incline for three hundred yards beyond, where it ended at a gated entrance to dense woodland. Amanda stopped on the home's characterful doorstep, a shopping bag in one hand. She jangled a free-hanging brass bell. Moments later, the pretty sky-blue door opened, revealing a fair-haired woman around ten years Amanda's senior.

"Mrs Barnes?" Amanda asked. "I'm Amanda Fairchild."

Mrs Barnes stuck out her hand. "Pleased to meet you. Call me Rachel."

"Rachel." Amanda passed her the shopping bag. "I picked these up at the shop on my way over as a small thank you. But, I must reimburse you for the trouble and expense this situation has caused." She reached into her handbag and lifted a purse halfway clear before Rachel stopped her.

"Please don't. It was no trouble. Laura and Belle are good friends, though it breaks my daughter's heart to see her playmate so sad and lost. Belle has suffered horrific nightmares, too. No surprise there, poor lamb." She opened the shopping bag and studied a decent bottle of wine and a box of chocolates. "These are lovely. No need for anything further. We were glad to put Belle up and are heartbroken at your loss."

"I can't tell you what your assistance means. I returned from America to find my brother and my sister-in-law dead and buried, with their daughter an orphan."

Rachel beckoned her inside. "My Laura is pleased you aren't whisking Belle away to another area. I admire you taking on Ravensbrook. That's quite a project."

"I saw it for the first time, around lunch. I've not explored the house, yet. The removal crew dumped my boxes in a couple of empty rooms, then I hurried over here." She coughed. "After a brief stop at the church."

Rachel gave an understanding nod. "The girls are upstairs. Let me call them for you." She leaned around to point her face up a steep, tight staircase. "Girls? Belle's Aunt Amanda has arrived. Time to come down."

Above them, a wrought iron latch lifted, accompanied by the dragging of a wooden door against the pile of a thick carpet. "We'll be there in a second, Mum," a female child responded.

Rachel escorted her guest into a heavy-beamed sitting room with deep-set inglenook. "Laura was going to help Belle pack her things. She brought a few clothes and a soft toy over in a bag after the accident. I've kept up with her washing, so we didn't need access to the house again."

"Jake and Karen would be grateful, as am I."

Two sets of feet thudded down the staircase.

Amanda pivoted as a bright-faced nine-year-old entered the room, stepping clear of her downcast peer.

Belinda stood in the doorway clutching a pink holdall. Big brown eyes fixed on her nervous aunt, but she said nothing.

Rachel broke the ice. "Amanda, meet my daughter, Laura. Laura, this is Belle's Aunt Amanda."

Laura smiled. "Pleased to meet you."

Amanda managed a lacklustre response. "Likewise. I'm glad Belinda has had such a good friend to support her during my absence. That's kind of you, Laura."

"Belle." The single word escaped Belinda's mouth like the gasp of a dying breath.

"What's that, sweetie?" Rachel asked.

Belinda remained focused on her aunt without blinking. Her mouth ground into a slow response. "People call me Belle, not Belinda."

Amanda flushed. "I'm sorry, darling. I haven't seen you in over two years." She slaked her dry lips with a cautious tongue. "Look at how you've grown. Mummy and Daddy sent me pictures, but it's not the same as meeting you again in person."

Rachel fidgeted on the spot, desperate to soften the tense atmosphere. "Amanda, you're welcome to stay awhile and get better acquainted before you leave, if that makes life easier?"

Amanda sighed. "You and your generous family have done enough, thank you, Rachel. I won't pretend returning to the house and working out our new relationship will be easy. However, we can't put it off any longer."

"Right you are." Rachel placed a hand on Belinda's shoulder. "You're welcome to pop over anytime you like, Belle. Assuming it's okay with your aunt."

Belinda flung her arms around the affectionate woman's waist and sobbed.

Red-faced, Rachel blinked at Amanda and mouthed the words, *'I'm sorry.'*

Amanda batted the incident aside with a casual wave. The ease of her gesture failed to match a gutted devastation at the unfolding scene. If anything could hammer out the obvious distance between her and her niece with clarity, this meltdown was it. She remembered that promise at the graveside, then stepped forward and lifted Belinda's bag from where the child had let it fall. Previous, motherly instincts she never knew existed surfaced to accompany her resolve. "Thank Laura and Mrs Barnes, Belle. We must head home for tea." Amanda brushed her between the shoulder blades with a delicate hand.

Belinda sniffed and let go of Rachel. Amanda walked to the front door and opened it, niece in tow.

Rachel followed, with Laura watching from the sitting room doorway. Rachel indicated a telephone in the hallway. "If you need anything, Amanda, please call. We're in the phone book."

Amanda nodded. "I'll try not to bother you. See you soon." She stepped out into amber rays of early evening sunlight, one arm dallying with Belinda's limp shoulders.

Laura joined her mother on the doorstep to wave, as aunt and niece wandered towards the village square and church beyond.

* * *

Amanda stirred beneath the bedclothes from a bizarre sensation of something burrowing into her forehead. With no other furnished rooms upstairs than Belinda's and the master belonging to the girl's late parents, Amanda was left with little choice but to sleep in Jake and Karen's bed. Every fidget disturbing the mattress felt like trespassing on their memory. She didn't know how the arrangement appeared to Belinda. The child spoke only when asked a direct question from the moment they left the village. Tea was a stilted affair. Amanda had toyed with asking Belinda to show her around the house, but that seemed a futile gesture unlikely to prise open her clamshell jaw and spark much-needed conversation. Amanda's eyelids fluttered open. She found her face drilled by Belinda's intense stare. Whether anger or resentment lingered behind those eyes, Amanda couldn't tell. This was their life now, for better or worse. They'd have to make it work, somehow.

Amanda propped herself up against the pillows. "Morning, Belle."

Belinda remained mute.

Amanda pressed on. "Listen. I can't imagine the awful stuff you're going through. I hurt too, although that's not your responsibility to bear. But I want to help you. I can't if you won't talk to me."

Belinda turned in a robotic fashion, then walked to the door in silence and closed it behind her.

Amanda rubbed her forehead. "Shit, this will take

work."

A curtain pole above the window collapsed with a clatter that made Amanda almost jump clear of the mattress. She clambered out of bed to inspect the damage. *This entire house is falling apart at the seams.* With the curtain pole stood in a far corner of the room out of the way, Amanda trudged along the landing to the bathroom.

When she came downstairs, Amanda found Belinda dressed and sitting at the dining table with a glass of water. Amanda maintained a warm and positive tone, regardless of the effort and pretence involved. "You fixed yourself up sharp."

Belinda swung her legs beneath the chair. "Time."

"What's that?" Amanda sat down opposite.

"I need time, Auntie Amanda. I'm so…" Belinda's head shook, lips trembling.

"Hey." Amanda reached across and grabbed her hands, half fearing the child would pull away. The coldness in those fingers surprised her. "It's okay. I'll look after you. That's what Mummy and Daddy wanted if something bad happened."

Belinda hung her head.

Amanda gave her chin a gentle flick, cracking the faintest hint of a smile on Belinda's face for the blink of an eye. "Why don't we dispense with the 'Auntie' business? That's awkward to say and rather formal. How about you call me Amanda?"

Belinda squinted. "Are you sure?"

"If I'm calling you Belle, that seems fair now, doesn't

it?" Amanda winked.

Belinda nodded. "I suppose."

Amanda looked through the nearest window. "It's a nice day out. How about popping over to Dolton? Have you ever visited the village shop there?"

Belinda shook her head. "That's where you and Daddy grew up, isn't it?"

Amanda grinned, pleased at making a little headway and receiving full sentences at last. "The village, not the shop. Although your father and I used to race down there on a Saturday morning with our pocket money to buy penny sweets and comics. You could say we grew up there too."

Belinda seemed hesitant, but a glimmer of hope ghosted her countenance. "Okay."

Amanda patted the table. "Great. You'll love it. That place is an Aladdin's cave; it goes back and back. They sell stuff you won't even find in a supermarket. We'll stock up, then come home and fix a nice meal."

A hilltop village of less than two thousand souls to the east of the River Torridge, Dolton's narrow, twisting streets gave it an intimate feeling. Lined with thatched cottages, stone and slate homes, plus occasional new builds, it provided layers of architectural history cheek by jowl like so many of its neighbours. Amanda found a parking area behind the village hall; new since her last visit. Walking through those tight, memory-laden thoroughfares with Belinda at her side, Amanda felt like her own mother in bygone days. Bar a lick of paint and some modern signage, she found Church Street Stores as well-stocked and exciting as she had in her youth. Aisles and rooms fell over one another, packed from floor to ceiling with everything from essential groceries and household items to maps, rudimentary kitchen utensils and car products.

Amanda chortled at an assortment of chamois leathers. "I'd almost forgotten how comprehensive their range is. What do you think, Belle?" She turned to find Belinda absent. Opposite the Post Office counter section, Belinda stood in the doorway. She watched a funeral procession's solemn gait towards the door of St Edmund's Church.

Amanda swallowed. "That's difficult to see after everything that's happened."

Belinda whispered. "The dead woman walks beside her husband."

Amanda noticed an obviously bereaved old gentleman keeping close to the coffin. "That's the spirit. Err, I mean the attitude."

Belinda stared until the procession left her field of vision. "Are Nana and Granddad buried here?"

"No, darling. My folks were both cremated."

"They got sick, didn't they?"

"That's right." Amanda's eyes reddened at the memory. "Within a short space of each other."

Belinda looked up at her. She reached out and gripped her hand. "Was it catching?"

Amanda shook her head. "No. Mum suffered a stroke. Dad went after a series of heart attacks."

Belinda released her hold. "Oh."

Amanda raised an eyebrow. "What's this about?"

Belinda turned away. "Bad things happen when sicknesses spread."

Amanda waited for more, but no other words followed. "I imagine they do. Hold up while I finish shopping, then we'll head home."

Back at Ravensbrook, Amanda fixed them a fine bolognaise with mince she'd purchased at Neals Traditional Family Butchers in Dolton. Conversation proved sparse and lacklustre, yet Amanda sensed the girl lowering her guard an inch at a time. Whatever else burdened Belinda's heart and mind, they were creeping forward in establishing a relationship.

With the meal settled, Amanda booked a glazier on the phone to fix the broken window the following week. Next she fetched a broom, mop and bucket and set about cleaning dirt from the floor where the wall had toppled with fatal consequences.

"I heard a crash." Belinda's voice from the doorway made Amanda jump.

"I thought you were outside, Belle." She frowned. "What crash? I've only swept so far."

Belinda gulped. "The morning Mummy and Daddy died."

Amanda's heart skipped a beat. "You were here?" PC Lucy Maitland had apprised her of such a possibility over the phone, the same way she'd told Oakdene Primary's head teacher in person.

Belinda shook her head. "I... I can't remember. It's all so fuzzy." Her face turned ashen, legs giving way.

"Easy." Amanda dropped her broom and pulled the girl close. "It's okay. Don't strain yourself to recall it. Things will come back in their own time."

3
Dreams and Visions

Amanda strolled through Oakdene on a bright afternoon, digital SLR camera slung over one shoulder and sunglasses perched atop her head. She'd spent the morning waiting for the glazier to arrive. Now the broken window at Ravensbrook featured a clean, new pane of glass. With Belinda at school and a sudden realisation she'd never explored the tiny but pretty village in any detail, a walk was in order. Even during her brief Christmas visits to Jake and Karen's previous home, she'd not paid Oakdene much attention. The bonus of it featuring abundant suitable subjects for her artwork settled Amanda's decision to get out of the house for a spell.

The SLR bleeped as she squeezed off shots from a variety of angles comprising the church tower, surrounding homes and woodland. She wandered on at a lazy pace, shielding the camera's rear screen with one hand to page through thumbnails of memory card images. *I must export those American photos, too. My feet haven't touched the ground since I reached Bristol.* She looked up in quiet awe at a characterful thatched cottage with an immaculate garden bordered by a low, sweeping stone wall. *Perfect. This will make a fabulous watercolour or acrylic.* Amanda backed further into the lane, framing the shot. A car honked its horn, and she jumped aside before wandering back to set up the picture again. "Say 'cheese,' little home." A male head appeared from behind the wall as she pressed the shutter button. "Bugger!"

"Oh, I'm sorry. Did I spoil your picture?" The thickness of the man's neck matched the width of his cuboid noggin to such an extent all facial features appeared stuck on a hot dog, poking from his dark grey, partially unbuttoned shirt. A carpet of tight, cropped brown hair in a centre V, combined with an even shorter, well-trimmed beard, might cause thuggish assumptions to be made from a distance. Yet misty, soft hazel eyes and a thin but gentle mouth - never rising above the horizontal around its edges - spoke of a tender, compassionate and introverted soul within.

Amanda's frustration evaporated into curiosity, disarmed by his immediate apology. "Is this your home?"

The early thirties fellow waved a trowel at her. "Nope. Gardener."

A half-smile crept up one side of Amanda's face. "That would explain why you were kneeling behind the wall."

The man shrugged. "Either that, or I'm a bizarre spoilsport who enjoys lying in wait to ruin tourist snaps."

Amanda's eyes glazed over. "I'm not a tourist."

The man set down his trowel and wiped his hands on a rag. "Photographer?"

"Artist. I paint bucolic English landscapes for a living."

"Then you've found a delightful spot. I'm sorry, I don't recall seeing you around the village before." He offered his hand across the low stone wall. "Craig Symonds."

Amanda accepted his handshake. "Amanda Fairchild. I'm new, of sorts."

"Of sorts?" Craig tilted his head.

Amanda shouldered her camera again. "Not to the area; I grew up in Dolton. My late brother and his wife were renovating an old farmhouse south of the village when-"

"Say no more." Craig raised a palm. "I should have twigged at the name Fairchild. That tragedy at Ravensbrook shook the community. I'm sorry." He rubbed his chin. "Have you moved into the old place, or is this a passing visit to take care of business?"

"I've moved in. Jake and Karen's daughter is mine to care for now. Did you know them?"

"Only to say hello. They had bigger concerns at their property than tidying the garden, so we weren't well acquainted. How's the girl bearing up? What an awful situation."

"Belle? Better than I would in her shoes. She's at school today."

"You've inherited a challenging environment. Were you living local before?"

"No. I had a place in Bristol."

"Strong art community?" Craig asked.

"Yes, although I moved up for university and then took a job in business management."

Craig folded his arms. "That's somewhat different to painting landscapes."

Amanda bit her lip. "Yeah. The job was something I thought I *should* do. Art is what I *wanted* to do. In the end, my heart won out. That and I grew tired of having neither time nor energy to paint, once the working week and life's chores were through."

"The classic conflict." Craig's vocal tone rang with sympathy.

"Have you always been a gardener?" Amanda leaned over the wall and examined pristine beds of colourful flowers.

"Nope. I worked in a high-flying IT job at a London law firm for a decade, until I couldn't stand it any longer. I became desperate to escape the rat race and save my sanity. So, I liquidated minor equity in my city flat, nabbed a manageable mortgage on a one-bedroom cottage here and set myself up as a gardener in the Torridge Valley."

Amanda snorted. "You lasted twice as long as me in the corporate arena. I thought your accent wasn't local."

"I'm an Essex boy by birth."

"How are you finding it?"

"I love the quiet simplicity here. People still have time for one another."

"Is there enough work?" Amanda regarded the surrounding homes.

"I get by. No chance I'll be dining on lobster soon, and I take all the extra odd jobs I can to stay afloat. Before I left London I was living a frugal existence, saving every penny into a nest egg for my escape."

Amanda smirked. "Did you go over the wire or under the fence?"

Craig laughed. "I've never looked back. So what's your medium? Oils?"

"Watercolour or acrylic for the majority. I play with pastels, charcoal and pencil sketches for my own amusement, but that's not a gigantic market. Once in a while I'll do a spot of clay modelling: foxes, birds, otters and other wildlife subjects. Again, more for pleasure. There are better modellers able to do it commercially. It's a narrow field."

"Wow. I'd love to see your work." Craig gave a nonchalant stretch at odds with his statement.

"I can see yours from here." Amanda admired the flowers. "You're an artist of sorts. That's a fine display of blooms."

Craig shook his head. "Alas I can't claim credit for this composition; only its maintenance. The actual artist was dear old Peggy, twenty years ago."

"Is she unable to tend the garden herself now? Forgive me, but anyone with such a particular aesthetic eye must have had a hard time handing over the reins to another person."

Craig pursed his lips. "She had little choice. Peggy went blind on account of diabetes when she was sixty-seven. Her husband passed away, so there was no-one to tend her beloved garden. My predecessors have also popped their clogs over the ensuing two decades. Like you, I've inherited something special."

"Have you tended it long?"

"A year. She's a lovely old girl. Would you like to meet her?"

Amanda checked the church tower clock. Belinda would be at school for another hour. "Okay, why not?"

Craig opened a waist-height wooden gate in the wall and welcomed her inside. "I left Peggy round the back. Do you have an aversion to being touched?"

Amanda flinched.

Craig chuckled. "I'm not hitting on you. Peggy likes to feel the faces of new people, so she can gauge their appearance in her mind."

"Oh, I see. No, that's fine."

"Good. This way." Craig led Amanda around the side of the cottage to a modest patio outside two open French doors.

Frail of appearance with blind, grey eyes set in reddened sockets, Peggy Greene always wore a lilac cardigan topped with a draped lavender shawl for extra warmth - even in summer. Short white hair atop dark grey roots in a virtual 'bowl cut' framed bags of heavy shopping on wan cheeks to match her bony frame. She shifted in a cushioned rattan chair as the pair approached, voice dry but sharp as a pin. "Who's that lady with you, Craig?"

Craig leaned closer to Amanda. "There's nothing wrong with her hearing."

Amanda nodded. "It's common to find other senses heightened in the visually impaired."

Peggy grabbed a walking stick leaning against the arm of her seat and banged it on the paving slabs. "I'm not *'visually impaired,'* young woman; I'm blind as a bat. Don't spout that PC language nonsense around me."

Amanda wrinkled her nose, taking an instant shine to the brusque pensioner.

Craig cleared his throat. "Peggy, this is Amanda Fairchild."

Peggy grumbled. "What's the matter? Doesn't she have a tongue? Is she dumb?" Peggy tapped her cane near Amanda's feet. "Or do you say *'vocally impaired'* in the mad outside world these days?"

Amanda couldn't hold in her smile, which transfigured into a playful gasp of amusement. She leaned over the seated old lady. "It's good to meet you, Peggy."

Peggy stuck one finger in her ear. "Not so loud, if you please. I'm blind, not deaf." Peggy cracked an open-mouthed grin of yellowing teeth and reached out a bony hand sporting pronounced veins. "Peggy Greene, love. It's good to meet you too. Are you one of Craig's friends?"

"We've just met." Amanda held still while Peggy moved questing hands up to touch her face with dry skin the texture of aged leather.

"Did you want something from me? You're not selling religion or double-glazing are you?"

"No."

Craig jumped in. "Amanda is sister to Jake Fairchild, who died with his wife at Ravensbrook."

Peggy's crimson eye sockets seemed to swell. Her voice rasped, and she pointed in the general direction of another chair nearby. "Won't you have a seat, my dear?"

"Thank you." Amanda sat.

Peggy adjusted her shawl and croaked. "It must be time you took a break, Craig. Would you be a star and fix us a pot of tea?"

"Of course. Back in a jiff." Craig disappeared through the French doors.

Amanda watched him go before addressing Peggy. "You've a lovely garden."

Peggy sighed. "I miss it so. The flowers are still here, of course. I can hear the wind teasing their petals and smell the fragrance of each bloom."

Amanda's tone became delicate. "You miss the glory of their colours?"

"Exactly. What I'd give to see my beauties in flower, one more time. I couldn't let them die, even though my sight failed."

"Craig told me the story. For what it's worth, he's doing a top job caring for them. I know I haven't visited your garden before, but the display is stunning."

Peggy folded hands across her stomach. "Thank you. Three things I long for in this world: my late husband, Harry; the sight of my glorious garden in bloom; and my cat, Thomas. He only died six months ago. A neighbour brought him to me as a kitten. I never saw the animal, though I'm told he was a tabby. Thomas was so affectionate, always jumping into my lap and curling up to sleep. How I loved to stroke him. He passed away in his basket one night after I went to bed. When he didn't jump on my mattress for a morning snuggle, I knew something was wrong. I got up and reached down where he slept in the kitchen, to find his soft body stock still and devoid of life. Craig came round later that morning and buried him under my favourite clump of peonies." She sniffed, then wiped her nose with a twig-like finger. "But here I am droning on about a dead cat, when you've lost your own brother and your sister-in-law to a horrendous incident. Forgive me."

"That's okay."

"How is their daughter, now? Or is that a foolish question?"

"Considerate not foolish. Polite to ask, but I'm sure you can guess the answer."

"Ah. I heard you've moved into Ravensbrook to care for her?"

Amanda shifted in her seat. "That's right. Gosh, you're better informed than your gardener."

"He's not one for idle gossip. Can't say I blame him; I was never a fan myself. But, when you're a blind old woman in a village of well-meaning people, folk pop round to visit and bring their wagging tongues along."

Amanda smiled again - a common occurrence in the short time since meeting Peggy. "How did you know I was a young woman when Craig and I approached?"

"The sound of your movements and snatches of conversation I caught on the air." Peggy lifted her nose to the sky. "There are many voices on the wind in

Oakdene. Whispers in the breeze for those who will listen."

"She's not telling your fortune, is she?" Craig appeared at the French doors clutching a well-laden tea tray.

Peggy scowled.

Amanda looked from one to the other. "Does she do that?"

"*She* has a name and is still present," Peggy grunted.

Amanda sat upright. "I'm sorry. Do you tell fortunes, Peggy?"

"From time to time. I've always enjoyed a certain sensitivity to the unseen world. In a strange and ironic twist of fate, I see some things clearer now than when I still possessed the use of my eyes. Your opening comment was more accurate than you realised."

"What do you see?" Amanda asked.

"Impressions. Scenes and pictures of what people will face. Sometimes images from long ago."

Craig set down the tray on a squat table. "I tease her about it, but Peggy has a surprising knack for calling things right."

Peggy's mouth crinkled. "Yes. How are your foundations now?"

Amanda shot Craig an inquisitive look.

Craig fetched an extra chair from inside. "One day Peggy told me I should check the foundations beneath my cottage. She claimed she could sense water flowing somewhere it shouldn't."

"And?" Amanda urged.

"And she was bang on. I had a local surveyor give

the place a once over. The earthen wall of a nearby culvert had eroded. Water began undermining my foundations. The authorities fixed it right away, but I'd have lost my home with the leak undiscovered."

Amanda puffed. "That's impressive."

Craig poured the tea. "So, do people call you Mandy?"

Amanda put on a deadpan stare. "Only if they want their legs broken."

Peggy erupted into a cackle. "I like her."

Craig flushed. "Noted." He changed tack. "How's life at Ravensbrook? Still much to do, I'll bet."

Amanda accepted the cup and saucer he offered her. "I had a glazier fix a window, this morning. My next job is re-erecting and re-pointing the internal wall that killed Jake and Karen." She grimaced. "Only problem is: I've no idea where to begin and can't splash out on builders right now."

"Would you like me to look? I mentioned I do odd jobs. I've put up a wall or two in my time."

Amanda fidgeted. "I couldn't pay much."

Craig thought for a moment. "I don't have a decent picture of my cottage. If you'll whip up a compact watercolour for the living room wall when you've a moment, that would suit. One hand greases the other around here. That's the way it's always been, I'm told."

Amanda pressed her knees together, relieved at a solution to her disheartening DIY dilemma. "Deal."

"Great. Due to the fine summer weather, I'm tied up with gardens most of the day. But since the evenings are lighter, I could pop round after work. Do you need extra materials?"

"There are surplus bricks. Jake and Karen kept a separate pile from other jobs they'd undertaken. Can you mix mortar? I've never done that. Clay or paint I'm at home with. This is a new arena for me."

"No problem." Craig caught Peggy's confused eyebrows butting together. "Amanda is a professional artist."

Children ran in gleeful abandon from the school gates at Oakdene Primary. Amanda waited outside, the camera slung over her shoulder again. She'd enjoyed her social with Peggy and Craig, then decided to meet Belinda for the last stretch home.

Belinda wandered from the building, a distinct contrast in demeanour to the ebullience exhibited by her peers. She walked alone, solemn and quiet, not noticing Amanda until she reached the gates.

"Hey, Belle. How was your day?" Amanda lowered her head to make eye contact.

Belinda looked back at the school, then raised her eyes to a thick canopy of woodland in the near distance. "It was okay."

A schoolboy of similar age, lingering across the road, clucked like a chicken towards Belinda. He rotated his finger in frantic circuits beside his head - the universal signifier of a crazy person.

Amanda frowned. The lad hesitated, then turned and ran up the road.

Belinda wiped silken blonde strands of hair away

from her face.

"What was that all about?" Amanda asked.

Belinda shook her head. "Nothing. Can we go home now?"

"Of course."

They set off down the lane leading south from Oakdene.

"Did you take any nice pictures?" Belinda nodded at the digital SLR bouncing against Amanda's hip.

"I hope so. Once I've downloaded them to my computer, we'll have a look on the screen." She reached out and touched Belinda's arm. "Thanks for asking, Belle."

Belinda remained silent, and the pair walked on.

* * *

Amanda scrubbed the interior of a large upstairs window at Ravensbrook with a soapy sponge. She'd already cleaned the outside on a ladder earlier in the day before Belinda came home from school, distracted as ever. Amanda washed all the windows to brighten their environment. This room, facing south to where the River Torridge snaked around the rear of the property, offered sufficient space and light for her new studio. Amanda endured pangs of guilt over not making the general home more comfortable, first. Beggars couldn't be choosers. Craig would assist her with the collapsed internal wall. If she didn't get back to work soon, there'd only be dry crackers and water to live on. Amanda scratched a stubborn stain on the glass with a fingernail. Light playing against her reflection dimmed, showing more of the room behind. A tall, dark silhouette lingered near the door. Amanda jolted and spun. The room lay empty. Fresh rays of evening sunshine poked between passing clouds. Amanda's tight shoulders relaxed. *A trick of the light. Crumbs, I can't wait to lift the gloominess in here with a decent coat of paint.* She studied the room's smart wooden floor. *I'm thankful Jake took care of that and sanded it.* She spread an array of old sheets across the floorboards, then opened a tray of emulsion. Roller in hand, Amanda hesitated near the half-open door. "Belle?"

Silence lingered a moment before a gentle reply carried along the landing. "I'm here."

"Are you doing your homework?"

"Yes, Amanda. What's the capital of Zimbabwe?"

"Err, that would be Harare."

"How do you spell it?"

"H-A-R-A-R-E." Amanda connected an extension pole to her roller, loaded it with emulsion, and started work on the ceiling first.

"Amanda?"

"Yes?" She walked the pole back and forth. After a few strokes of application, the room already blazed with new life.

"What did the capital used to be called?"

Amanda paused from her labours. "Your teachers expect a nine-year-old to know that?"

"No. It's a geography quiz. They want us to research the answers, but Dad's old laptop is broken. I was worried about asking to use yours. It's for your work, isn't it?"

Amanda leaned out of the room. "The capital used to be Salisbury, like the cathedral city in Wiltshire." She hesitated, then added, "Back then the nation was referred to as Rhodesia, or the Republic of Rhodesia. Make a note of any answers you're unsure of and we'll look them up together on my computer later, okay?"

"Okay."

"Good girl." Amanda continued coating the ceiling before progressing to the walls. Daylight remained sufficient to illuminate her work until the job was done. *I'll tackle the skirting board and door frame with some gloss in the morning.* She backed onto the landing and examined her work. *Nice one.* A terse series of comments from Belinda's room caused her to listen hard.

"No. I don't know where it's gone. Leave me alone." With every phrase, Belinda's voice grew more agitated.

Amanda crept along the passage and pushed Belinda's door open with cautious fingers. "Belle?"

Belinda sat cross-legged on the floor, school books scattered about her. She lifted a pale face to meet Amanda's curious expression.

Amanda slipped inside the room, checking nobody else was present. "Who were you talking to?"

Belinda fidgeted. "Nobody."

"It didn't sound like nobody. Why were you upset?"

"I was frustrated with my homework." She averted her eyes.

Amanda squatted and examined the completed

geography quiz. "Which question? You appear to have completed the remaining answers; although, the capital of Turkey is Ankara, not Istanbul. That's the largest city."

Belinda clasped nervous fingers together. "I must have been thinking out loud about something."

"Who did you want to leave you alone? Has someone bullied you at school? I noticed that boy the other day, when we walked home together."

"Sometimes they're mean because I'm sad and don't play like I used to. I'm okay, Amanda."

"Hmm. Have you finished all your homework?"

"Yes."

"Right then. I'll fix us a bite to eat."

"Amanda?"

"Yes?"

"I'm not hungry and I'm tired. Can I go to bed please?"

Amanda pushed aside rising concern distorting her face. "Don't you want anything at all?"

"Not tonight. I'll have a big breakfast before school in the morning. Mummy always said that was the most important meal of the day."

Amanda sighed. "Okay. If you change your mind, come and find me."

"I will."

Amanda kissed her on the forehead. "Night, darling."

"Goodnight." Belinda watched her leave, a haunting loneliness lingering in her pupils.

Amanda rolled over in the still night watches, jarred awake by a horrified shriek. *What on earth was that?* A follow-on series of deafening screams echoed down the hallway from Belinda's room.

"Good God." Amanda tumbled out of bed in the darkness, fingers scrabbling for the nightstand lamp switch. It clicked on, supplying the master bedroom with a cold cone of white light. Amanda inserted her feet into a pair of slippers and dashed for the door. Belinda screamed again.

"Belle? It's all right, honey, I'm here." Amanda burst into the child's bedroom and flicked the ceiling lamp on.

Belinda sat bolt upright, eyes wide. Her expression suggested disorientation, as though she didn't recognise her surroundings. Sweat poured down her neck and soaked into a crumpled nightdress.

Amanda perched on the mattress edge and held her close. "Shh, I've got you. It was only a dream. A terrible nightmare."

Belinda quivered in her grasp, chilled to the bone. Her words shook with the same vigour as her limbs. "It was so real."

Amanda lifted a glass of water from the bedside table. "Here, try a sip."

Belinda complied.

"Do you want to talk about it? Sometimes that helps." Amanda took the glass away and set it back down.

Belinda stared at the wall. "I saw them again."

"Saw who? Who did you see?"

"The old people from Underwood."

"Old people? Underwood? Is that a nursing home you've visited with school?"

Belinda shook her head. "The village in the woods."

"I haven't heard about that."

"Long before Oakdene, there was another village. Its people got sick, and many died, centuries ago. Then the new village was built nearby."

Amanda thought for a moment. "The Black Death; it must have been. I've heard similar tales from other counties. Relocated and abandoned villages abound. How do you know about it?"

"The ruins are still there. Some friends and I explored them, the day before Mummy and Daddy died."

Amanda shivered. Was it an errant draught from the creaky structure closing in about her, or the sudden vague association of a devastated, ancient village with the death of her sibling? "What do you mean you saw the old people again?"

"The people from long ago. They were there the day we played in the ruins."

"How did you see them?"

"Laura, Jane and Anton had gone ahead. They left me behind at a spot where a home once stood. Children lay dead on straw mattresses. They were covered in horrible dark spots and had swollen bodies."

Amanda stifled a sad exhalation. "That sounds like the bubonic plague for sure."

"A woman cried outside, while a man hung by a rope from the beams above me."

"Like when someone is executed?"

Belinda gave a furious nod.

"That makes little sense, unless it was suicide on account of despair. Those children were nearby?"

"Yes."

"They must have belonged to him. What a horrible dream. Did you fall asleep in the woods or just imagine it while exploring?"

Belinda's limbs stiffened. "I *saw* it, like I was there with my eyes wide open."

"Did you tell your parents any of this?"

"Not on the day it happened. I might have later, had they…"

Amanda squeezed her. "It's okay. Have your teachers taught you about the old village and what happened to it?"

"No. Anton's mother told him the story. I overheard him discussing it with my friends."

"Did she tell him about the swelling and dark spots you described?"

"He didn't mention those."

"How did you know about them? Was there a documentary on TV?"

Belinda touched her forehead. "I didn't know about them. I didn't understand what I was seeing or why. Then the hanging man opened his eyes and hissed the word 'vengeance' at me."

Amanda started, unsettled by a resolute insistence in Belinda's eyes and vocal tone. "Vengeance?"

Belinda's face paled. "It frightened me."

"And you dreamed that scene again tonight?"

"Yes, but this time, I was asleep. There was something different to begin with."

"Different how?"

"The villagers were happy. A cart arrived carrying wrapped parcels of beautiful fabric. People handed the cloth around every home like Christmas gifts. Then I watched them fall sick. More men were hanging in their huts. I felt sad, then angry." She squinted. "No. *They* felt sad, then angry. The dead men cut their ropes, climbed down, and chased me. I was terrified."

"That must be when you started screaming." Amanda pushed the silken locks away from Belinda's forehead. "What a terrible addition to everything else that's happened."

Belinda neglected to mention Anton and the cross, though it still played on her mind. "Amanda?"

"Yes?"

"Are you going to send me away?"

"What?" Amanda pulled back.

"Some boys at school caught me telling Laura what I'd seen. They said I was mad and that you'd send me away to be locked up in a padded cell and never see daylight again." Tears welled up in her eyes.

Amanda gritted her teeth. "Did they?" She patted Amanda's clasped hands. "You listen to me, my fine old friend. Nothing on this earth would make me send you away. Jake and Karen asked me to look after you. Even if they hadn't, you're my niece and I love you." She scanned the ceiling, desperate for the right words.

"I know this is a big change. It is for me, too. With all the horrible things you've suffered, bad dreams are inevitable. Sometimes that's how we process difficult situations and work through them. But I'll always be here to wake up to and offer comfort. I'll always be here to listen, if you need me. No more of this sending away talk, okay?"

Belinda gulped. "Okay."

"Maybe your mind pieced together those images from snatches of stories and things you've heard. They're a collage based on the bad times you're going through."

"But why did I see them before Mummy and Daddy died? Life was happy then."

A stinging shard of Amanda's soul wanted to respond with, *'and it's not now?'* but she knew she couldn't take Belinda's comment personally. The child meant nothing by it, other than she'd enjoyed a carefree life with her parents. "Stories and those ruins may have fired your imagination. The pain that followed brought it up again in your dreams." She eased Belinda down under her covers. "Lie back, now. Try to rest and dream of happy times, nice places and all the things you love. No more sick and dying children, or hanging men. Nobody is coming after you, Belle. I won't let anyone hurt you."

Belinda's eyebrows raised high onto her forehead. "Promise?"

"I promise. Get some rest." Amanda kissed her cheek and retreated to the doorway, where she extinguished the overhead light. After pulling the door to, she waited in the hallway, listening for Belinda's breathing to slip into the telltale first stages of approaching sleep. A bright moon shone through the landing window. It cast silver highlights upon the treetops of distant, thick woodland. Its dark outline lurked across the meadow, reaching up into hills behind. Amanda drew nearer to the glass and whispered. "Underwood."

4
Girl in the Water

Amanda and Belinda watched from the lane in Oakdene while the Sunday faithful left church. Reverend Julie Clement shook hands with each parishioner in the porch at All Saints. Their wandering observers continued past the churchyard wall. Amanda's SLR jostled from her shoulder - a now common sight that had earned her the nickname: '*The woman with the camera*' among those yet to make her formal acquaintance. In her hands she clutched an old picnic basket she'd bought years before while dallying with still-life art subjects. Today it contained food, ready for use as per its intended purpose. Muted organ music carried on fragrant air; a poor substitute for the symphony of summer birdsong in the trees outside.

"Where is this spot you suggested?" Amanda swung the basket in a playful curve, keen to stoke embers of childish excitement evident in Belinda's manner this morning. A picnic proved an inspired idea to lift her spirits.

"A short way along this lane, up the valley beyond the village. There's a meadow past the stone bridge that crosses the river." Belinda pointed in a vague, northerly direction.

"I drove over that bridge on my way into Oakdene, when I arrived. I've been meaning to explore the area. We never ventured down this way much from Dolton as kids."

Belinda managed a momentary skip. "It's a spot otters come out to play, if you're lucky."

"Maybe I'll capture some shots to inspire a clay wildlife model."

Belinda shielded her eyes from brilliant sunlight with one hand. "Like that cat you made the other day?"

One corner of Amanda's mouth crinkled into a teasing sign of amusement. "Oh, so you've looked in the studio, have you?"

Belinda clamped arms tight either side of her own body. "I didn't touch anything."

Amanda ruffled her hair. "Curiosity saw the cat, rather than killed it."

"It's lovely. There's so much detail in the fur."

"Thank you, sweetie. I'm making it as a present for a blind lady I met in the village. She had a cat called Thomas she loved stroking, who died a while back."

Belinda stopped in the lane. "But how will she see it?"

"She won't; hence my focus on texture. Clay isn't the same as fur, of course. But Peggy likes to picture things in her mind based on touch. I thought when she misses Thomas, she could feel the model. That's why he's curled up asleep. There's less chance of a leg or tail breaking, if they're all tucked against his body."

"When will you give it to her?" Belinda started walking again.

"The model needs to dry. Then I'll source a local potter with a kiln who can fire it. There'll be one somewhere in the vicinity."

The burble of a meaty car engine disturbed the rural Sabbath tranquillity of their stroll. Heavy revving from a V8 feeding a booming exhaust, roared somewhere on the other side of the river, drawing nearer.

Amanda struggled into a narrow gap between bramble bushes on the water side of the lane. "Quick, Belle. Tuck yourself in behind me. This idiot is going way too fast."

Belinda reached her side in time to catch a glint of sunlight winking on a car windshield and reflective bodywork. A British Racing Green Aston Martin Vantage executed a right-hand turn onto a single-track stone bridge over the river. Its driver didn't slow into the sharp left bend on their side, cornering the prestige motor as though it ran on rails. Belinda squashed herself against Amanda's torso. She flinched at a spray of gravel and dirt kicked up by the super-sized, low-profile tyres passing inches from their fragile sanctuary. The Aston roared around another corner, like an arrow in flight to the heart of Oakdene. Its brake lights flared for an instant, then vanished from sight.

Amanda listened for the sound of other traffic, then stepped back into the lane, shaking her head. "Some people have no consideration." She noticed Belinda still crouched amongst the brambles. "Are you all right, Belle?"

Belinda's earlier buoyant nature appeared to have vanished, much to Amanda's chagrin. "Uh-huh." She coughed and brushed dirt from her blouse. "That car wasn't stopping for anyone."

Amanda surveyed the pretty arch of the stone bridge with its low side walls. "I didn't realise how handsome a feature it is. You don't see any of this from behind the wheel." She reached in and helped Belinda clear of the gap. "Nor walkers on the lane, if you're driving like a nutter."

Belinda regained her confidence and hurried forwards. "The meadow is on the other side of the bend."

"What's the rush?" Amanda quickened pace to keep up with her.

"I want us to reach the track before another car comes."

They darted across the tight corner leading onto the bridge. Belinda led them through another gap in some hedgerows, marked by a faded green sign declaring the way a *'Public Footpath.'* Beyond, the trail sloped downward, bearing right towards the broad, gentle flow of the Torridge. Its languid waters slipped by this spot with scant, telltale ripples of current. Smooth and clear, with a dark, stony bottom, its mirror surface painted a perfect picture of the cloudless, azure heavens above.

"Is it damp?" Amanda reached a level patch of tall, lush grass.

Belinda squatted and allowed the succulent blades to

sough through her fingers. "No."

Amanda set down the basket and opened it. She passed a folded tartan blanket that had rested between its handles to Belinda. "Spread this out." A kingfisher caught her eye, its flash of brilliant blue plumage shimmering as it rocketed by faster than the Aston. "What a splendid spot. After lunch I'll take snaps of the river and bridge." Amanda displaced to seat herself and the basket where Belinda laid the covering. She doled out cold chicken salad on plastic plates, then poured apple juice into accompanying beakers.

A rustling disturbed the undergrowth while they ate, followed by a curious, whistling squeak. Belinda whipped her head around, then pointed. "Look."

Two sleek otters lumbered out of the swaying foliage, nipping at each other and rolling around in a playful fight.

Belinda's face lit up. "Like Tarka."

Amanda smiled to herself. "This is '*the Country of the Two Rivers*' Henry Williamson wrote about."

Belinda leaned towards the rambunctious animals, stretching out an eager hand.

"Easy," Amanda cautioned. "They're nice enough, but those teeth are like razor blades."

Belinda held still and watched the pair scamper to the water's edge. She put down her plate of food and scrambled up for a closer look. At first her giggles warmed Amanda's heart as much as the sunshine did her limbs. Then the amusement plummeted into gaping silence.

"What is it?" Amanda asked, about to bite into an

apple.

Belinda stood on the bank facing towards the stone bridge, cheeks pale and wan. Midway between her and the attractive crossing, an even paler female face stared from beneath the lazy water's surface. Long, submerged hair swept outward in slithering strands that appeared to move in time with the river's whims. Piercing blue eyes watched Belinda, while a silent mouth spoke unheard and unfathomable words from the depths of her watery grave.

"Belle?" Amanda stood from the blanket, sending nearby grasshoppers into a flurry of activity.

Belinda whispered. "There's someone in the water."

"Where?" Amanda dropped her apple and darted over, worried a child might have tumbled in.

Belinda froze. "Near the bridge."

Amanda's face struggled against the sun's glare. "I can't see. Is it an adult?"

"No. A girl like me."

Belinda shut her eyes to push away the apparition. A collective whisper of voices carried over the treetops, sweeping around the hill from woodlands beyond.

Amanda continued staring at the river, oblivious to any sight or sound out of the ordinary.

Belinda covered her ears, but the whispers continued in her head. *Make them stop. Someone, please make them stop. Why won't they leave me alone?*

Amanda looked away from the bridge to find Belinda's face twisted in discomfort, with both hands clamped either side of her head. "Hey." She reached up and pulled her arms clear. "What's going on?"

Belinda's face fell. "I'm sorry. I thought I saw a girl in the water."

Amanda felt her forehead. "Are you unwell? Do you want to go home?"

Belinda slouched back towards the blanket. "I can't eat another thing."

Amanda observed the chicken salad Belinda had barely started. Part of her wanted to scold the child; part to wrap her in cotton wool like a delicate porcelain doll. The former idea would only cause Belinda to shut down; the latter to postpone whatever she'd have to face eventually. She settled for a compromise of mild disappointment in her voice, hoping to guilt her niece into trying a little more food. "You've not eaten much. That's tasty chicken. I put a lot of effort into it. The vegetables are sweet and full of flavour, too."

Belinda flopped down and popped a cherry tomato between her lips.

Amanda retrieved her camera from next to the basket. "That's a start. Why don't you relax and take your time over lunch while I grab some pictures?"

Belinda responded by nibbling at a chicken drumstick.

Amanda removed her lens cap and returned to the riverside. She squatted to frame a shot, then clicked off several more in different orientations and postures.

Belinda tidied plate scraps away and sipped her juice. "Are you going to paint the bridge?"

Amanda backed up for a broader perspective, squinting into the viewfinder. "No question about it. This will make a fine subject."

* * *

Fast-drying, easy to clean and lacking a strong odour while producing bold, vibrant colours from heavy pigments; these were some benefits that made acrylic one of Amanda's favourite artistic mediums. The ability to over-paint dried areas without consequences and not have your paint spread, didn't hurt either. She stood in her bright new studio at Ravensbrook, mixing colours with a palette knife. A primed Gesso board stood on an H-frame tabletop easel in the centre of the room. Amanda's laptop computer rested on the same sturdy table alongside, her favourite photograph of the stone bridge filling its screen. Light washed in from the pristine window behind as Amanda settled herself on a comfortable high stool and set to work. Across the room, the clay, curled up, life-sized approximation of how she imagined Thomas the cat, continued drying in the warm rays of sun. Amanda tested a sturdy cup of brushes next to her palette, locating a favourite tool. The Gesso board already featured a simple under-drawing she'd laid down earlier, before Belinda rose for school. With the compositional aid in situ, work commenced applying mid-tones of paint to capture shape and form. She put down the brush and spritzed drying paint on her palette with a spray bottle.

Time drew on with a brief pause for lunch, while the painted representation of their Sunday picnic spot sharpened like a photograph coming into focus. In the afternoon, Amanda worked on the finer details, picking out stonework and light on the water.

The front door banged downstairs, causing Amanda's head to pop up like a meerkat. The sound of familiar, childish footsteps creaked on the staircase. "Belle?"

"I'm home," came the reply.

Amanda set down her brush and checked the laptop's clock. *Goodness, time flies. Where did that day go?*

Belinda appeared in the doorway. "Can I have tea at Laura's house?"

A firm fist banged on the front door. Amanda climbed down off her stool and made for the staircase. "I wonder who that is?"

Belinda called after her. "How's work on the bridge coming along?"

"I'm almost done. You can take a peek if you'd like." Amanda reached the hallway, twisted a wrought-iron handle and tugged open the heavy, studded front door.

Craig Symonds stood in the driveway, peering up at the gable from beside an aged but well-loved red Land Rover Defender. A flash of movement in the doorway grabbed his attention. "Amanda, Hi. I finished my last job of the day earlier than expected. Since I promised you help with that internal wall, I thought I'd check if this is a good time?"

Amanda joined him outside. "Even if it weren't a good time, I'd drop everything to accommodate you. This is such a relief." She examined the upstairs portion of Ravensbrook, upon which Craig's attention had been transfixed. "What's wrong with the roof?

Don't say that's about to collapse too?"

"No. Doesn't look like it from here. I could swear I saw a young man watching me from that window, when I pulled up."

"I've no young men tucked away in upstairs cupboards. My life is hectic enough without all that nonsense."

Craig grinned. "Probably some coat or object in a bedroom reflecting on the glass."

"Or your imagination," Amanda added.

Craig opened the Defender's tailgate. "I've brought enough supplies to mix mortar, plus a couple of trowels and a spirit level."

Belinda appeared on the doorstep. "Amanda, you didn't say whether I could have tea at Laura's?"

"Of course you can, darling. Be home before it gets dark though."

Belinda hesitated, watching Craig. "Who's this?"

Amanda beckoned her over. "Belle, meet Craig Symonds. Craig is a local gardener, who also knows about bricklaying. He's come to help re-erect our wall."

"Hello," Belinda spoke in a detached voice.

"Hello, Belle."

Belinda prodded Amanda. "Can I go now?"

Amanda nodded. "Hurry along. Give my regards to Rachel and Laura."

"I will." Belinda waved a hand as she launched into a happy run along the driveway.

Craig watched her go. "She seems full of beans. You must be doing something right."

* * *

"How are you getting on with your aunt?" Laura Barnes sat cross-legged on her bedroom carpet at The Old Bothy.

Belinda shrugged, grooming the mane of a model horse with a miniature plastic replica of an equestrian brush.

Laura tried again. "She seems friendly."

Belinda's chin sunk into her chest. "I want Mummy and Daddy."

Laura watched her friend with compassionate eyes and then moved another horse into a playful canter across the carpet. She put on a silly voice, pretending to be the pony. "Don't worry, I'm here."

For a moment Belinda managed a weak smile, which faded as though some unimaginable horror had intruded into their playtime. She stared at the bedroom window, shaking her head.

"Belle?" Laura touched her arm, but Belinda recoiled before shuffling on her bottom towards a dark corner. Lattice panes blew open, causing a startled thrush to swoop away from the overhanging thatch in a flurry of wings.

Laura scrambled up and ran to the casement. "How did that happen? There's no wind inside the house. Nor out." She reached for the latch, only to reel across the room as though punched in the gut.

Belinda fought to shut out a mass of whispering voices again. Since covering her ears proved ineffectual, she tried an obvious, desperate alternative to drown out the incessant throng.

Rachel Barnes' feet pounded up the staircase the moment Belinda started screaming. She burst into the room where Laura lay winded and clutching her stomach, eyes awash with fear. The window panes opened and closed at a continuous rate, while an unseen and unheard internal cyclone blew papers around the room in a silent vortex. One of the toy ponies flew from its resting place on the carpet to strike Rachel on the forehead. She staggered back onto the landing from a mixture of the impact and shock. Belinda stopped screaming and watched her with puffing cheeks and confused eyes. She shouted a tremulous rebuke at the whirling papers. "Leave them alone. They haven't hurt you." The other toy horse struck Rachel in the solar plexus this time. Belinda grizzled and cupped both hands across her mouth.

An inserted key rattled in the downstairs front door. Christopher Barnes called out for his wife. "Rachel? I'm home early. Rachel?" He ascended the stairs where Rachel lay crumpled against the landing wall in a seated position. The vortex of papers fluttered to the carpet and lay still, while the window panes ceased their repetitive flapping.

"Chris?" Rachel fought for breath and tried to stand.

"Careful. What happened?" Christopher helped her up.

The sound of Christopher Barnes exchanging heated words of concern with his wife seeped through the wood of a closed dining room door. Belinda waited in the hallway, listening to the parents of her best friend discuss their verdict, while Laura accompanied the scene inside with whimpers and tears. She'd recoiled from Belinda when she offered to help her up in a copycat gesture of the two adults. Her face had contorted into a cocktail of confusion, terror and heartbreak at the inexplicable encounter centred around her playmate.

"I know she's suffered a tough time, but I won't allow my wife and daughter to come to harm on her account. What was it, some sort of poltergeist or psychokinesis?" Christopher fumed. "I thought that was all guff until I found you just now."

Rachel rubbed her forehead. "I don't know, Chris. The experience terrified Belle, too."

"Yet you say she spoke to it like a person?"

"Spoke to *them*," Belinda corrected under her breath, outside in the hall.

Christopher paced the room. "We'll send her home." He addressed his daughter. "Laura, I don't want that girl in this house again. I'm sorry. You're not to visit Ravensbrook either. I know you're good friends, but this is unacceptable." He sighed. "What's going on at that old farmhouse?"

"I've not served them any tea yet," Rachel protested.

Christopher grunted. "Fine. Fix the girls a sandwich, let Laura say goodbye to Belle, and then pack her off down the lane." He tugged open the dining room door and eyed Belinda with an exasperated stare.

Belinda looked past him to where Laura sat cuddling her mother, eyes moist and puffy.

Rachel studied the lonely, sullen girl standing in her hallway for a moment, then faced away and stroked her daughter's hair.

* * *

"Now that is a proper job." Craig Symonds stepped back to admire a pristine internal wall reconstructed from recovered or re-purposed historical bricks.

"It looks sturdy," Amanda commented. "I can't believe how fast it shot up." She patted the brickwork.

Craig set down his trowel. "No doubt the section that crumbled failed without warning. Jake and Karen wouldn't have picked up any danger indicators. I'm sorry."

Amanda sat on a rough wooden chair. "Thanks. It was a dreadful accident." She hesitated, face weighing up an obvious internal dilemma.

"Something on your mind?" Craig asked.

Amanda scratched flaking skin behind one ear. "It's possible Belle was here when they were killed."

"What makes you think that?"

"Something I was told by the police and something she said later. I daren't push her over this."

Craig crouched at her side. "What would it achieve, anyway? If Belle was here and saw or heard the wall collapse, that's doubly awful. Maybe she hinted at it because she wants to talk about it, but doesn't yet feel able."

"That's what I was hoping." Amanda propped her chin on an upturned palm.

Craig straightened as the front door banged. "Keep giving her space. If she's ready to talk, you'll know."

Belinda appeared in the open doorway.

"Come and see the new wall, Belle." Amanda gestured for her to approach.

Belinda took two steps into the room, studied their handiwork for an instant, and then turned before disappearing upstairs.

Craig blinked. "A mite different to when she left. Perhaps the friends had a row?"

Amanda frowned. "I've no idea, but it's rude. I'll make her come down and apologise."

Craig grabbed her arm as she marched towards the hallway. "Let it go this time, yeah?"

The fire extinguished in Amanda's belly. Her shoulders slumped. "Whenever I seem to make progress, I find myself back at the start." A flare of setting sun permeated the window. "I haven't served you anything. Not so much as a biscuit."

"Forget it. We've been busy." Craig started packing away. "I've leftovers ready for bubble and squeak in the fridge at home. I'll hold you to your promise, though."

"What promise?"

Craig placed both hands on his hips. "That painting of my cottage. It's called Cosicott. Across the square from the church; you can't miss it."

"If I don't already have a photo to work from, I'll grab one in a day or two and get cracking."

"Splendid." He tapped the wall and smiled to himself.

Amanda woke in darkness to find she'd nodded off on the downstairs sofa. A supper tray rested on the coffee table before her. Its plate of cracker crumbs and an empty bowl with a telltale soup tide mark reminded her of the hasty repast consumed in solitude. Her busy day of painting, culminating in unexpected building work and the emotional toll of her ongoing situation with Belinda, had cost more energy than she'd realised.

A sudden clatter from the rear upper portion of the house sharpened Amanda's sleep-muted senses. She hurried upstairs, where the door to her studio remained open. Its overhead light clicked on in her hands to reveal the tabletop easel lying flat. Amanda approached, closing the screen of her laptop, which had long since gone to sleep. *The easel has never fallen over before. I can't have secured it in place. Draughty old house.* She lifted the painting. *Thank goodness that didn't happen when this was still wet.* Her eyes swept over the image to rest upon a section where water met the bridge stonework. Amanda let go of the Gesso board with an involuntary squeal. The pale, forlorn face of a young girl peered from the depths, hair sweeping out around her like current-dragged underwater weeds. "How is that possible?" Amanda spoke in a hoarse whisper to the walls of her studio. *I didn't paint that face in there. Could Belle have done it? That's too detailed for a nine-year-old.* She gulped and forced herself to lean over the painting for a closer inspection. *It's a watercolour wash. Fuzzy edges applied while the acrylic was still wet.* She rubbed her chin. *Thing is, for that to work the face must have already been painted in white acrylic underneath.* She massaged quivering fingers against the effects of a chill on her upper arms. *Belle said there was a girl in the water. I'll ask her about it in the morning. Man, that's creepy.*

Amanda was already sitting at the dining table with a plain white mug of coffee when Belinda came downstairs for breakfast next day. "Good morning, Belle."

"Morning." Belinda spoke with a non-committal tone of voice and matching facial expression.

"Why don't you sit down and let me fetch you something?"

Belinda paused, holding onto the back of a dining chair. "Am I in trouble?"

Amanda raised an eyebrow. "Are you aware of any impolite behaviour that might land you in trouble?"

Belinda gripped the chair tighter. "I had a lot on my mind when I came home last night. I meant to look at the wall longer and not run upstairs. Sorry."

Amanda lifted her mug between both hands. "Did you and Laura have a disagreement?"

Belinda's face fell. "We're not allowed to see each other outside of school now."

"What?" Amanda restrained an instinctive urge to stand. "Why?"

Belinda shook her head. "I don't want to talk about it."

"But she's your best friend, isn't she? Would you like me to speak with Rachel Barnes?"

"Please don't."

So pathetic was the petition in those eyes, Amanda let the subject drop. *Another item on the list of topics she won't discuss with me.* She sipped her coffee, then set the mug down. "Did you go into my studio after you arrived home?"

"Only when I first got in from school. I wanted to see your river meadow painting, remember?"

"And?"

"It's lovely." Belinda pulled out the chair and finally took a seat.

Amanda hummed. "You didn't think it lacked anything or needed tweaking?"

Belinda shook her head. "Oh no, it was perfect."

Amanda's eyes half closed. She repeated the word in a distant murmur. "Perfect."

Belinda flushed. "I'm not the best person to ask. I can't draw or paint. Not even stick figures like kids half my age."

"Is that so?" Amanda's mouth dried up.

"Your river meadow painting looks wonderful to me. I'm sure it will to others."

Amanda stood. "Do you remember at the picnic, you thought there was a girl in the water?"

Belinda glanced out of the window as though distracted. "I must have been mistaken. There wasn't one, was there? You looked for yourself."

Amanda watched the evasive child, a distinct unease knotting her stomach. "I didn't see one." She waited without success for a further response, then grabbed her mug. "I'll fix your breakfast."

Amanda wasn't sure how long she stood in the sunlit studio after Belinda left for school. The acrylic painting lay where she'd let it fall on the collapsed tabletop easel the night before. That ghostly image of a drowned child peered out at her in silent panic. *I can't sell the original or prints with that in it. Not if I ever want to be taken seriously again.* She secured the easel into an upright position and reached for her tubes of acrylic. *Thank goodness for over-painting. I'll mix light and shadows on the water's surface to remove her.* Amanda set about the work. Burning questions fought for attention in her brain as she adjusted the image. *Who is that girl? Someone who drowned in the river? Did Belle see her? If so, what's she doing in my painting and how did she get there? To produce a result like that requires knowledge of how paint works, let alone an eye for detail. Belle couldn't have done it. Why was she covering her ears and staring at the woods on Sunday afternoon? Did Jake and Karen take her to the river in times past?* Amanda pulled back, happier to no longer endure the underwater apparition's stare. *Difficult memories, I guess. I hope this new strain on her relationship with Laura is temporary. Kids fix things fast and become firm friends again. It'll blow over.*

At various points throughout the day Amanda wandered back into the studio, half expecting that face in the water to reappear. The painting remained as she'd left it. She threw herself into art business admin and addressing a positive response from a gallery owner in Great Torrington, keen for an in-person meeting and closer examination of her work. The distraction proved welcome, yet every time the house creaked or a gust of wind found its way inside, Amanda felt alone and vulnerable. *Some publishers use ghostwriters. Have I a ghost painter, in the literal sense?* Amanda's new life course was set and Ravensbrook her home. *I guess there are things I'll ignore and hope they go away. I'm understanding my niece a little better, it seems.*

5
Startling Compositions

Amanda started her Avensis and rolled down the undulating driveway, across the brook beside the meadow. Belinda had left for school an hour earlier. The car slowed to a crawl through the pretty streets of Oakdene. Amanda honked her horn at Craig, bent double in someone's front garden. He almost jumped out of his skin, causing her to snicker before picking up speed along the lane beyond the village. She wound through a narrow series of bends, following contours of the wooded hill on her left. The River Torridge sparkled on the opposite side, not rushing in its course as one that has accompanied the flow of time since before recorded history. Flashing headlights reflected in the Toyota's rear-view mirror. A deafening burble and engine roar crept through the driver's window she'd lowered for a breath of fresh air.

Amanda grimaced. *It's that bastard who nearly ran Belle and I down on our Sunday picnic. Almost the same spot, but racing in the opposite direction.* She caught sight of the bridge ahead, resisting an urge to be bullied into driving faster than comfort allowed. The Aston Martin's sleek lines were unmistakable now. Its horn blared, a mocking karma of her teasing action against Craig. Amanda growled and made a wanker gesture at the impatient motorist. The steering wheel lurched round to the right in her other hand, as the front offside wheel struck a pothole near the narrow lane's edge. Amanda attempted to recover, but the car barrelled into the section of brambles she'd used as a sanctuary with Belle, wiping them out. "Shit!" She stomped on the brake, bringing the car to a skidding halt three feet from the water's edge. Blood pumped in her ears like a raging winter torrent, the polar opposite of the Torridge's current state. She ran a hand shaking from adrenaline down her face as the Aston pulled up near the bridge, hazard lights blinking. Amanda reached for the door handle, checking she wasn't about to put a foot straight underwater. Lush grass stood tall enough to be pushed aside by the opening door.

A clipped voice rang out from the lane above. "You should learn to drive, old man."

Amanda poked her pretty feminine head above the Toyota's roof, followed by a corresponding sharp intake of breath from the Aston's driver.

The patronising man's tone vanished like smoke on a stiff breeze. "Oh my goodness, I'm so sorry. Are you all right?"

Fit, but with the rosy-cheeked evidence of life enhanced in the company of a decanter; at forty-two, Julian Asbury prided himself on a well-to-do country gent lifestyle. An orphaned only child, the business of running his family estate kept him occupied as a heritage guardian. Yet for all that, Julian loved the attention wealth and position afforded. Attention he milked, from the suave dimple in his chin beneath gelled, short dark hair to the red and white checked shirt peeking out of a brass buttoned navy blazer. Immaculately pressed trousers and well-polished Oxfords completed his signature ensemble. Both added a touch of class to an overconfident swagger. He displayed no qualms about soiling his clothing in a hurried descent of the bank to reach Amanda.

Amanda scowled, face like thunder. "Bloody idiot. What the hell were you doing back there?" Her cheeks reddened in concert with her raised voice. "Are you some kind of maniac? Who drives like that on a single-track series of S-bends?"

Julian reached the other side of the vehicle and cleared his throat, lest the following introduction be confused with a response to her rhetorical question. "Julian Asbury." Since extending a hand in greeting seemed likely to have it bitten off or slapped aside, he motioned at her legs. "Can I help you round?"

"You've done quite enough." Her eyes fell upon the wheel that had struck the pothole. Its twisted rim stuck out with a punctured tyre hanging off. Amanda clutched her head. "Fuck." She kicked the tyre. "I'm supposed to be meeting a gallery owner in Great Torrington. Look at my car; it's not going anywhere, ARSEbury."

Julian rounded the bonnet and surveyed the damage. "That's Asbury. You can call me Julian."

"I'll call you something," Amanda almost spat. "What am I going to do now? I need this meeting for my business."

Julian's facial hue mimicked Amanda's passable impression of a raspberry, although borne of embarrassment rather than anger. "Do you have much to transport?"

Amanda folded her arms. "An acrylic painting of that bridge, a watercolour of Oakdene and a print portfolio."

Julian adjusted his crimson tie. "Right then. I'll drive you to Great Torrington for your meeting." He read the concern in Amanda's eyes. "At a more sedate pace. Afterwards I hope you'll allow me to buy you lunch as an apology. In the meantime, I'll phone the garage and have them tow your car in for repairs. No insurance claim necessary. The bill is on me."

Amanda had been gearing up for a tirade of pithy insults, but his offer stole the wind from her sails. There was a glint to his eye that unsettled her, though she'd not find a better offer to escape this predicament or reach the gallery in time. "Won't they need the keys?"

"Leave them in the boot with the car unlocked. I'll let the mechanics know where they are." Julian pulled a top-flight mobile phone from his smart blazer. "You said it yourself: the car isn't going anywhere. No chance of it being stolen. This area is quiet. Zero vandalism I'm aware of and no carbecues."

"Carbecues?" Amanda's eyebrows lifted.

Julian flicked up a number from his electronic address book. "Setting a car on fire. You can't have visited Paris lately. Carbecues are a weekend epidemic there."

Amanda sniffed and put on an exaggerated La De Da voice. "I must have spent too much time at the casinos in Monte Carlo instead."

Julian ignored her as someone answered his call. "Hello, it's Julian Asbury…"

Amanda tuned him out, opened the car boot, and retrieved her artwork samples. She took a deep breath, then noticed her would-be rescuer waving. "What is it?"

"Oakdene Motors need a name and address, so they'll know where to deliver your vehicle after it's repaired."

"Amanda Fairchild. I live at Ravensbrook, south of the village."

Julian looked her up and down. "I see."

Amanda made a show of dropping her car keys into the open boot and slamming it shut.

Julian turned towards the river, phone clamped to his head. "Ravensbrook." He hesitated. "That's it, the old farmhouse. The vehicle is unlocked; keys in the boot. Quick as you can, please. Thank you." He hung up.

Amanda leaned against the vehicle's bodywork. "You spoke to that garage like you know them."

"They work on my Aston, from time to time."

Amanda blinked. "Isn't Oakdene Motors a local outfit? I'm surprised you trust them with a monster like that." She nodded at the Vantage squatting in the lane, begging to be driven.

"There's none more reliable or skilled than Brian

Taylor. Since I'm local, he's the obvious choice."

"You live in the village?"

"On the outskirts. Atop the hill, yonder." Julian drew nearer. "May I take those for you?" He reached towards a black, waterproof portfolio case and A3 zipped folder propped between her legs.

"Okay. We'd best shove off before I'm late." She handed the items to Julian. "That's not an excuse to put your foot down."

"I wouldn't dream of it." Julian probed the inside of his cheek with his tongue. "Pardon my intrusion, but I assume you're a relative of the Fairchilds? The couple who owned Ravensbrook before?"

"I am." Amanda accompanied him up the bank towards his vehicle. Its waxed British Racing Green paintwork glimmered with a satin finish. "Jake was my brother. His orphaned daughter is my charge, now. I've moved into Ravensbrook."

"That's an old property. It predates Oakdene, you know. Might even have a year or two on my estate."

"Estate?" Amanda almost choked on the word, though she didn't know why. No way this guy lived in a three bed semi.

"High Stanton. It's a 17th century manor." He deposited Amanda's luggage inside the Aston.

"Of course it is." Amanda tried to disguise her sarcasm.

Julian pursed his lips. "Look, I realise we've got off to a shaky start…"

"Remind me whose fault that is?" Amanda cocked her head.

Julian flushed. "Yes, well I hope you'll allow me to make amends and we can begin again in a civilised fashion." This time, he extended his hand. "Bygones?"

Amanda sighed and shook it. "Bygones."

Julian beamed. "Marvellous. In you hop. Next stop, Great Torrington."

The smart but compact market town of Great Torrington followed a right-hand bend in the Torridge, eight miles as the crow flew northwest from Oakdene. Partially clinging to an inland cliff top, its lower sections suffered occasional watery wrath from the river. This site of ancient forts and castles provided abundant amenities, yet with a proud populace protective against conquest from the larger commercial chains. The verdant hillsides proved steep here, with panoramic views across the unspoilt valley and river whence the settlement took its name.

Amanda dug her nails beneath the passenger seat of the Aston's compact cabin. Sleek as a cruise missile, it felt like a piece of automotive engineering that suffered sedate travel under protest.

Julian swung into South Street Car Park, Amanda almost pressing her foot through the floor to make him apply the brakes before they hit a wall. She wiped her brow as Julian killed the engine with inches to spare. He leaned over the centre console. "Where is this gallery?"

"Dove's Fine Art, on Cornmarket Street. I can't remember which road that is. I haven't been to Great

Torrington in years."

"A short stretch up South Street and around the corner. Perfect. We'll stow your wares back in the car and stop for a bite at The Black Horse afterwards. That's nearby, on the High Street."

Amanda produced a faint smile. "That I do remember. Mum and Dad used to bring us to The Black Horse for birthday celebrations as kids."

"The character and emotion conveyed are striking, right across the board." Angela Dove, the mid-fifties gallery owner, sat at her desk turning pages in Amanda's print book. One well-manicured nail rested on a watercolour of a large, half-timbered coaching inn.

Amanda leaned over from where she sat opposite, beside Julian. "The George Inn, Norton St Philip. One of our nation's oldest public houses."

Julian made an approving sound. "Outside Bath. I know it. Some friends and I drive over there for drinkies after the horse racing whenever I'm in Somerset." He waved a confident finger at Angela. "You know, Ms Dove, I've many fine acquaintances in my circle who'd appreciate fresh artwork of this quality. It's just the ticket for their flavour of home decor." He half turned to Amanda. "I must commission you for some pieces featuring my country estate." He stressed the last two words more for Angela's benefit than Amanda's. Amanda realised he was fluffing her talent to Angela, but hoped he wouldn't blow this. Such opportunities weren't two a penny.

Julian reached for the print book, one submissive hand raised towards the gallery owner. "May I?"

"Of course." Angela slid it across to him.

Julian flicked through the pages, face contemplative but serious. He made various thoughtful hums in his throat, moving his head from side to side at each new picture. "Oh yes. Once my chums discover these, orders will fly out the door." He smiled at Amanda. "Good for your online business." He opened his attention out to include Angela. "Or any gallery owner savvy enough to stock her wares."

Angela laughed under her breath. "Amanda had already sold me on the quality of those acrylic and watercolour originals. That was before the book even came out." She sat back in her seat. "Not that I wouldn't appreciate a visit from those well-heeled friends of yours." She addressed Amanda. "I'd say we can do business."

"Cheers." Julian lifted a straight glass of lager towards Amanda over lunch.

A traditional 16th century coaching inn, The Black Horse featured a white double gabled frontage with black timber framed, leaded windows. This hostelry, set in the middle of town, was believed to have formed the headquarters of both royalist leader Lord Hopton and parliamentarian Thomas Fairfax during the English Civil War. A wealth of exposed beams, part cobbled floors, open fires and exposed stonework suggested little had changed since that time but the menu.

Amanda clinked her glass of shandy in acceptance of the salute. "Thanks for the embellishment."

Julian took a taster, then set down his glass and thumbed the list of culinary offerings. "What embellishment was that?"

"Those country estate commissions." Amanda bit her lip.

Julian shook his head. "No embellishment. I was serious. I'd love some new artwork of the old place. Would you be willing to pay a visit and look round? You'd be well compensated for your work, of course."

Amanda fidgeted at the charming glint in his eye again. Asbury was smooth, but single. For an early forties member of the landed gentry with an Aston Martin, that set alarm bells ringing. But she couldn't afford to refuse an offer of well-paid work, such a short distance from home. "Okay, if you're sure?"

"I am." Julian's mobile phone rang beneath his blazer. He lifted it out to read the incoming caller's name. "It's the garage. I'd better take this in case there's important news about your motor." He answered the call and listened. "Okay. Good work, Brian. Yes, if you can drop it off at Ravensbrook, that will be splendid." He listened again. "I'll let her know. Bill me for parts and labour - the whole deal. Thanks, goodbye."

Amanda wrinkled her nose. "How bad?"

"The front offside wheel, tyre and shocks need replacing. He's also going to sort out some under body welding on that side. Your car will fail the next MOT without it."

"That's good of him. Any idea how long?"

"It should be with you at the end of the week. Will that be a problem? Do you have other engagements?"

Amanda shook her head. "No, it's fine. I don't need to drive anywhere. Oakdene's shop is well stocked for essentials. If you like, I'll visit your home for a recce with my camera."

Julian banged the table with a flat palm, causing Amanda to jump. "Outstanding. You see: a tough start to the day ended better than expected."

Amanda shrugged. "Yeah, I guess it did."

* * *

Added to over the years with grand extensions from humble beginnings, the 17th century manor house of High Stanton would be any film director's dream setting for a costume drama. Leaded light windows across three floors, set in stone mullions amidst ornamental masonry, were interrupted partway along with a breathtaking, triple-storey example of the same. This twelve panelled, sixteen foot glass and stone monstrosity started at average head height above the ground and allowed copious sunlight into the estate's great hall. Topiary hedges lined a sweeping path to the central oak and iron studded front door. Amanda didn't like to guess how much that sturdy portal weighed, nor how long it had served its purpose, but the feature looked original. It reminded her of the smaller - if equally sturdy - door at Ravensbrook, and dated from the same period. She halted on the path, wondering whether to backtrack and begin snapping off pictures. *No, that's rude. I'm sure Julian wouldn't mind, but I'll not forget my manners.* She pulled a stiff bell cord beside the impressive door. Far away, a faint jangle sounded inside. It took an age for a reverberating clip of footsteps to draw near. Amanda didn't care. It gave her time to recover after a steep climb from the village. High Stanton sat in a recessed position on a clear patch of the hill's summit above Oakdene. The estate lay far back enough to neither see nor be seen from the village below, and was bordered with ornamental trees blending into the hillside woods. This visit on foot had been a trek, with the added energetic cost of her puffed ascent. Amanda adjusted wayward hair and straightened her clothing.

A massive bolt slid back inside the hallway, allowing the door to swing wide on well-oiled hinges. Julian Asbury stood there, a near carbon copy of his appearance when they'd met the day before. Amanda amused herself with playful visions of his wardrobe containing twenty identical outfits hanging in a row. She wiped a secretive smile from her chops and offered a polite nod. "Good morning, Julian. Here I am as promised."

Julian beamed. "Amanda, welcome." He reached out both hands to clasp hers, setting Amanda's teeth on edge. His touch lasted a moment, so she let it go without obvious signs of discomfort. Julian joined her on the doorstep and craned his neck backwards. "What do you think of my humble abode from the outside?"

Amanda's eyes narrowed. "Fabulous. Does it have a library?"

"It does." Julian looked surprised. "Is that significant?"

"Not to my painting. But, you might want to look up the word '*humble*' in one of its dictionaries."

Julian roared. "I can see we'll get along fine. Let me take you on a whirlwind tour. Or would you like tea first? That's quite a hike up from Oakdene."

"Even further from Ravensbrook. I'll manage a quick gander. Then some tea before I get down to serious photography. I don't paint interiors, if that's what you're looking for?"

"Not at all." Julian ushered her into an expansive stone hallway with high ceiling. "Your portfolio suggested an intimate connection to the subjects you paint. I thought if you got a feel for the manor inside, it might help you capture its spirit while painting the exterior."

Amanda pivoted to face him. "That's a reasonable assumption. You've thought about this."

"Thank you. I'm not a complete novice when it comes to the artistic mind, even though I'm a duffer with a pencil or brush."

This uncharacteristic flash of modesty caught Amanda off-guard. Julian demonstrated an ability to flatter and make people feel the centre of attention whenever he wanted. Amanda doubted this was ever a selfless gesture. But the fact remained he was now a client. She noticed an oil portrait of a man in an old

English Cavalier outfit, standing proud with High Stanton in the distance. Confidence and superiority dripped like liquid emotional pigment from his waxed moustache, as though the painting weren't dry, despite its age.

Julian sidled up to her, admiring the portrait. "My most prestigious forebear, Oliver Asbury. He built High Stanton."

"It's an achievement." Amanda scanned the echoing hallway. "Even today it would be an achievement, with modern equipment and building methods. How long ago was this?"

"Over three and a half centuries. He's also responsible for founding Oakdene, after The Black Death almost wiped out its predecessor. Did you know there was an abandoned, older village in the valley?"

Amanda gave a gentle nod. "My niece mentioned it. Underwood?"

"That's right." Julian folded his arms. "Its etymology arose from the settlement's position at the foot of a wooded hill. These days the term is a joke. What little remains, lies beneath woodland. Thus: 'Under-wood,' you see?"

"I was already there before the explanation, thanks." Amanda rolled her eyes.

"Of course. I'm sorry."

"What happened?" Amanda asked. "You mentioned The Black Death?"

"The Great Plague of 1665 reached into many English shires. In a strange twist of fate, the capital enjoyed some relief when The Great Fire of London killed off rats infested with fleas carrying the disease, the following year. In a close-knit community like Underwood, the tiny populace stood little chance." Julian took a breath, eyes misting at the portrait. "Dear Oliver took pity on the area and its few survivors. He purchased land for Oakdene and gifted it as a freehold to any residents who settled there. The decent chap even paid for a new church - All Saints - so villagers would have somewhere to worship."

"You must be proud," Amanda said.

Julian's cheeks rouged a fraction. "I don't claim any saintly genetic association, but it swells the chest to think of my ancestor using his fortune in such a benevolent fashion. *'Noblesse oblige,'* as the French say."

"Nobility obliges," Amanda followed with the English translation. "The social responsibility of wealth, status and entitlement."

"That very same," Julian muttered. "A cynical historian once argued with me that Oliver required a nearby populace to staff his estate. That's nonsense. We have tied cottages and accommodation aplenty in the home and wider grounds. I run with lesser personnel these days, but those who remain still live close by."

"So Underwood went back to nature?" Amanda asked.

"With a little help. Oliver had difficulty attracting sufficient residents to Oakdene, after the original group settled. Its worrying proximity to a visible site of tragedy, I suppose. People can be quite superstitious. More so back then."

"Small wonder after what happened," Amanda interjected.

"True. To make the fledgling settlement viable, it required trades and fresh blood. So Oliver bought the old village and its surrounding land, tore down most of Underwood's structures, and then planted the area as an extension to the hillside woods already owned by his estate. Saplings turned into trees and Underwood faded into the landscape; or so the tradition goes. Everything I've told you was orally handed down through my family line. Whatever the specifics, Underwood vanished."

"Out of sight, out of mind?"

Julian stuffed hands deep into his trouser pockets, jangling keys and loose change. "I imagine that was his thinking. Who can say? But, we've dwelt on Oliver long enough. Let's look around. We'll begin with that library." He started walking. "You'll be pleased to learn it contains a fine selection of dictionaries." He cast a mischievous glance backward as Amanda followed. "Even if their present owner is less familiar with the contents than you'd like."

Julian winked, and Amanda shook her head, trying not to smirk.

Amanda felt as though she were receiving an exclusive, personal tour of some National Trust or English Heritage property. High Stanton didn't disappoint. The cost of maintaining and running the estate must have been eye-watering. She wondered what Julian did for income, or if the family vaults were packed with gold, silver and other treasures belonging to the Asburys for generations. Such an impertinent question wasn't on the cards, so she allowed the old property's atmosphere to invade her soul. This act of surrender carried with it no small amount of discomfort. At various points, hairs rose on the back of her neck. An overwhelming and all-pervasive aura of sorrow and anguish followed her from room to room, making Amanda glad when Julian suggested tea on the veranda.

After a stop for refreshments, she called a polite halt to Julian's ramblings about the extensive home and his declared vision for *'a vibrant Torridge Valley, meeting human expectations of the 21st century'* - whatever that meant.

Alone at last, Amanda moved about the grounds, filling a memory card on her digital SLR with scene after scene of exquisite imagery. The real difficulty she faced wasn't doing the place justice in paint, but choosing which views to cherry pick as the finest.

Mid-afternoon saw Amanda slip between those ornamental trees on the estate's periphery and commence a descent through thick woodland. She'd left her departure too late and was anxious to beat Belle home from school. A direct plunge south downhill, rather than following the driveway and lane back to Oakdene, offered a suitable choice.

Birdsong faded to a dead calm as she fought against momentum induced by the gradient. Her frantic feet reached a staggering halt on level ground near the foot of the hill. Above and to her left, ivy-clad stonework of an old tower poked above the treetops. *Good heavens, that must be the old church at Underwood.* She checked the clock on her phone. *I'm making good time. I can take a picture or two. Such a view will form a romantic composition in sunlight like today. It's a perfect fusion of nature and the artificial. Lovely.* She pushed through snagging bracken and reached a spot where afternoon rays dappled the stonework and its clinging greenery to perfection. She lifted the camera's eyepiece to her face and rotated the lens zoom.

"What the...? Belle?" A familiar white blouse and mop of tangled blonde hair darted into the abandoned house of worship. Amanda swept her reticle across to the old church door and zoomed further. "No."

Belinda stood facing her in the crumbling entrance, a cruel open slit across her throat. Blood pumped between parted flaps of skin, drenching her clothes in a sea of crimson. She choked on a fountain of vital fluid rising from her lips like a sanguine spring or some arterial artesian well.

Aghast, Amanda lowered the camera to find the doorway empty. She crashed through the undergrowth in a panic, stumbling against wonky tombstones slick with moss. Inside, the open-roofed church lay silent and devoid of any visible soul. Her breath came in short, grating rasps. Disordered thoughts tumbled over one another the way she'd tumbled over the graves. *No wonder Belle found this place creepy.* She strode for the doorway and headed south as fast as numb legs would carry her.

Breaking through the woodland barrier into the top end of the daisy filled meadow brought precious relief. Ravensbrook brooded in the distance, while a flash of white on its approaching lane to her left caught Amanda's eye. "Belle," she called at the child wandering home from school in a world of her own.

Belinda looked up and waved.

"Thank God," Amanda panted under her breath. She surged across the meadow, running to hug a confused Belinda with trembling arms.

* * *

Amanda worked with loving strokes on an acrylic composition of High Stanton's primary elevation. A shot of the main exterior proved the obvious choice for her first painting. Julian Asbury was eager for multiple pictures, but she'd wade through the copious volumes of secondary images at a later date. If this initial piece met his expectations and the cheque cleared, she looked forward to seeing how far his enthusiasm (and wallet) would reach. Already the stately home burst forth from the picture's background in breathtaking splendour. Amanda admired her progress so far. *I've got to hand it to that toff: his home makes an incredible subject.*

A rattling diesel engine clattered to a halt outside, followed by a quieter motor. Seconds later, someone hammered on the front door. Amanda put down her brush and hastened to the staircase.

"Car's all done for you," A thirty-something male mechanic in dark overalls bearing the name tag '*Andy,*' dangled the Toyota's keys before Amanda's nose after she opened her door. Behind him, the blue Avensis gleamed like a new pin. A red and white tow truck emblazoned with the logo '*Oakdene Motors*' sat alongside; a mid-twenties colleague of the mechanic waiting at the wheel.

Amanda stepped outdoors and performed a circuit of her car. "Did you wash it too?" she gawped.

Andy grinned. "All part of the service."

Amanda crouched and inspected the previously damaged wheel. "It looks good as new."

"It is new," Andy replied. "New wheel, shocks and tyres. Our boss insisted on tackling random welding on the underside, too. He's a stickler for doing a proper job on anything that needs fixing."

Amanda straightened. "An attitude that'll win my custom in the future. Speaking of which, I understand the invoice is being taken care of?"

"Already done." Andy moved towards the tow truck's passenger door. "Mr Asbury paid this morning. You have a good day now."

"You too." Amanda coughed at a cloud of diesel from the truck's exhaust. She watched the vehicle reverse in a semi-circle, then rumble towards the village.

Belinda appeared on the doorstep behind her, clutching a book. "Your car is back."

"And it looks better than ever." Amanda studied her. "What are you reading?"

"The Wind in the Willows." Belinda held up an E. H. Shepard illustrated hardback copy of Kenneth Grahame's classic story.

Amanda inclined her head towards her car. "I won't jump in my motor and roar off up the lane like Mr Toad." She fought back a wicked grin. "Though the gentleman who paid for this seems a near perfect human version of him."

Belinda bobbed at the thought of Toad's motoring antics. "Poop Poop."

As if on cue, the Oakdene Motors tow truck reached the end of their meadow and honked its horn twice.

Amanda and Belinda laughed in unison.

"Would you like to see my latest painting, Belle?" Amanda followed her niece inside.

"Is it of that big house you visited?"

"Yes. Have you ever been to High Stanton?"

Belinda shook her head. "There was a summer party in the grounds last year, but I was sick and couldn't go. I've never seen it."

Amanda started up the stairs with her. "I've plenty of photos and an acrylic picture well on the way. Come on, I'll show you."

They reached the landing and entered the studio.

Amanda made a big flourish with her hands. "And here it…" She never finished the sentence, mouth agape at the picture.

Belinda reached her side. In the open outline of the main doorway - yet to be filled with a wash of colour and feature details - stood a clear (if hurried) portrayal of a man dressed as an English cavalier. Even at such a diminutive scale, his mouth stretched wide in pain and horror, reflected in flat eyes. Belinda reached one hand up to touch her forehead, voice a trance-like hush. "Oliver Asbury."

Amanda almost bit her own tongue in half. The child was right. "How do you know that?"

Belinda fidgeted. "I must have seen a picture somewhere."

That suggestion wasn't beyond the realm of possibility. However, Amanda detected signs of withheld truths sweeping the girl's body language as they had so many times before. Amanda gripped both her shoulders, fixing Belinda with a firm but desperate stare. "I didn't paint that man in my picture, Belle."

Belinda's lips quivered, desperate to protest her innocence over what felt like an accusation. "I didn't do it. I can't even paint."

Amanda gulped. "I know, honey. How do you think it got there?"

Belinda's eyes looked anywhere but into those of her anxious aunt.

Amanda tried again. "You know more than you're telling me, don't you? Please, Belle. I'm worried and I want to understand what's going on."

Belinda looked down, tone sheepish. "Jonathan might have done it."

"Who's Jonathan?"

"The young man who used to live in the house."

"Used to live in the house? I thought it was derelict when your mum and dad bought it. Does he have a key? Is he a squatter?" Amanda gave her a gentle shake. "Belle, if you're hiding a homeless guy here, I won't be cross, okay? But I need to know."

Belinda ground one foot into the sanded floorboards. "I only met him the night before Mummy and Daddy died."

Amanda's brow creased. "Was he here when the wall collapsed?"

Belinda shrugged. "I hear him sometimes. When the police came to see me at school, he told me Mummy and Daddy were dead before Mrs Masters fetched me from class."

"Jonathan is a boy at your school?"

"No. Jonathan is grown up. Sometimes he comes to me when I'm feeling all alone. Nobody else can see him."

A dawning realisation soothed Amanda's troubled brow. "Ah. He's an imaginary friend. I see."

Belinda stamped her foot and shouted. "He's not imaginary. Why won't anyone believe a word I tell them?"

Amanda jerked back, releasing Belinda's shoulders. "Hey, it's okay. I had an imaginary unicorn when I was your age."

Belinda's eyes darkened, and she thrust a sharp finger towards the tabletop easel. "Did it paint pictures too?" She stormed out of the room and slammed the door behind her.

Amanda stood in breathless silence, unable to take her eyes off the anguished figure darkening High Stanton's empty doorway.

6
Fuel to the Fire

A blank expression and bulbous brown eyes beneath permanently raised, bushy black eyebrows gave Sam Peebles a look of constant anxiety. A tiny, tight mouth set in his pudgy round face added a vacant sense to the thirty-one-year-old's visage. Odd job man and grounds keeper at High Stanton, Sam could be relied upon to do whatever he was told without asking questions. The more sarcastic wit attributed this to him lacking sufficient intelligence. Any who dared vocalise such views tasted the stocky fellow's fiercest knuckle sandwich. Simple though not innocent, Sam wasn't an influential thinker, nor yet a calculating rogue. He considered himself the 'hands' of greater and more important men. Julian Asbury employed Sam because he was cheap and desperate for work. His old grounds keeper and odd job man had passed away. Producing results sometimes sloppy and lacklustre in quality, Sam always got tasks done in reasonable time. Each day he left for work, visited the pub, and then retired to his tied cottage on the High Stanton estate. A nagging voice inside urged Sam to be more than he was. If the ponderous fellow ever listened, he either paid it no heed or lacked the drive or direction to affect significant change.

Sam loaded a chainsaw and safety mask into the rear of a bronze Ford Ranger pickup that went with the job. He laid them beside a wheelbarrow resting on its side.

Julian Asbury's Aston Martin rolled to a halt outside the weathered cottage Sam called home. Its electric driver's window slid down and the driver stuck his head out. "Morning, Sam."

Sam brushed dirt from his hands. "Morning, Mr Asbury. What can I do for you?"

"Are you off tree felling?"

"Yes, Sir. There's a suitable patch of ash down below. I'll saw one up and bring it back to season in the firewood store."

Julian nodded. "Good man. Listen, when you're done there's a ragged patch of box hedge near the great hall window. Tidy it up, would you?"

"Yes, Sir," Sam replied with less enthusiasm than before, knowing how weary he'd feel after the day's forest operations were completed.

Julian raised his window again and lurched off down the main drive towards High Stanton's entrance pillars.

Sam drove up to a large, softwood five-bar gate on an inclined, no-through road west of Oakdene. Its tarmac surface ended in a rough turning circle. He reversed the truck before hopping out to release a padlock, giving access to a woodland track beyond. As he climbed back into the cab, his thoughts turned to the village. *I could murder a pint at The Royalist about now.* He licked his lips. *Save it for later, Sam. You've a full day of work ahead.* He crunched the gears and eased the Ford as far into the woodlands as the track allowed. *Good job I brought a barrow. Carrying individual lumps of wood from that stand of ash could be a pain in the arse.* He switched off the engine and slipped out beneath a green canopy swayed by a whisper of fresh air. *I hope there are no kids kicking around. Saturdays are always a gamble.* He paused beside the tailgate. *Not long and they'll be around every day, once school breaks up.* For a moment his thoughts wandered to a younger, carefree Sam and childhood days during summer holidays that seemed to last forever. He swept one palm through stiff, brush-like short hair, then unloaded the wheelbarrow and rested the chainsaw and safety mask inside it.

Two minutes along the track, Underwood's ruined church tower poked between boughs to his left. Sam ambled a hundred yards further before setting the barrow down. He checked the area for signs of juvenile mischief or discreet lovers, likely to suffer a fatal rude awakening once the tree fell. All appeared quiet, so he donned his mask and set the chainsaw on level ground. Chain brake applied with the switch on and choke opened, he primed the fuel pump and gave the starter cord several brisk tugs. The peaceful stillness of that woodland glade broke asunder; herald of one woodland sentinel's approaching fate. Sam let the engine run a spell, then closed the choke and released the chain brake. His chosen tree presented a perfect specimen with room to fall unhindered and space for disassembly work. Sam pulled the throttle and moved in for the kill, sending a cloud of sawdust whipping about like arboreal confetti. He stepped back as telltale cracks from the trunk and a splitting rasp announced an impending collapse. The ash fell with a sigh of leaves morphing into a rumble as its trunk pummelled into the soft woodland floor. Sam set to work removing branches, until his thick, sweat-slaked neck and damp collar suggested it was time for a break. He rested the chainsaw on the sawn stump, then wandered away and lifted his mask visor, blotting perspiration from his eyes with a dirty handkerchief. A welcome breeze caused him to raise his head, eyes closed, waiting for nature to wick away the salty by-product of his labours. He took a deep breath of cool air.

A twig snapped among the trees behind, close to the fallen trunk. Sam's eyes blinked open, and he turned, rubbing a crick in his neck. A meek, feminine figure watched from beside the toppled ash. Sam placed both hands on his hips. "Well now, what are you up to, then? I didn't see you there. You might have been hurt."

Playful attempts at a fatherly expression dropped away with his jaw into an impossible, open-mouthed scream of horror.

Birds fluttered from the treetops as the chainsaw

engine gunned, followed by Sam's desperate shriek ending in a sudden gurgle and silence.

Martha Hall slid down a steep section of the hill below High Stanton. Here, a footpath followed one of several new rights of way laid down by Torridge District Council to encourage recreation and tourism. She caught hold of a gnarled root, slowing her involuntary tumble, and dug a single red walking pole into loose earth on the other side. *They should have put a gradient warning on the promotional pamphlet for this trail. Note to self: e-mail the council when you get home.* Martha sat up straight and brushed twigs from a tight blonde bun in her hair. She squinted in mild discomfort from new contact lenses she was breaking in. One of her late thirties office worker pals suggested she ditch the glasses and take up walking if she ever wished to meet new people and snag a possible mate. Well-intentioned advice to cast off the unwanted bonds of spinsterhood before they imprisoned her for life. The only problem was: she didn't enjoy walking in groups and couldn't remember the last time she'd met an attractive, single man in the quiet folds of the rolling Devon landscape on her own. That and the contact lenses made her pull the most contorted faces to relieve the irritation they caused. Not the best combination for a lonely, socially challenged singleton on the lookout for love.

A resounding swish and thud rocked several treetops below her position. Martha peered through the greenery in hopes of a better view. *Tree felling. I'd best be cautious. This area is private land - despite the path - so they might dispense with warning signs.* She struggled aloft and wiggled both shoulders, correcting her shifted backpack, then set off with great care to avoid another fall. A chainsaw roared in a series of short bursts. *They must be stripping branches.* Martha stopped and removed a water bottle from her belt, uncapped it and took a thirst-quenching mouthful. The sawing ceased, replaced by a faint, resonant burble of the power tool on tick-over. Martha secured her bottle and moved further down the steep, winding trail. *It looks to be levelling out further on. Thank goodness for that. I... Wha-?*

Her thought process stalled at a sudden revving from the chainsaw engine, followed by a terrifying male shriek and choking rasp. Martha remained fixed to the spot. *What's happened? Has someone been hurt? What if they require medical attention?* She spurred herself into action, crashing in a straight line through heavy undergrowth towards the source of the disturbance. She almost fell headlong over the fallen ash tree, then lost her footing on one of the free-rolling branches beside it. Martha's walking boots slid out from beneath her. She found herself horizontal on the ground, staring straight up through a neighbouring tree's crown at a lazy blue sky. A heady metallic aroma mixed with petrol fumes acted like smelling salts upon her dazed brain. She lifted her head off the spongy ground and reached a sitting position, in what was starting to feel like a habit.

Ahead, tree trunks dripped with splattered gore,

running in viscous rivulets to irrigate their roots. Gobs of mangled viscera adorned the motionless torso of a portly man a few years younger than herself. He lay staring up at the cloudless firmament, sporting a raised safety mask visor, mouth wide. A broader, savage tear, like a second, evil grinning mouth, opened at his throat. The now-stalled chainsaw rested on its side nearby, blade soaked in a dark wash of blood that pooled beneath its motor. Most shocking of all, a young girl in a summer blouse and skirt stood before him, staring like a statue at his lifeless corpse. Red highlights that must have sprayed from the deceased man's opened throat tinted her unkempt blonde locks. The pretty but simple clothing she wore had received a thorough dousing of human dye, like a fur-wearing debutante splattered with red paint by some animal rights activist. As if the sickening weirdness of that image didn't prove haunting enough, the entire scene played out against the peaceful backdrop of an overgrown, ruined church tower a short distance beyond.

Martha fought an urge to pass out from shock and the overpowering, pungent aroma of carnage. She scrabbled up and stumbled over to the catatonic child. "Are you hurt, young lady?" Martha pawed at the girl's limbs. "Can you speak? What happened? What's your name?"

A single muttered syllable escaped her frozen mouth. "Belle."

Martha retrieved a mobile phone from her jacket pocket and dialled 999.

"Which service please?" the emergency operator asked.

Martha forced herself to look at that pathetic figure sprawled across the ground with his throat ripped open. Her first instinct was to ask for an ambulance. *Too late for that. This guy needs a mop and bucket.* Martha chastised her own mental callousness; a sudden defence against near overwhelming urges to flee or faint. Now it remained for someone to uncover what had transpired during those fateful minutes of her hill descent. A fresh stench of urine and excrement from the dead man's voided bowels and bladder wrinkled her nose. She spluttered into the phone. "Police."

Amanda Fairchild stepped out of the village shop at Oakdene, wicker basket dangling from her right forearm. Under normal circumstances it would be difficult to feel depressed or troubled on such a glorious day amidst the splendour of the Torridge Valley. However, recent circumstances had proved anything but normal. Try as she might, Amanda couldn't find a reasonable explanation to hang her hat on regarding the interference with her artwork. When rationality failed and all logic avenues reached dead ends, where did you turn next? There was no simple solution, and she still struggled to blot out the scene of Belinda standing in that ruined church doorway with her throat cut. *Did I dream it? Are there magic mushrooms or something in that clearing that cause hallucinations?* A police car tore past, lights and siren going great guns.

She looked up as a door opened on a tiny thatched cottage bearing the carved wooden sign: *'Cosicott.'*

Craig Symonds stepped outside and shut it behind him.

"A late start for gardeners on a Saturday morning, wouldn't you say?" Amanda's teasing voice belied her inner turmoil.

"Who said I was working?" Craig shielded his eyes and glanced across the road.

Amanda smirked at his threadbare shirt and dirty, torn trousers. "If that's your social, going-out finest, remind me not to be seen at a public event with you."

Craig chuckled. "Okay, you've got me. I've a spot of weeding to do for someone I missed yesterday."

Amanda crossed after another passing police car. She admired the exterior of his quaint home. "I haven't forgotten your painting, by the way. It turns out I've a photo of Cosicott taken the day we met."

Craig folded his arms. "You mean the day that handsome bloke popped up behind a wall in your shot, further down the lane?"

Amanda chewed a pretend cud. "I don't know about that, but you're in it."

Craig snorted. "Nice." He set off south through the village.

Amanda punched his arm. "Sourpuss."

"How's life at Ravensbrook? Is Belle riding on a more even keel yet?"

Amanda's jovial manner evaporated, and she lagged behind.

Craig stopped. "What's wrong?"

Amanda flinched. "I wish I had a way to explain it. Craig, I'm at a loss."

Craig licked his lips, then wrinkled his nose. "I find successful explanations comprise two important components: words and the truth. Which of those are you struggling with?"

Amanda clamped her spare arm atop the one holding the basket. "Both. The truth, or what it is. How to compose thoughts into words that make sense to anyone. I include myself in that."

Another emergency siren wailed in the distance, north of the village.

Craig pulled Amanda out of the lane as a third police car tore past and hung a sharp right at The Old Bothy. "Something must have happened in the woods."

Amanda drew a sharp breath. "That place is weird. Have you ever been?"

"To the woods? Of course, it's right on my doorstep."

"How about Underwood?"

Craig raised an eyebrow. "You sound wilder than Peggy. Your face is a picture. Not one you'd want to paint, either."

Amanda frowned. "I do landscapes, not people." Her voice grew distant. "Never people."

Craig grabbed her arm and pulled her along.

Amanda gasped. "Where are we going?"

"To the woods."

"What?"

"Someone's probably had a fight or found something illegal. We'll see what's up with the police. Then I'm taking you for a stroll around, so you can see it's nothing but a bunch of old trees and crumbling foundations from long ago."

Amanda dragged her feet. "What about your weeding?"

"The weeds will be there when I return. Come on."

As the pair reached the ill-defined turning circle, it became apparent the incident was more serious than Craig had suggested. Two police cars occupied rough tarmac beside the gate, while a third had driven a short way along a track beyond and parked nose-on to a bronze Ford Ranger pickup. Two male officers stretched blue and white police tape between tree trunks either side of the gateposts, forming a makeshift cordon. One of them noticed Amanda and Craig approach. He stepped forward and raised his hand.

"Sorry, folks. You'll have to turn back."

"What's going on?" Craig asked.

"There's an incident in the woods. I can't say any more for now."

Amanda peered through the undergrowth without success, then heard a familiar girlish voice shout in protest. "I don't know what happened. Leave me alone. Stop grabbing me."

Craig read the fear in her eyes. "Belle?"

Amanda nodded and ran forward.

Craig intercepted the officer, who tried to grab her. "She's that girl's guardian. For God's sake man, let her pass."

The other officer drew nearer, addressing Amanda. "You're the Fairchild girl's aunt?"

"Yes. How did you know that? Is she all right? What's happened?"

"I'm PC Eric Walker. My colleague, Lucy Maitland, spoke with you on the phone after you got home from America." He glanced into the lush woodland. "There's been an accident with a chainsaw involving a local labourer. Either that or a suicide. Young Belinda must have happened upon him at the fatal moment. Her clothes are a mess, but she appears unharmed - physically, anyway."

Amanda covered her mouth. "No. Not on top of everything else."

"I'm afraid so. A hiker heard a man cry out as she was descending the hill. She found your niece staring at the deceased, drenched in his blood."

Amanda's eyes watered. "I must see her."

Eric grimaced. "You don't want to go down there."

Amanda sniffed and clasped her hands together. "Please."

Eric scrunched his face up. He stepped aside and spoke into his radio.

Two minutes later, a stern-faced female officer strolled up the track away from the scene. "Amanda Fairchild?"

Amanda recognised the force number on her badge from follow-on e-mails the pair had exchanged. "PC Maitland?"

Lucy Maitland motioned for the pair to approach.

Eric frowned. "You're not taking them down there,

Lucy?"

Lucy sighed. She addressed Amanda as Craig stomped up behind. "Is this your chap?"

Amanda fidgeted. "No. But he's someone I trust."

Lucy hesitated. "Belinda is upset. Small wonder; I almost lost my breakfast after we arrived. From the state of her clothes, she must have witnessed the suicide at close range."

"How do you know it was a suicide?" Craig asked. "Your colleague said it might have been an accident."

"That's possible. From the body's position away from a tree he'd felled, I'm leaning towards the former. When you've attended enough suicides, you realise most people use whatever they have to hand that'll get the job done, whenever life gets too much. Careful planning is rarer than many believe. That guy had stepped aside for a break and wasn't using the chainsaw to cut trees during his last moments. I'd stake my pension on it."

"Not a murder, then?" Amanda asked.

Lucy shrugged. "We can't rule that out. The chap's throat was cut, but he wasn't decapitated. That's common with accidents and suicides. The moment unconsciousness occurs after severing the carotid artery, they drop the chainsaw."

Craig studied her deadpan face. "You sound like you've encountered chainsaw suicides before." His eyes widened as she stared back, unblinking. He coughed. "Oh, you have."

Lucy's face softened. She squinted at sunlight streaming through the swaying greenery. "Belinda must know what happened; but it's locked away inside. She's suffering from shock. That sweet, unfortunate girl won't talk, nor budge from her spot at the scene where a hiker found her. She becomes agitated the moment we try to move her. There's a doctor on the way. If you're willing, I wonder if she wouldn't respond better to seeing you first?"

"Thank you," Amanda replied.

Lucy set her jaw. "Don't thank me yet. Not until you've witnessed that grisly scene. I hope you've both got strong stomachs." She set off down the track with Amanda and Craig close behind.

* * *

Amanda tucked a silent, pale-faced Belinda into bed at Ravensbrook. When she and Craig reached her near the church at Underwood, Belinda's eyes flitted around the trees, then fixed back on the dead labourer. It took a minute for her to register their presence, whereupon she clutched tight to Amanda like a limpet. By the time a doctor arrived on site, Amanda had shepherded her niece several paces distant to sit on the ash stump. After a check-up and some questions, the doctor advised she be taken into hospital for examination and temporary monitoring. By nightfall, Craig and Amanda were able to bring her home in a taxi. All that time - including while speaking with a clinical psychologist - Belinda's details of the incident remained limited and prone to intermittent bouts of silence.

"It was horrible," Belinda clutched her bedclothes, repeating a phrase she'd used multiple times at the Royal Devon and Exeter.

Amanda touched her. "You mustn't be afraid of that man who died, Belle. Sometimes people grow sad and lose the will to live. It was an awful thing to see, but he's in a better place. The dead can't hurt you."

Belinda stared right through her. "Are you sure?"

"Of course I'm sure. Settle yourself down."

Belinda pressed her head back into the pillow, voice trembling in a nervous whisper. "They did it."

Amanda's stomach muscles clenched. Was she about to receive a nugget of vital information or testimonial evidence leading to a court case? "Who did it, Belle?"

Belinda swallowed hard. "The villagers."

Amanda's complexion turned ashen. "Someone from Oakdene killed that man?"

Belinda shook her head, pulled the covers over it, and remained still.

Amanda sat there a moment longer. Did Belinda's statement represent a revelation or the fanciful product of shock and trauma? Either way, attempts at extracting further information tonight would prove a lost cause. She got up, walked to the door, and clicked off the light. "Sweet dreams." Her statement felt callous, however well-intentioned. What normal human being - even an adult, hardened by a life of hard knocks - could escape nightmares so soon after witnessing such a horrific death? Belinda was an innocent child.

Down at the dining table, Craig stirred a mug of hot chocolate. He looked up when Amanda trudged into the room. "I fixed myself another. Hope you don't mind?"

Amanda plonked herself on a chair opposite. "It's the least you've earned after today. Thanks, Craig."

Craig hunched over. "Will you tell me what else has been going on? You've not been yourself since we bumped into each other this morning."

"I haven't, have I?" Amanda rubbed her eyes. "Where to begin?"

"Why don't you just make a start, then fill in any blanks as you go? I'm a smart bloke; I'll make sense of it."

Amanda snorted. "Then you're better than me, because I haven't a clue." She sighed. "Okay, here goes. Before her mum and dad died, Belle claims she saw a vision of disease-infested dead people while playing at Underwood. She says others were hanging from the roofs of their houses."

"Underwood was all but lost on account of The Black Death. She might have learnt that at school."

"Not the details she relayed to me. And what about those hangings?"

Craig lifted his mug of chocolate. "Suicide from despair?"

"I thought that too. Belle said one of the dangling victims opened his eyes and hissed 'vengeance' at her."

"Sounds like a violent daydream to me. How did you get onto that subject with her?"

"She had a nightmare about it. Not long afterwards, we took a Sunday picnic near that old stone bridge over the Torridge. Belle was convinced she saw a girl her own age in the water."

"Another vision?"

Amanda puffed. "I don't know. The next week events took a sharp turn towards the inexplicable."

"How so?"

"Do you remember that evening you helped me rebuild and re-point the wall?"

"Of course. I gave it another pat earlier; it's solid as a rock. That was the night Belle ran off happy then came home a changed girl."

"Yeah. Well, earlier I'd painted an acrylic from a photo I took at the bridge. After you left, I dosed off. Later, I awoke to a noise upstairs in my studio and discovered someone had painted a girl into the picture. A girl under the water."

"What?" Craig almost spilled his drink. "Can Belle draw or paint?"

"No, and this was good; I mean *really* good. There's a technique where artists paint details with white acrylic and then apply a watercolour wash to bring them out. That appeared to be the method employed."

"Have you still got the painting?"

"Yes, but I've removed the girl." Amanda clasped her hands together.

"Didn't you take a photo first?"

"Why? Who would I show it to and for what purpose? When I dropped hints about the painting and my studio to Belle, she became evasive. Something similar happened after Julian Asbury commissioned me to paint his manor. This time his ancestor appeared in the doorway. I showed Belle, and she knew who the guy was."

"Did Belle go with you to the manor?"

"No, she's never been. She suggested a guy called Jonathan might have painted it."

Craig finished his drink and set the mug down. "Who?"

"Someone she insists used to live here."

Craig laughed. "In this old ruin? Is he a tramp?"

"I thought so at first. When she said nobody else could see or hear him and that he'd informed her Jake and Karen were dead before the police did, I figured he was an imaginary friend. That or a random personality conjured from her subconscious anxieties after their death."

"You mentioned the police thought Belle might have been here when the accident occurred. So this Jonathan became a way of telling herself what she already knew but struggled to accept? A safety net to distance herself from the pain?"

"I'm no mental health professional, but…"

Craig grunted. "That doesn't explain your painting alterations though."

"Nor the weirdness of Underwood."

"You were wigging out over that place before we rocked up at the police cordon. Did something else happen there?"

Amanda nodded. "To me, on my walk back from High Stanton. I stumbled across the ruins and fancied that old church would make a decent painting."

"I believe it would. Minus the gore splattered trees in front that we saw today, of course."

"When I set up a shot with my camera, Belle was standing in the doorway with her throat cut. The moment I looked up, she vanished. I ran inside, but the place was empty."

Craig blinked. "I've heard a few odd stories about it before now, but nothing like that. Where was Belle at the time?"

"On her way home from school. I caught up with her afterwards. She'd not been to the woods that day."

Craig sat back in his chair. "Do you know why she went there today? If I'd suffered scary dreams and visions about a place as a child, I'd be inclined to stay away."

"She said she started walking, but can't remember how she got there. When I tucked her in just now, she whispered to me that '*the villagers*' killed that man."

Craig straightened in an instant. "Which villagers? People from Oakdene?"

Amanda hesitated. "No."

Craig slackened again. "People from Underwood?"

"Who knows? After this morning, that place will always be associated with the macabre and unexplained in my mind."

"I don't blame you. We could all use serious counselling, I should think. I never liked Sam Peebles, much. That's who the body belonged to, although they'll jump through the formal identification malarkey hoops before admitting it, no doubt." Craig drummed his fingers on the table. "He could be a pain after a few pints at The Royalist, when his blood was up. But, I'd never wish something like that on him. I don't know of anyone else in the village who would, either. It's odd Belle saw people hanging that we associated with suicide; then Sam took his own life there. Maybe the atmosphere got to him?"

"And Belle's claim about the villagers?"

Craig shifted in his seat. "Could she have undergone another vision or dreamed up a story to cope with stumbling upon Sam as he cut his throat?"

"I suppose. Who was Sam Peebles? What did he do?"

"One of Julian Asbury's workers. Asbury owns those woods."

"He told me the story of how his ancestor purchased them."

Craig guffawed. "Right. That's one thing I can't stand about that toff. Whenever he meets someone from the village, there's this sense he expects them to bow and scrape in gratitude over the actions of his benevolent ancestor. Either that or I just don't like him because he's almost flattened me with that bloody sports car of his once or twice."

Amanda managed a faint smile. "That's how I met him: he ran my car off the road. He paid for the repairs and took me to Great Torrington, by way of an apology. It was an eventful week."

Craig got up. "Your life is anything but dull. I'd better head home and you should get some rest."

Amanda walked with him to the door. "Do you need

a lift?"

"Nah, it's a short walk, and you've given me a lot to mull over. I'll stick to the lane though. Some of this nonsense is too ghostly for comfort, whatever happened to Sam."

"You don't think I'm nuts or traumatised by loss?" Amanda stood beside him on the doorstep.

Craig folded his arms across his chest and eyed her with a serious expression. "No. If you're strung out, you hide it well. Sure, I've only your word to take for the painting stories and what not. All I've seen is the aftermath of Sam's supposed suicide and poor Belle drenched from head to toe in his blood. That was horrible, if not supernatural. I'd suggest all we can do is keep living everyday life. These weird goings on might wither away in time." He made to leave, then turned back. "Now you've opened up, will you tell me if anything else odd happens?"

Amanda nodded. "It'll be a relief. I've no-one else to talk to. Alone, I felt like I was losing my mind."

Craig winked. "If you dribble or mutter to yourself, I'll let you know."

Amanda scowled. "You're all heart."

Craig brushed his lips against her cheek. "Take care of that kid. She's stronger than she looks."

"I know. Night, Craig."

"Night." He set off down the drive and didn't look back.

7
Primary Purgatory

Belinda sat at her school desk during the last week of the summer term. A class of warm, playful friends had grown chillier ever since she'd first investigated Underwood with Laura, Jane and Anton. It didn't take long for word to circulate the tiny village of how she was found standing over the corpse of Sam Peebles, washed in his blood. Whether the tale got out after a careless disclosure by the hiker who found her or through some other means, didn't matter now. Laura Barnes had been instructed to stay away from her former best friend, ever since the incident in her bedroom at The Old Bothy. Jane Perkins, their joint bosom acquaintance, felt like piggy in the middle for a time. Now, with these latest horror-filled tales to fire a child's imagination, she kept close to Laura and left Belinda alone.

Mrs Myers, the class teacher, wiped a board at the front of the room. "Playtime. Get plenty of fresh air blowing through your brains, ready for our maths quiz afterwards."

A half-hearted groan mellowed into the anticipation of immediate recreation. The scuffling of feet hurried along the corridor and out into the playground.

Belinda followed her peers at a slower rate. Several girls eyed her with a frown, speaking to each other behind raised hands, then looking away.

The bellowing shouts of raucous boys filled Belinda's ears when she reached the main door. Outside, their rising chant alternated between obvious attempts at chainsaw noises (each with hand gestures pretending to cut another's throat) and a catchy - if cruel - chorus.

"Bloody Belle, Queen of Hell. Bloody Belle, Queen of Hell."

Belinda hastened toward a quiet, flower-bordered corner of the quadrangle. One girl from a lower class stumbled during a game of hopscotch. She grazed her knee on the tarmac, which left enough of a cut to spill blood. Her friends ran to her aid when she cried, and then watched Belinda pass with grim suspicion.

Across her shoulder, someone from Belinda's own year hissed, "She did it," under her breath.

Belinda wanted to help the injured girl stand. Anything to demonstrate her innocence or show she wasn't a monster. The moment her course veered back a fraction towards the hopscotch markings, a tensing of agitated limbs amongst the junior huddle made her revert to plan.

The teasing boys hurried behind, still chanting, "Bloody Belle, Queen of Hell."

Belinda reached the corner. Having no other place to

go, she whirled and stared down her tormentors. The boys hesitated, no longer so cocky or self-assured. Was the Ravensbrook Witch about to cast a spell on them? Belinda shook back an urge to cry and blurted out, "Why are you saying this? What have I done to you?"

The boys jeered. Belinda scowled at Anton Webb, huddled in their midst and swept up in the unpleasant game like a raft caught in white water.

Helen Masters burst out of the front doors with her assistant, Kelly Poole, in tow. She waved towards the crying girl, still nursing her bloodied knee. "Take Michelle inside and patch that up with some cream and a plaster, Kelly."

"Yes, Mrs Masters." Kelly obliged, soothing Michelle's tears with her matronly manner, familiar to every young student at Oakdene Primary.

Helen's onward beeline towards Belinda hushed the spiteful male bullies in an instant. She drew up to her full, intimidating height and let loose. "What on earth do you boys think you're doing?" She allowed the words to hang midair for a second. "I heard you through my office window. Your language was bad enough, but did you not consider for one moment the cruelty you were inflicting on Belinda?"

The boys lingered, red-faced with hunched postures. Several young observers who'd stood by without participating melted away.

Helen went on. "Can you imagine what it would be like to set off for school one morning, then be told later that both your parents were dead?"

Silence reigned in the formerly noisy playground.

Helen pushed through the boys and pivoted, one hand resting on Belinda's right shoulder. "What if you also took a walk in the woods and stumbled upon the terrifying scene of a man taking his own life? Then afterwards, when you returned to school the following week, your classmates called you names as if everything was your fault. How much would that hurt?"

One lad piped up in an indignant, self-righteous tone. "Belle is a witch. She attacked Laura and her mum by making things fly."

"Don't be absurd, Kieran," Helen chided.

"But it's true," Kieran protested. "Ask Laura. She's not allowed to be friends with Belle anymore because of it."

"That's quite enough. I'll not endure another word." Helen fixed Kieran with a gorgon-like glare. "Each of you will wait in the corridor outside my office until called. One at a time I want you to come inside, where you will apologise to Belinda under my supervision. Is that clear?"

Silence.

Helen spoke louder, with an authority that brooked no refusal. "I can't hear you."

"Yes, Mrs Masters." The jumbled response rippled from each reluctant mouth.

"If I catch anyone taunting Belinda again, there will be serious trouble." Helen tapped her foot. "Well, what are you waiting for? The corridor outside my office, now!"

Those condemned transgressors shuffled back

inside, followed a minute later by Helen and Belinda.

Call it luck of the draw or some unfathomable universal design, but Belinda found the last bully to apologise was none other than Anton Webb. He'd learnt a valuable lesson about the price of peer pressure today, yet struggled to make eye contact with her while mumbling hurried regrets.

Helen Masters looked to Belinda, sitting beside her on one of the office chairs. "Do you accept his apology?"

Belinda gave a silent nod.

"Very well." Helen stood. "Anton, you may accompany Belinda back to class. In the future, if you've nothing nice to say to a classmate you used to play with, I suggest you leave them in peace. But I'd rather you offered her friendship and support, even if she isn't the bubbly companion you're used to. Try understanding why that is and be kind." Helen drew breath. "You may go."

Anton opened the door and let Belinda leave first, before closing it behind them.

Out in the corridor, the pair walked side by side towards their classroom.

Belinda stopped halfway. "Anton, I realise you're not speaking to me these days, but I need to know if you still have that cross?"

Anton regarded her with a sulk initiated by the humiliation of discipline. "Why?"

"You should put it back."

"Not that again, Belle. Finders keepers; it's mine. I'm keeping the cross safe until I'm old enough to sell it. I'll be a rich treasure hunter and won't have to work like my mother or stepfather."

Belinda's eyes darkened. "It's not yours; it belongs in the church at Underwood. Anton, you must return it. I've kept quiet about your find until now, because I didn't want any of us getting into trouble."

Anton folded his arms. "Who are you going to tell? Would anyone care?" He shuddered. "Besides, I'm not going back to Underwood unless someone makes me. Not after what happened to you with that dead man."

Belinda presented the uncertain appearance of one who wanted to reveal more, but held her tongue. If this onetime friend - albeit casual - could go along with playground insults, how would he use what little else she understood about this predicament to her further detriment?

Anton left her standing. "I'm going back to class. Are you coming?"

Belinda waited a moment longer, and then followed with heavy, dragging steps.

* * *

Explaining the unbelievable details of recent events to Craig had lightened Amanda's burden a fraction. After Belinda left for school midway through her last week before summer, Amanda busied herself with basic household chores. Mind free to roam, she continued her mental quest for logical explanations, however impossible they proved to grasp and hold on to. The floorboards above her head creaked while she pressed bed linen in the kitchen. Amanda set the iron down and listened, a peach pillowcase hanging limp between lithe fingers. No further noises disturbed the ensuing silence. *This house is full of creaks and groans. It's old and only semi-renovated; what do I expect?* She began work again, before her eyes lit up at a bright idea. *What if Belle was hiding a homeless guy in the attic?* She let the pillowcase drop back onto the board. *Don't be daft, Amanda. Jake and Karen would have noticed that. She's only nine. Oh God, I wish there was another option regarding those mysterious people in my paintings. Anything other than ghosts or my own unconscious madness.*

The hall telephone warbled to life. Amanda hurried to answer it. "Hello?"

"Ms Fairchild? It's Helen Masters, Belinda's head teacher."

Amanda drew a sharp breath. *What can have happened now?* "Is everything okay?"

Helen made an uncomfortable grunt in her throat. "There's nothing to worry about. Would you be willing to collect Belinda at the end of school today?"

"Sure, I can do that. Is she unwell?"

"Some boys were mean to her in the playground. I caught them chanting, *'Bloody Belle, Queen of Hell,'* if you can believe it."

Amanda almost spat. She clenched her teeth and gripped the receiver so hard her knuckles whitened. "What did she do?"

"To initiate such an outburst, or do you mean in

response?"

Amanda snorted. "Either."

"To initiate it: nothing I'm aware of. It pains me the story of Saturday's events spread through Oakdene like wildfire. I appreciate you detailing particulars of the incident in that private note you sent in with Belinda, as a precaution."

"I wrote to you in case she suffered an episode of distress at school. Mental pictures or memories setting off a meltdown. I didn't expect her peers to cause it."

"Yes, I realise that," Helen replied. "I'm sorry. When I noticed what was taking place, I hurried into the playground and tore the lads off a strip. Their lack of empathy and compassion pains me. A by-product of the modern, selfish 'me culture' we live in, I suppose. But, I'll not have it run rampant through my school."

"Thank you, Mrs Masters."

"Each boy apologised to Belinda in my office. She's in class now. But, having someone escort her home later might be advisable. I can't imagine what she's going through."

Amanda sighed. "And at her age. Who of us can?"

Helen hesitated before speaking again. "Are you aware of difficulties between Belinda and the Barnes girl, Laura?"

"Yes. I've asked Belle what happened, but - like so much else - she keeps it bottled up inside. All I know is they don't play together anymore. Such a shame. The Barnes family were wonderful after my brother and his wife died. I offered to speak with Rachel Barnes, but Belle begged me not to, so I've let it go. Rachel avoids me in the village now. Don't ask me why."

"That's curious. I'd noticed they're no longer close. Ah well, school breaks up on Friday. Eight weeks of holiday is a long time in childhood friendships. Laura and Belinda may reinstate their relationship before returning in September. Time away will offer Belinda space."

Amanda leaned against the wall. "That's what I was hoping. Sometimes *in*action is the best course of action. I realise that's a paradox."

Helen chuckled. "You should have been a teacher."

Amanda smirked. "I doubt I'd have enough patience. Thanks for calling, Mrs Masters. I'll be waiting for Amanda at the gates after school."

"Splendid. Have a good day." She hung up.

Amanda finished her ironing, then placed the clean linens in an upstairs cupboard. Floorboards in the attic above her creaked this time. *I haven't investigated up there yet.* She gulped. *Get a grip, Fairchild, it's an attic. The quicker you dispel supernatural notions, the happier you'll be.* She retrieved a heavy duty torch from the kitchen cupboard below, then made her way back upstairs to a smaller, dirty plain wooden staircase in a rear corner of the building close to her studio. Dusty and filled with more cobwebs than usual, the expansive top floor storage area lacked any kind of natural illumination or electric lighting. Amanda swept her broad torch beam across old boxes of assorted junk, then lifted flaps to peer inside. Some items she recognised as knick knacks from Jake's childhood he couldn't bear to part with. Others must have belonged to Karen. Amanda secured them again, then pushed through the keepsake containers towards the chimney stack. Loose mortar lay in piles about it on the grimy floorboards. *Crap. Is Craig up for another brickwork job? If that chimney comes down, it could finish us while we're sitting downstairs or walking outside the building. I can't take the risk of it disintegrating further from a winter of open fires.* A lack of spectral encounters or weird chills in the dark, atmospheric space boosted Amanda's confidence a fraction. She retreated downstairs and stowed the torch back in the kitchen before checking the clock. *I'd better hustle if I'm going to reach the school before kicking out time.* She yanked open the sturdy front door, closed it with a bang and hurried up the drive towards Oakdene.

Amanda got within a hundred yards of the school, in time to see Belinda run across the lane into the heart of the village. Yelling schoolchildren - all concerned with their own affairs - bustled behind, oblivious to her flight.

"What now?" Amanda spoke under her breath while giving chase.

Belinda darted beyond the square and disappeared through the church gates at All Saints.

She must be seeking solace with Jake and Karen. Amanda slowed to allow the child time. When she reached the graves of her brother and her sister-in-law, she found them unaccompanied. *Where can she have gone?* Amanda continued along one side of the church, with its wraparound graveyard. Twenty yards from a thick-trunked yew tree around the corner, she found Belinda sitting cross-legged on the lush sward, head bent forward over her lap.

"Hey," Amanda spoke with a timbre of soothing balm to underscore her words. "I thought you were visiting your mum and dad. Mrs Masters phoned me about what happened during playtime."

Belinda looked up. "Mummy and Daddy aren't here."

Amanda blinked. "Why sure they are, sweetheart. They're right around the corner."

"That's their bodies. Cold and empty. They've gone."

Amanda sighed as she drew nearer. "That's true." She touched her own heart. "But we'll always keep both in here, where no-one can ever take them away. They'll listen whenever we've troubles to unburden."

Belinda remained still.

Amanda crouched before her. "Were you seeking a quiet place away from your classmates?"

Belinda pursed her lips. "I came to sit with Jonathan, before going home."

"Your imag… I mean, your friend?" Amanda caught and corrected herself. "Does he visit here often?"

Belinda rubbed the tops of her legs. "His body also lies here, but he hasn't gone. Not like Mummy and Daddy."

"How do you mean?" Amanda pushed down an immediate cloud of butterflies in her stomach.

Belinda rose, revealing a low, moss stained grave

marker bearing a simple inscription:

'Jonathan Dowland, 1648 - 1667.'

Amanda's palate withered to an arid desert while she calculated the dates. "Nineteen. A young man. Do you think this is the Jonathan you've seen at Ravensbrook and who talks to you sometimes?"

"It *is* him," Belinda insisted without raising her voice. "He lived in our house, long ago."

Amanda read the dates again, casting her mind back to Julian Asbury's re-telling of local historic events. "The Jonathan buried here was alive before Oakdene existed. He must have been one of the earliest people laid to rest in this churchyard, after they abandoned Underwood and settled the new village."

Belinda watched her without a word.

Amanda straightened. "Honey, I don't want to question what you believe or destroy any comfort drawn from it. The world is full of unexplained mysteries. I came to walk you home, because I'd also like to be a source of comfort. What do you say?"

Belinda forced an uneasy smile. "I'm ready to go now."

Amanda put on a playful expression and nodded at the grave. "Is Jonathan coming too?"

Belinda glanced back. "He'll go on ahead. Jonathan appears and disappears as he wishes."

Amanda's shoulders knotted at the certainty of Belinda's reply to a question she'd intended to lighten the mood with. Together they set off back around the church.

"Good afternoon." Reverend Julie Clement, the middle-aged vicar of All Saints, stepped out of the porch as they passed.

"Hello," Amanda replied.

Belinda nodded a soundless greeting.

Julie extended a hand. "You must be Belinda's aunt?"

Amanda accepted it and shook. "That's right. Amanda Fairchild."

"Julie Clement. I'm sorry you missed the funeral. It was a rainy day, but the community gave Jake and Karen a caring and tearful send-off."

"Thank you. I wish for all the world I could turn back the clock and attend."

"Regret is a painful emotion, but you weren't to know. It took everyone by surprise."

Amanda twisted towards Jake and Karen's grave markers. "Regret is a pointless emotion too, because we can only change life's outcomes going forward, not those past."

"But it's no less real or troublesome for that realisation," Julie added. She changed the subject. "Have you visited the church before?"

Amanda thought. "No. Not inside. Silly, when you think about it."

Julie motioned to the doorway. "You're welcome to take a peek, unless you've pressing business elsewhere."

Belinda decided the matter, despite having attended for her parents' funeral. She wandered into the structure, Amanda close at heel. A simple yet elegant whitewashed interior with attractive wooden roof beams echoed the format of churches from the period across the land. Amanda's focus fell upon a roster of parish vicars painted in gold lettering on a large, dark wooden board. Sure enough, the current entry read:

'Julie Clement.'

Julie reached her side. "That panel bears every minister's name, dating back to James Carrick. He was the first vicar of Oakdene, and formerly of the old village during its last days."

"The Black Death? That must have been a tough assignment," Amanda commented.

Julie nodded. "I don't envy him that one. James died of consumption within two years of Oakdene's birth, according to records. Such a tragedy after surviving the plague that afflicted Underwood. Our church was still a wattle and daub affair at the time. It took several years to complete the stone structure we're standing in today, though it occupies the same parcel of land. You'll find James among the older graves out back."

Amanda watched Belinda wander the aisles, studying biblical imagery in the stained glass windows and various carved wall decorations depicting the Stations of the Cross.

Julie picked at her cardigan. "May I ask how Belinda is coping? I heard about the incident at the woods on Saturday."

Amanda folded her arms. "Belle has drawn the short

straw on bad luck of late." She jerked her head towards the roof. "Either that or someone up there doesn't like her."

Julie wrung her hands. "I'm sure it's not tha-"

"I'm being facetious. Sorry," Amanda interrupted.

"Ah." Julie's agitated limbs calmed. "Are you settling into life here?"

"Jake and I grew up in Dolton, over the hill across the river, so it's not a huge change. I'd never spent long in Oakdene, for all that. His death and my effectively becoming an instant mother... Well, that'll take a little more time."

"No doubt." Julie offered a warm smile. "If I can help in any way, please let me know."

"Thank you." Amanda waved at Belinda. "Come on, Belle. Home time."

* * *

Belinda tossed and turned in another fit of restless slumber, troubled by sinister dreams. The church of All Saints, Oakdene, stood black against a crimson sky. Between each stone of its construction, mortar seeped out as blood, presenting the transfigured house of worship like some macabre jam sponge. Stained glass figures in the pictorial story windows fell to their knees and wept. A familiar hissing of angry whispers whipped about Belinda's legs. Their utterances stabbed at her heart, though she failed to grasp why. "Guilty. Guilty. Guilty."

Belinda's eyes snapped open in bed at Ravensbrook.

Her room lay doused in early morning sunlight. She mouthed the word under her breath. "Guilty."

Sitting by herself in the warmth of their daisy-filled summer meadow stole anguish from Belinda's troubled mind. The last couple of days at school had passed, empty and alone. It relieved her not to suffer further torment from the other kids. Few wished their onetime companion a pleasant holiday at the end. Even Laura and Jane's temporary farewell felt false and stilted. She'd trudged home friendless and solitary, with little positive anticipation regarding the next two months other than more time spent alone. Now, making daisy chains into a garland for her hair provided a carefree distraction.

"Whatcha doin'?" A young lad's voice startled Belinda. She hadn't heard anyone approach through the soft, swaying grass.

Belinda shifted round. "Hello, Kevin."

Kevin Lloyd was one of the quieter boys in her class. He enjoyed playing with the other kids, but refused any part in taunting Belinda. Of medium height with a pudgy countenance his mother described as *'a good face for radio,'* he was an average student. Average height, average build, average appearance, average grades. Yet one thing Kevin possessed which separated him from the hoi polloi: he was his own person and not one of the mindless sheep.

Belinda set the floral crown atop her messy blonde locks. "I'm making daisy chains. What are you doing here?"

Kevin plonked himself on the ground beside her. "I haven't seen you playing with any of the other kids since we broke up." He scratched his head. "Do you want to take a walk with me?"

Belinda clutched both arms across her chest. "Really?"

Kevin shrugged. "Sure. Why not? I sometimes swing by Oakdene Motors to look at the cars Mr Taylor and his mechanics are working on. If he's not too busy, he teaches me stuff from time to time. Do you know how to reset the auto-wind on Honda power windows? I do."

Belinda looked impressed, and tried not to giggle. "No." Kevin Lloyd was honest and uncomplicated as the summer days were long. "What else have you learnt?"

Kevin thought for a moment. "I know how to change an air filter." He indicated Belinda's floral crown. "It's different from making daisy chains, though."

Belinda got to her feet. "I'd like something different today. Thanks, Kevin."

If Kevin experienced any emotions over her enthusiastic response, they didn't register on his unremarkable face. Offering a friendless classmate companionship was the right thing to do, so he didn't think further about it.

Together they crossed the meadow and followed the lane into Oakdene.

Down at the village pub, locals often teased Brian Taylor that he could remove bolts from his neck to fix cars at the garage he owned. Such comments referred to a tall, oblong head and laughing (yet down-turned) eyes that suggested some comic Frankenstein caricature. The early fifties mechanic took it all in his stride. Patience and an even temper were his forte. Brian prided himself on the loyal customer base he'd built at Oakdene Motors. A quarter century had passed since he'd purchased a run-down shed with little more than a dream and a modest business loan. His outfit handled vehicles from eager customers as far removed as Bridestowe; such was their reputation for outstanding service and honesty. Brian's late father was a self-employed engineer who'd serviced agricultural machinery. He'd grown up in the village where his family had dwelt for centuries.

When Belinda and Kevin appeared in the open workshop doorway, the chief mechanic stood shining a lamp across the underside of Julian Asbury's Aston Martin on a ramp above him. Their flash of movement dispelled his attention.

"Kevin? Hello there. Have you come to help me locate this oil leak?"

Kevin left Belinda's side and hurried to join Brian beneath the ramp. His mouth dropped open. "A V8 Vantage. I've seen Mr Asbury drive it around the village, but I've never been this close."

Brian grinned. "You like Aston Martins, hey?"

Kevin encircled the ramp's exterior, gazing upward. "4.7 litre V8, 420 bhp, 0-60 in 4.4 seconds."

"How on earth did you know that, young man? I'd have had to look those statistics up."

Kevin examined its exhaust system in awe. "I have one on a card in my Top Trumps set."

Crow's feet of amusement stretched around the corners of Brian's eyes. "I see. Do kids still play Top Trumps? That's great. Not everything is mobile phones and computers, then?" His gaze shifted to Belinda, lingering by the open double doors. "Who's your friend?"

Kevin remembered his manners. "This is Belle. She's in my class at school."

Brian hung his lamp from a hook and wiped greasy hands on a rag. "Pleased to meet you, Belle. Feel free to come inside. You're safe as long as you don't touch anything."

Kevin stood on tiptoe and wiped clean oil from the bottom of the vehicle with one finger. "Belle lives down at Ravensbrook."

Both Brian's eyebrows raised in unison. "The Fairchild girl?" He gave Belinda a warm smile accompanied by sympathetic eyes. "We fixed your aunt's Toyota a while back."

Kevin held up his hand to show the oil.

Brian passed him the rag. "It's fresh, not dirty sump oil. My money is on a faulty gasket between the engine block and timing cover. If I find any gunk greasing the engine belts and pulleys, I'd say it's a definite. I'll have to replace the breather."

"Is that expensive?" Kevin asked.

"The gaskets aren't, but the labour will run into a

couple of thousand pounds. It's a heavy task. I'll check around some more, then get cracking once my guys return from a delivery job. Extra hands are a must." He addressed Belinda again. "How are you enjoying the summer holidays?"

Belinda offered a non-committal head wobble and remained by the doors.

Brian took the rag back from Kevin and put it down. "What I'd give to be running around as a kid again. Roaming the hills, woods and fields; catching bugs in jam jars down by the river; making rubbish bows and arrows, and playing Robin Hood. We used that old church at Underwood as the Sheriff's pretend castle, once upon a time." His eyes twinkled. "Happy days."

Another boy the same age appeared outside the workshop beside Belinda. "Oi, Kev, do you fancy a bike ride? Mum said she'll fix us pizza afterwards."

Kevin met the striking blue eyes of his friend, Jason Tong. Tall and thin with wavy blond hair, Jason was tipped to be Oakdene's next heart-breaker when he grew up. For all that, he was a loyal friend with a good spirit. He elbowed Belinda.

"Hey, Belle. I haven't seen you around, much. Are the girls playing with you, or are they still acting dumb?"

Kevin left Brian and joined his friends. "I reckon they're still acting dumb. She came for a walk with me."

Jason grimaced and shook his head. "I could have flattened Kieran and those idiots in the playground last week. Sorry about what happened, Belle." He tweaked

Belinda's homemade headdress. "Nice daisies."

Belinda smiled at the pair of them, then nudged Kevin. "You can head off with Jason. Thanks for bringing me here, Kevin. It was kind of you to remember me."

Kevin flushed, torn between two choices. "Are you sure?"

"Yes. Enjoy your bike ride and pizza."

"Thanks, Belle." Kevin called back through the workshop doors. "See you again soon, Mr Taylor. Good luck with that oil leak."

Brian Taylor waved one firm, work-calloused hand, the other clutching his lamp again for further inspections. "Have fun, Kevin. Keep learning about cars. Maybe one day I'll give you a job."

Kevin beamed and hurried away with Jason, leaving Belinda to linger beside a stack of old tyres near the door.

As she watched them disappear down the lane, an uneasy feeling trembled her arms. A gentle waft of air carried with it the jumble of voices she'd fought hard to resist and shut out whenever they emerged. "No," she spoke the defiant word to herself, afraid of being overheard and facing more rumours and derision. Saliva thickened in her throat, tinged with a fight-or-flight stirring of adrenaline and rising panic.

Inside the workshop, Brian Taylor remained focused on his task with legendary attention to detail.

Unseen forces swirled about Belinda, rippling the material of her dress like an unwelcome gust of wind. She stood firm in the garage doorway, eyes fixed upon its owner with emotionless morbidity.

8
Destructive Developments

Andy Mears and Greg Hansard drove through tight lanes in the Oakdene Motors tow truck. Andy frowned at his younger colleague, who crunched the gears as he downshifted through a hairpin.

"Is that jam on your collar?" Andy rubbed his finger through a bright red blob clinging to the driver's dark overalls. He sniffed a sticky smear of it, then wiped the mess on a tissue. "Strawberry, I'd wager."

Greg squinted. "I had a doughnut for breakfast."

Andy laughed. "When are you going to get yourself a wife? If I started the day on a jam doughnut in my work clothes, then put it all down myself, Trish would chew my ears off."

Greg adjusted his seatbelt for comfort as he pulled over to let an oncoming vehicle pass. "You're not selling me on the merits, Andy."

Andy shook his head and watched the river slip by out of the passenger window. "That's because you haven't experienced the joy of being cared for so much that you get scolded. Flippin' heck, didn't your mother ever pull you up on your appearance or eating habits?"

"All the time," Greg moaned.

"Doesn't that warm your heart, thinking back to it?" Andy leaned into his face.

Greg frowned. "No, it annoyed the crap out of me then and it still does."

Andy sat back, flicking a dismissive hand. "You're hopeless."

Greg pulled away again, passing a boundary sign for Oakdene on the village perimeter.

Andy hunched over the dash when they rounded a corner to the garage. "It's unlike Brian to close the workshop doors. Especially on a lovely day like this."

Greg pulled up the handbrake on its ratchet. "Maybe he doesn't want anyone disturbing him while he works on the Aston?"

Andy released his belt. "When did you ever know anything break Brian's concentration after he started work? He's like a bloomin' laser once he focuses on a job. Julian Asbury brought his car in with an oil leak. It's hardly the automotive equivalent of brain surgery."

Greg hopped down from the truck. "That posh guy doesn't strike me as a car fan. When he phoned to book, he couldn't answer basic questions about what was wrong. In the end, Brian gave up and reserved a slot to check it out."

Andy slammed the passenger door. "Asbury is no petrol-head. He's a great big show-off, that one. I've no doubt he enjoys driving the Vantage, but it's more about prestige and image than anything else, if you ask me."

Greg smirked. "I didn't, but I agree. Do you think Brian has popped out?"

Andy opened the office door. "We'll soon know." He pushed past the unattended front desk with its computer, printer, and two chairs positioned opposite for customers. Abundant paperwork heaved in trays, the largest pile weighted down by a discarded carburettor. Andy released a catch on an internal door into the workshop, then stepped through with Greg almost on top of him. Both stopped on a sixpence, though not sharp enough to avoid a sudden collision.

In the centre of their primary workspace, the hydraulic inspection ramp lay almost fully lowered. Electrical cables sparked from a control unit, while the sturdy metal uprights twisted over distorted pistons, drenched in escaped fluid. The British Racing Green Aston had slid sideways to hang halfway off the supporting platform. Beneath it, one overall-clad leg poked out, surrounded by a crimson puddle. A sickly smell of blood mixing with whiffs of oil and axle grease accentuated the gruesome sight. Greg retched. Andy forced himself towards the decimated vehicular lift. He rested one hand atop the Vantage's offside front tyre, then lowered himself and craned his neck beneath the ramp. Brian Taylor's pulverised head pressed into the workshop floor, less than half its usual width. Both eyeballs squashed together amidst a bloody mass of hair, flesh, and bone. His detached tongue lapped at the puddle of blood where he'd bitten it off during the sudden collapse. Further down Brian's mangled torso, his chest cavity had collapsed from the effects of blunt force trauma. Ribs poked out at assorted angles, accompanied by the rancid, acidic stench of burst stomach contents beneath.

Greg stumbled into a nearby cupboard-like staff toilet and lost his own stomach contents in a single, heaving volley. It marked the second time in ten minutes he'd encountered doughnut remnants from breakfast.

Andy leaned against the car's silky smooth polished bodywork for support as he rose and turned.

The toilet flushed and Greg reappeared; smeared puke daubing one corner of his mouth. He eyed the shattered platform. "What on earth can have happened?"

Andy reached towards the control unit, then recoiled at a fresh shower of sparks. He stepped away and touched a twisted metal upright. "Fatigue in the supports? There had to be more than some electrical failure to distort the lift and drop it like that."

Greg hobbled towards the workshop double doors. "I'll let a breath of fresh air in."

Andy barked at him. "Don't be an idiot. Do you want a kid or passerby to see this? We should call the police without delay." He forced numb limbs to carry him back into the office, where he collapsed into a chair and picked up the desk phone receiver. A silent tear escaped from one duct as he dialled. Working for Brian Taylor - the greatest mechanic and best boss in the world - had been his first and only job.

* * *

Amanda got up from the breakfast table where

Belinda sat picking at a bowl of cereal. The nine-year-old had forced a meal down under protest the night before, nixing Amanda's hopes time away from school would have a positive effect. A red postal van drew up outside, its driver almost clear of the cabin before the engine died.

Amanda opened the front door of Ravensbrook and waited for the whistling, cheerful postman to retrieve a pile of parcels from the vehicle's loading bay.

"I've a stack for you this morning." Stuart Neat rounded the van's side with his burden. "Home improvement materials?"

In other places under different circumstances, Amanda might have told the postie to mind his own business. Oakdene and rural Devon were different. Besides, she'd yet to thank him for breaking into the house after discovering Jake and Karen beneath a pile of rubble.

"Art supplies."

Stuart's next whistle became a drawn-out one of admiration. "You must be a regular female Rembrandt."

Amanda pursed her lips, concealing a smile.

"Pop them on the step here, shall I?" Stuart reached the doorway.

"In the hall, if you'd be so kind." Amanda stepped aside.

Stuart set the pile down upon shiny black flagstones beyond the mat. "There you go." He glanced into the room with its rebuilt brickwork, but said nothing.

Amanda noticed his expression and cleared her

throat. "The wall is back up now."

Stuart looked sheepish and averted his eyes. "So I see."

Amanda offered him her hand. "I never thanked you for trying to help my brother and my sister-in-law. It means a lot."

Stuart flushed. "What an awful day. I was on first-name terms with Jake and Karen. Finding them like that... Well, you must be suffering enough without me dragging it all up again. My heart goes out to Belle. She was full of life, once." He accepted and shook her hand. "Stuart Neat."

"Amanda Fairchild." She attempted to lighten the atmosphere. "That's a smart name you've got there."

A half-smile crept up one side of his face, as one who'd endured such jokes regularly since childhood. "What a tidy quip. It's a pleasure to meet you."

"Likewise."

Stuart was about to leave, then pulled himself up short. "Have you been into the village since yesterday lunchtime?"

Amanda tilted her head. "No. Why?"

Stuart gritted his teeth. "Um, I don't want to add to your worries, but forewarned is forearmed over grim news."

"Has something else happened?" Amanda pressed into the door frame to counteract unsteady legs.

"Brian Taylor, the mechanic was killed at Oakdene Motors yesterday."

Amanda covered her mouth. "That's awful. You said *'was killed.'* I assume you're not referring to a medical condition?"

"Workplace accident. A hydraulic ramp collapsed on top of him with a motor fully loaded." He tugged at his shirt collar with a pudgy finger. "I wasn't going to mention it, on account of it being another person crushed. But, I guess you'd find out soon enough. Sorry to darken your morning."

"That's okay. What a terrible tragedy."

Stuart inclined his head towards the parcels resting beside Amanda in the hallway. "Paint something nice. That'll cheer everyone up a touch."

"Have a good day, Stuart."

Stuart secured the van's rear doors, hopped back into the driver's seat, and then sped away towards the village, leaving a cloud of dust in his wake.

Amanda waited until the disturbance settled, then crouched and lifted her parcels. A creaking of internal threshold wood caused her to look up. Belinda stood in a nearby doorway, watching.

"Who were you eavesdropping on?" Amanda carried the packages into the dining area and set them on the table.

Belinda followed her. "I was interested in Stuart's story."

Amanda sat opposite the place where Belinda's still uneaten cereals rested. "Sit down a moment."

"I'm not hungry," Belinda protested.

"It's all right, Belle. You don't have to eat that if you don't want to. I'm curious about what you overheard."

Belinda pulled out her chair and slid onto its seat. "Something about Mr Taylor being squashed at his garage."

"That's right. Brian Taylor died yesterday." She rubbed her eyes. "I wish you didn't have to face more news like that. So much death in such a small village, and all within a short period."

Belinda's eyes glazed over. She stared through the wall and spoke with empty detachment. "It's not the first time."

By mid-morning, Belinda's endless strolls along the brook and sojourns in the meadow led her cabin-fevered feet in search of fresh terrain. She skirted east of Oakdene, keeping close to the River Torridge. The clock at All Saints chimed eleven as she wandered hither and thither with no preferred destination or course. Girlish giggles rippled between bushes surrounding a clump of elm. Jane Perkins stumbled out of the undergrowth, oblivious to Belinda's presence. She called back into the tangle of leafy flora. "I told you I'd find everybody before they reached base. I'm the queen of 52 Bunkers."

Laura Barnes, plus two of their other friends, Molly Weeks and Julia Drummond, pressed into the open air. They stopped upon spying Belinda, watching them a short distance away.

Molly tugged leaf matter from thick, wiry red hair. "What do you want?"

A rubbing noise of bicycle brakes whistled to a halt on the cracked, dry mud of a public footpath beside them. Kevin Lloyd and Jason Tong put steadying feet down, but remained astride.

Kevin looked from the crowd of girls across to Belinda. "Are you okay, Belle?"

Julia huffed and folded her arms. "Is *she* okay? What about us?"

Jason grunted. "Belle wouldn't hurt you. Anyway, that's not what Kev meant. Haven't you heard about Mr Taylor at the garage?"

"Of course we have." Molly stuck her nose in the air.

Jane Perkins' eyes became saucers. "It was terrible."

Jason motioned to Belinda. "Kev asked if Belle was okay, because the two of them visited the garage yesterday. They spoke with Mr Taylor right before it happ…" He winced, aware of how Belinda's kangaroo court of female peers might react to his well-intentioned truth.

Julia pointed an accusatory finger at Belinda. "She was there when Mr Taylor died?"

Kevin almost fell off his bike in frustration. "We were all there: Belle, Jason and myself. Mr Taylor was fixing an oil leak when we left."

Molly's eyes narrowed. "Where did the three of you go next?"

Kevin missed a cautionary stare from Jason; so innocent was his nature. "Jason and I went for a bike ride. Belle must have gone home, or off for a walk."

"Must she?" Julia said. "You left her alone with Mr Taylor, and the next thing his mechanics found him dead."

Jason scowled. "Will you get off Belle's case? Hasn't she suffered enough? Mr Taylor's vehicle ramp collapsed. What's that got to do with Bel...?" When he twisted to highlight the helpless defendant, Belinda was nowhere in sight.

Tears stung Belinda's eyes as she ran without care back the way she'd come. With the cork out of the bottle over her presence at Oakdene Motors, she knew word would spread. What about when Amanda heard the news? Would she rush to her defence or draw back in suspicion? Belinda's mind whirled with horrific images she could neither annunciate nor understand. Ever those vicious whispers pursued her, appearing without warning and calling from beneath the trees with their insistent summons. Why did they pick on her? How could she stop their anger and blood lust haunting her steps?

* * *

Amanda strolled towards the village from Ravensbrook the following lunchtime, a canvas bag held tight by the handles in her eager grasp. Its stretched outline suggested a stiff rectangular item and some other object eliciting a more organic bulge.

Craig Symonds reached Peggy Greene's front gate at the same moment.

Amanda grinned. "Hey. That's a stroke of luck. I thought this might be a regular gardening day for you."

Craig opened the gate for her, then set down a bag of tools beside the path. "Weeding and dead heading. The lawn could use a trim, but the other jobs take priority. Did you want me or Peggy?"

"Both." Amanda lifted her bag. "I have something for each of you."

"Intriguing." Craig proceeded to the front door and jangled a brass bell beside it.

The slow report of Peggy's cane tip against stonework approached, followed by a clunk from the solid old latch. The door swung back. "Come in, Craig."

"How did you know it was me?" Craig asked.

"You're due. Anyway, I recognise your smell."

Craig flinched. "I hope it's a pleasant one."

Peggy cackled, looking from side to side with unseeing eyes. "You've someone with you."

"It's me, Peggy," Amanda piped up. "Amanda Fairchild."

Peggy's confused face brightened. "You've come to visit the crazy old bint again? That's nice."

Amanda wrinkled her nose. Peggy's blunt nature proved a tonic, like last time. "I've brought you a present. Something I made for you."

Peggy sniffed. "Is it a cake? I'm partial to coffee walnut, if you ever experience a sudden urge to bake."

"No. You'd break your teeth if you tried biting into this. Shall we go inside?"

Peggy headed back down the hallway, calling over her shoulder. "We'll sit on the patio again. Craig, would you-"

"Already ahead of you, Peggy." Craig pressed one hand into the small of her back as he hurried past to open the French windows and arrange exterior seating.

Amanda closed the front door behind them. "Shall I fix a pot of tea, Peggy?"

Peggy continued towards the patio. "You're a sweetheart. Thank you, Amanda."

Ten minutes later, the trio sat outside once more. Amanda reached into her canvas bag and retrieved the glazed and fired clay cat. "My bread and butter is painting, but I make models for pleasure sometimes." She placed the curled up animal figurine in Peggy's lap.

Peggy felt the shape and texture with trembling fingers. Her red eyes watered. "To remind me of Thomas?"

"That's what I was hoping. It's not fur of course, but…"

"Such a thoughtful gift." Peggy leaned over, waving a questing hand in Amanda's direction.

Amanda clasped it. "I'm glad you like it. A commercial potter near Holsworthy fired it for me."

Peggy let go and stroked the clay pet again. "So many fond memories to comfort me on lonely evenings. Thank you, Amanda." She set 'Thomas' down on the table.

Amanda reached into her bag again. "And this is for you, Craig."

Peggy perked up. "Does he have a present too?"

"Not as such," Amanda replied. "Craig helped me rebuild that fallen wall at Ravensbrook." She handed over a framed watercolour of Cosicott. "This is a return favour."

Craig addressed Peggy. "It's a painting of my home." He held it up to the sunlight between both hands. "It's perfect, Amanda. You've captured the cottage's character to a tee. Cheers."

"No problem. Glad you like it." She poured out the tea and handed a cup and saucer to Peggy.

Peggy inhaled a deep lungful of air laced with floral aromas from her spectacular garden. "No doubt you've both heard about Brian Taylor?"

Amanda passed a cup to Craig. "Stuart Neat, the postman told me yesterday."

Craig shook his head. "What a way to go. At least it was quick. Thank goodness Belle wasn't there, like with Sam Peebles."

Peggy dropped a sugar lump into her tea and stirred it. "Craig told me what happened with your niece, Amanda. Not that the story wasn't already doing the rounds in Oakdene."

Amanda grimaced. "I can imagine. Of all the people to encounter a scene like that, why did it have to be her? First the village lost Jake and Karen; then those other two. Our population has taken a serious pruning of late, not unlike your roses."

Peggy shifted in her seat. "We've one new resident, though."

"We have?" Amanda asked.

"Of course. You."

"I hadn't thought of that."

Peggy sipped a mouthful of tea between loud, cracked lips, then placed the cup back in its saucer.

"The stain of past deeds hangs over Oakdene like a black mark. Some of its populace have encountered a wrath that burns unseen against the guilty."

Amanda studied her face. "Are you talking about our recently deceased? I thought Brian Taylor was known for his honesty? The worst thing Jake ever did was pull the legs off a spider when he was seven. Dad gave him such a stiff talking to, he almost became a naturalist afterwards. I've no idea about Karen, but she was lovely all the times I met her." She looked aside into a patch of flowerbeds sporting vibrant blooms. "I never knew Sam Peebles."

Peggy tugged at her shawl. "I meant past, as in long forgotten. Restless, angry souls reach out their hands towards those they deem responsible. Even our sainted local estate owner isn't immune from scrutiny."

Amanda placed both hands in her lap. "What do long forgotten deeds have to do with the living? Why would anyone, dead or alive, wish to harm the descendant of Oakdene's founder and benefactor?" She caught Craig's eye. "Something hasn't happened to Julian Asbury as well, has it?"

Craig shook his head. "Not that I've heard."

Peggy raised her cup, finished the tea, and then put her china down with a clatter. "Founder and benefactor? At what cost? There's nought as slippery as false altruism."

Craig coughed. "More of your stories, Peggy? This talk of the deceased is a little close to home for Amanda, remember?"

Peggy felt for the clay model again. "I didn't mean to

upset you, Amanda. You've been so kind. Ignore the silly blind woman and her vague fancies."

"You're not silly, Peggy." She stood. "I'd best hurry along and let Craig do some work."

Craig grinned. "Spoilsport. I rarely start my day with a tea break."

Amanda placed a gentle hand on Peggy's shoulder. "No need to see me out; I'll leave through the garden."

"Sorry about that," Craig muttered as they approached the gate again.

"Forget it. That wasn't your fault, and she meant nothing by it. You know I've encountered weirder stuff than Peggy's ramblings in recent weeks." She spied Rachel Barnes walking home from the village shop. "Speaking of which... Will you excuse me, Craig?"

Craig bent down and rifled through his tool bag. "Go easy."

"Rachel? Rachel?" Amanda repeated the name with a lilt, after receiving no response.

Rachel stopped in the lane and composed herself before facing Amanda. "Hello."

Amanda maintained an evenness of expression and tone. "Your greeting is cooler than our first encounter. Erm, is something wrong?"

Rachel's cheeks rouged. Her eyes flicked down to the road. "I don't mean to be rude."

"Have I upset you?"

"No." An inner conflict between self-preservation and propriety strained her facial muscles.

"I thought you'd been avoiding me. Listen, I promised Belle I wouldn't talk to you about her and Laura, but the sudden change in their friendship worries me. Can you offer any clues about what happened? When Jake and Karen died, your family took her into your home like absolute sweethearts. Then one day Belle told me she's not allowed to play with Laura anymore. Did she misbehave? If Belle has been naughty, I'll be sure to discipline her, Rachel. Just tell me, would you?"

Rachel's shoulders sagged. "Something happened when she last came to play at our house."

"Yes?"

Rachel waved her hands about in exasperation. "I ran upstairs after I heard Belle scream."

"Scream?"

"Uh-huh. Papers were flying around the room. Windows opened and closed. It was a calm day without a breath of wind. I found Laura lying winded on the carpet. She said an unseen force punched her in the stomach."

"Not Belle?"

"No. She insists it came through the window. Some of Laura's toys launched off the floor and struck me. Belle sat staring. Then she spoke to... whatever it was and pleaded with it not to hurt us."

Amanda stood open mouthed, the empty canvas bag hanging at her side.

Rachel continued. "My husband arrived home at that moment and hit the roof. That's when we decided it was best if Laura and Belle broke off contact. I'm sorry, Amanda. I know your niece has been through hell. But, you've got to admit the weird circumstances are growing in number."

Amanda blinked. "How do you mean?"

"First that hiker discovering Belle drenched in Sam Peebles' blood. Now with Brian Taylor at the garage..."

"Whoa, whoa, whoa, back up and hold the front page. What about Brian Taylor?"

"Belle visited him at the garage on the day he died."

"How do you know that? I thought she was making daisy chains in our meadow." Amanda took a step nearer.

"Laura overheard Emily Lloyd's boy and his friend talking about it yesterday. They were also with Belle at the garage."

Amanda's cheeks paled. "But they didn't witness the accident?"

"The boys didn't. They left Belle and fetched their bikes for a ride."

Amanda glared. "What are you suggesting, Rachel? Brian died from a catastrophic equipment failure. Do you seriously believe Belle ha-?"

"I don't believe anything definite, Amanda," Rachel interrupted, no longer on the back foot. "All I'm saying is: a lot of horrible things have happened around Belle. Laura misses her, but she's also frightened. Her playmate isn't the girl she once was."

Amanda's eyes flashed. "Can you blame her? Jesus, would you be?"

"I don't blame her. But, after what happened in our

house, I'll not put my child at risk either. I'm sorry. Maybe when all of this has calmed down, those two can reconnect in the future."

Amanda folded her arms and put on a sarcastic, girlish voice, impersonating Laura. "Yeah. Sorry I wasn't there when you needed me, Belle. Now you're normal, we can be friends again if you like?"

Rachel gritted her teeth. "I have to go." She turned without another word and walked away.

Amanda stood in the middle of the lane like a statue.

"Getting to the bottom of the friendship mystery?" Helen Masters stepped up beside her. "I've seen you around and we've spoken on the phone, but we haven't been properly introduced. I'm Belle's head teacher."

"Mrs Masters? Hello." Amanda bit her lip. "Right when I've accepted one bizarre, unanswered question, two more pop up."

Helen regarded her with a sympathetic expression. "If it's any consolation, Laura didn't take part in the name calling at school. She and Belle don't talk, but I'm not aware of any nastiness on Laura's part."

"Rachel Barnes said Laura misses Belle but is frightened of her. Something about objects flying around the room when Belle visited their home."

"One boy at school made a comment like that. Children can be cruel when they hear and believe wild stories about their own."

Amanda puffed. "What about when a child's mother claims to have witnessed the same incident?"

"What?" Helen stiffened.

Amanda shook her head. "Never mind." She chuckled in a heartless attempt at mirth. "There's nothing like an escape to the country for some peace, eh? Bristol is looking more like heaven by the day."

"You're not thinking of leaving us, are you?"

Amanda read genuine concern on her face. "No. I appreciated that phone call the other day. I'll not take Belle away from her home. Not unless she begs for us to go. Changing the subject: how are your plans for the autumn term progressing? I'm not one of those people who think teachers sit idle and twiddle their thumbs during the summer holidays."

Helen's face softened. "Thank you." She glanced around. "If the latest rumours are true, my job is about to get a lot busier."

"How's that?"

"Abigail Webb, who works in the village shop, let slip her husband is drawing up plans for a new housing development. He's an architect."

"I didn't know she was married?"

"Re-married. Abigail kept her previous surname. Her husband, Paul Gilbert, is stepfather to a boy Belle used to hang around with. Anton was one of her tormentors, I'm sorry to say. A reluctant one, though. The lad has his own problems at home. It's not a happy environment."

"And that's making your job busier?"

"No. Abigail hinted that the housing development will be sited right here."

Amanda gazed up and down the quaint street of cottages, flanked by wooded hills and the river.

"Where?"

"She was worried about disclosing too much, lest Paul find out. He has quite a temper. A group of ladies pumped her for sufficient details. Developers are planning to level the woods west of the village, bulldoze what remains of Underwood and build on every patch of level ground available. If that's true, it would almost double the size of Oakdene."

"With modern, box-like monstrosities a bazillion to an acre?" Amanda shut her eyes. "They'll ruin the place. How can this be on the cards? Don't the developers require a public consultation or something? Isn't that Julian Asbury's land?"

Helen threw up her hands. "Abigail wouldn't say anything else. All I know is, I can't sit around until those houses are up and sold before we consider school capacity and resources. I need answers and fast, if we're to offer families with young children educational places. Then there are revised teaching staff requirements, new budgets, etc. The list is endless." Her face fell. "If this goes ahead, Amanda, you may wish to reconsider that move after all. Oakdene will never be the same."

"Can you let me know if you learn anything further?"

"Yes. Once this gets out - and it already has, after Abigail's disclosure - the council will call a meeting. As a resident, you'll be welcome to attend and lend your voice to proceedings."

"Good. Gosh, what a bloomin' day. Okay, thanks for telling me. Speak soon." Amanda wandered back down the lane towards Ravensbrook in a semi-daze. From Peggy Greene's talk suggesting forgotten guilt repaid in blood; to Rachel Barnes and her assertions of violent, unseen forces surrounding Belle; there was so much to digest. Not to mention the revelation Belle was at the garage before Brian Taylor's accident. Now came news of a potential, massive housing development dominating the village. One that would replace the tree-lined view at the end of her meadow. She trudged into the living room and flopped into an armchair like a lifeless rag doll. "Whatever next?"

9

Conspirators

Julian Asbury yanked open the main door at High Stanton. Three male figures lingered on the doorstep, low mutterings silenced by the fury written across their host's face. Julian took a deliberate, loud breath in through his nostrils to highlight brimming annoyance. "You'd better come through to the library. I don't want anyone overhearing us." He shot a sharp glance behind as the trio followed him through the hallway. "How did the news break?"

Brandon Beeching answered first. "It seems Paul's wife let her tongue wag in the shop." A corpulent, self-serving tub of lard, forty-seven-year-old Brandon Beeching's balding head was a consequence of rampant obesity he'd fallen into over two decades. Brandon's long-suffering wife tolerated the slug-like appearance of her husband on account of his well-respected and prosperous position as a local councillor. As long as she was invited to the right socials, her spouse's ever expanding waistline could be overlooked. Brandon's close-set, dark eyes were always scanning for opportunities to pad his bank account. A career in local government represented rich pickings for an unscrupulous, grasping opportunist lacking any semblance of honesty or good character. Brandon had started out in an admin post at the council, before climbing the greasy local authority career pole to take advantage of any trick that would enrich him. Corrupt, brash and unfeeling, he looked down his nose at everyone in his path. Yet for all that, he could turn on the charm when it served his purposes and present a charismatic facade, faking solidarity with voters.

Paul Gilbert clenched his teeth. "I'll thrash the life out of her. Why couldn't she keep her big mouth shut?" Paul was a serious bastard with a phenomenal talent for hiding it well. A blond buzz cut rising into a spiked topper above a playful grin and large, twinkling eyes hinted at anything but the abusive control freak pulling levers inside. He'd never married before getting hitched to divorcee, Abigail Webb - a single mother from the village. Even Paul realised this was due to no woman sticking around once they knew him. A stable job as an architect and boyish attractiveness couldn't compensate for the emotional and physical assaults he delivered with just enough restraint to avoid legal consequences. Pushing forty, it amazed Paul the day Abigail accepted his marriage proposal. How lucky that the woman was weak, desperate and eager to avoid rocking the leaky relationship boat in which she now found herself stranded. An easy mark for a bully to capitalise on.

"Do nothing rash. This was bound to happen eventually," Gary Cripps responded. A stubbly shadow clinging fast to Gary's jawline and upper lip suggested an eternal five o'clock. Swept back hair atop a short back and sides outlined a square, high-brow cranium cresting beady but emotionless eyes. His apparent coldness and indifference served the mid-thirties planning officer from Torridge District Council well. Especially when it came to rejecting applications from hopeful developers or home improvement seekers. Nicknamed *'The RED Officer,'* on account of his position in charge of *'Rural Economic Development,'* that informal nickname also mocked the particulars of his post. Certain disgruntled planning applicants suggested every drop of ink in his pen ran with human blood. Gary was beloved of councillors for bringing in money, while riding roughshod over the concerns of locals or sweeping them under the carpet. Bullied at school, he'd developed an inferiority complex. Now, flaunting his professional authority over the public, offered a form of control and self-esteem management. Single, sullen and miserable, Gary avoided the limelight wherever possible. Prosperity far beyond his meagre salary appealed, and he didn't care who suffered to attain it. If denying inoffensive property updates to the populace within his sphere of influence delivered a semi-sexual thrill of superiority; pocketing backhanders from wealthy developers to afflict the same with unwanted new housing initiated a full-blown psychological orgasm.

Julian ushered them into the library, grabbing Paul's arm as he passed. "Have you tackled those updates I requested?"

Paul tapped a document tube slung over his shoulder. "I've brand new plans plotted and ready to roll, once Gary signs them off. I squeezed in another two semis and a coach house on that corner plot. By cutting the neighbouring gardens down to courtyard affairs and creating a mews beyond the coach house arch, we'll add a few hundred thousand to the bottom line. Garden space isn't that profitable in this day and age. Housing is where it's at."

"Splendid." Julian released his arm.

Paul uncapped the tube and spread out his revised plans for the group to peruse. He tapped the aforementioned updated area with an index finger. "There."

Julian nodded his approval, then caught Brandon's eye. "What's the mood in Oakdene since the news broke?"

Brandon shrugged. "About what you'd expect. They're grubby 'Little Englander' NIMBY types. Some people resist change at all costs."

Gary hummed. "Let's look at what they're losing: a patch of tangled woods most people avoid and some crumbling ruins. No great sacrifice, is it? I'll bet the few random visits villagers make there are down since your grounds keeper topped himself with a chainsaw, Julian."

"Did Sam display any warning indicators of mental health issues?" Paul asked.

Julian tweaked an eyebrow with plain disinterest over the topic at hand. "We didn't engage in drawn out discussions about life. He was my lackey; a member of staff. Who knows what went through his head? Not much, I'd say."

Brandon smirked. "That was the general consensus at The Royalist. Did Sam know about any of this?" He waved a hand, palm up, across the unrolled plans.

"No," Julian replied. "To him it would have been one less parcel of land to manage, after the bulldozers rolled in. I doubt Sam would've cared."

Gary rested his backside against a leather Chaise Longue. "That was a rum business about Brian Taylor at the garage. At first I thought his accident would mask our activities and make life easier. A helpful diversion while we rolled out the plans at a time of our choosing."

Julian tutted. "It's bloody inconvenient. I'm not sure I'd trust Brian's subordinates with my motor. I'll have to consider somewhere in Great Torrington, or Fore Street Garage over in North Tawton. On the plus side, Brian was a sentimental old fool. He'd just the rose-tinted view of the area to rally dissenting voices against our development. That vehicle ramp of his did us all a favour." He studied the faces of his compatriots. "What about the public consultation?"

Gary locked his fingers together. "Brandon has reserved the village hall for a meeting on Friday. There'll be angry questions about you selling off the land."

Julian pulled himself erect, chest swelling. "It's mine to sell."

"I realise that," Gary replied. "What I'm saying is: you should attend and speak at the meeting, having already anticipated its Q & A component. Expect a tense atmosphere and a blemish or two on that halo you wear."

Julian scowled. "Watch your mouth, Gary."

Gary held up his hands. "Be prepared, that's all."

Julian flicked a savage hand in the air. "What do I care for the plebs? Small people with insignificant lives."

Paul rolled up his plans. "Hey, *we* live in the village, too."

Julian remained unmoved. "I was referring to people's outlook rather than their domicile. Besides, once we pull this off, you'll trouser enough cash to move wherever you please."

Paul countered his curt reply, still affronted. "And you can fix up your country pile before it topples about your ears or you go broke."

Julian pulled out a chair and sat at the table. "What happens after the meeting?"

Brandon's eyes twinkled. "A charm offensive. Gary and I will go door-to-door offering reassurances and selling the benefits."

"What *are* the benefits?" Gary asked.

Brandon took a breath. "A shit-load of money for the four of us. As far as Oakdene is concerned, we'll concoct some waffle about increased prosperity for everyone. All the usual guff councillors have lied to residents about since time immemorial, whenever they're gearing up to destroy a community. Jesus, how long have you been in this game? You're bent as a right-angle; use your imagination."

Gary straightened. "After the door-to-door visits and

formal receipt of written objections, we'll draft a wealth of bogus internal meeting minutes indicating careful deliberation and attention to villager concerns. That'll be available on-line, so residents will know they've been heard. Then we'll green-light the project anyway and start building. All nice, neat and by the book."

"Will there be protests?" Julian cocked his head.

Brandon chuckled. "From grey-haired agitators and bumpkin dropouts? If there are, they'll disperse once they need the loo or the pub opens. Don't underestimate geriatric bladders or the pulling power of cider." He tapped his finger against the table. "If objections become too loud, we'll run a press piece about this being the least destructive option to support HMG's required development quotas. That or other bollocks woolly enough to make a measured response impossible. Once the wider populace think we're looking out for their best interests, they'll ignore further rumblings from Oakdene."

Julian pondered the proposal. "Good. My ancestor purchased that land after buying (and donating) another parcel for the village. Three-and-a-half centuries later, why shouldn't I liquidate that useless scrap of ground to preserve the manor?"

Brandon gave him a thumbs up. "Right. It's not like we're building a nuclear power station on Oakdene's doorstep. They're houses, for God's sake."

* * *

Once the chairs ran out at the village hall, it was standing room only. A meeting to discuss the proposed Oakdene housing development drew such a crowd they were peering through windows from the car park.

Craig Symonds agreed to escort Peggy Greene so she could listen and take part. For the first time since he'd met her, Craig envied the blind eyes that would never see such a modern blot on the landscape come to fruition. Facial expressions and body language among the attendees ranged from fear and anger to grief and confusion.

On a raised platform at the back, Julian Asbury, Paul Gilbert, Brandon Beeching and Gary Cripps stood in a corner huddle, ignoring dagger eyes stabbing at them from the assembly.

Amanda entered the building and stood on tiptoe, surveying the sea of heads. Gary caught her eye and waved. He indicated a seat he'd saved on Peggy's opposite side. She squeezed into the row, apologising to those who half-stood to let her pass.

"It'll get hot in here." Craig tugged at his open-necked shirt collar.

Amanda smirked. "Was that hot or heated?"

Craig nodded. "That too. I can't believe this is happening." He waved at some gardening customers who acknowledged him. "Is Belle staying in? You didn't ask me to reserve her a spot."

"She's at home. Quiet and lost in her own thoughts. No change there." Amanda teased her hair through unconscious fingers. "I haven't seen you since that day at Peggy's. I'm still reeling from the stuff Rachel Barnes told me."

Craig fidgeted upon observing wigging ears all about them. "We'll get into that later, if you like."

Peggy placed both hands on her cane and slammed it into the floor. "They can't build on Underwood. They mustn't."

Amanda noticed Julie Clement milling about at the back. "I wonder if she'll speak up about the old churchyard?"

"Who's that?" Peggy lifted her head.

"The vicar," Amanda replied. "Are there still human remains in those graves at the ruin?"

Peggy bowed her head. "So we were always told."

"What will happen to them?"

Craig leaned over Peggy's lap. "I imagine they'll transplant them to another site. All Saints, if there's room. Otherwise, a general cemetery nearby. They must have de-consecrated the church at Underwood when the village moved. So soon after the plague, nobody could blame them for leaving its graves alone. Time moved on, like in many other long-forgotten churchyards. It's never been an issue until now."

Peggy shook her head with surprising vigour. "That won't bring them peace." Her chin wobbled. "There's a price still to pay. A terrible price."

Craig sat back. "Yeah, for everyone who lives here, with a modern brick goitre like that development disfiguring our homes. At the end of my tiny back garden, the ground slopes upward beyond the fence into beautiful green woodlands. After this man-made disaster, I'll be lucky if I'm not overlooked by half a dozen pigging ugly semis."

"Have you seen the plans yet?" Amanda asked.

Craig shook his head. "They're going to unveil them during the meeting. Your view from Ravensbrook will be diminished, too; albeit at a greater distance."

"I know. It's occupied my thoughts since I heard the news." Amanda straightened in her seat as Brandon Beeching called the meeting to order.

"Good evening, Ladies and Gentlemen. Thank you for attending. I'm sorry the hall doesn't have capacity to seat everyone, but the details we discuss will be available on-line along with our full proposal."

A gravelly male voice piped up at the back of the room. "Bloody Judas."

Brandon raised both his hands. "Please. I realise this is a sensitive subject. News of the development escaped earlier than intended, so we've put this meeting together in a hurry." He eyed a sheepish Abigail Webb. Casual onlookers might wonder at a woman wearing a scarf - even a light silken one - in such a warm environment. For Abigail, it provided the only solution to the problem of disguising cruel neck bruises. Paul had lost his temper after visiting the manor for a meeting earlier in the week.

"I thought you're supposed to represent our interests?" a woman declared.

Brandon let the comment hang, then settled into his stride. "I'd like to begin by introducing my fellow speakers. You're all familiar with Mr Julian Asbury, owner of High Stanton. It brought much relief at the council when Mr Asbury offered a patch of unproductive land near the boundary of his estate for development consideration. Every county receives housing quotas from Westminster we're obliged to action. At this point I should introduce Paul Gilbert, our architect, and Gary Cripps, the planning officer. Many of you know them from village life. I derive great comfort with both men working on this project in our back yard, so to speak. When it comes to ensuring the development meets strict planning regulations and doesn't spoil Oakdene's aesthetic appeal, we couldn't be in better hands. As residents, they have personal, vested interests in seeing every consideration addressed."

The tense atmosphere continued, but occasional murmuring subsided while Brandon launched into a display of charisma on steroids. The hall's subdued audience remained calm until Gary put the housing estate layout proposal on an overhead projector screen. Even untrained eyes noticed every available inch of land stuffed with characterless boxes. Quaint local references in the proposed street names, like *'Asbury Gardens,'* and *'Underwood Close,'* did little to lighten reddening faces.

The gravelly voiced man leapt to his feet and shouted at Julian Asbury. "Why have you foisted this monstrosity upon us? It's all very well for you in your fancy country estate, but what about everyone else? Have you any idea what this will do to the village?"

Julian took to the podium, working hard to control his boiling fury and abject disdain for those he addressed. "The patch of land I'm making available has lain dormant far too long. Our family timber business folded long before my time, leaving that weed-choked parcel at the foot of the hill an unrealised asset. Meanwhile, modern running and maintenance costs on the exquisite stately home built by my forebear - the founder of this village - continue to skyrocket. 17th century manor houses aren't cheap. Mr Beeching assures me every aspect of this proposal is in line with government guidance and requirements. Change is never easy in a place that has resisted it for so long." A sickening smile spread across his face. "I like to think of this as the completion of a loop in time. That land was abandoned to build a new village, while the old was torn down and forgotten. Many foundation stones in your own houses came from its predecessor. Now the old land is re-joining the new, making our settlement one."

Peggy Greene shot up like a rocket and swayed against her cane. She called towards the podium. "You're as reprehensible as your forefather. It's all about money, isn't it?"

Julian fixed her with an icy stare. "As I've already indicated: if it weren't for my forefather, there would be no village, Mrs Greene." He noticed Amanda sitting beside her, so chose his next words with care. "Forgive me, but we're all aware of your penchant for wild observations. They're legendary in our community; even up at the manor. No doubt many in Oakdene have sought - and found - comfort from your unorthodox advice." He forced a pointless disarming grin, which didn't quite come off. "Such is your standing. However, we must weigh up pressing requirements for development with our available options in a rational, unemotional frame of mind." He coughed. "You said it's about money. I've been transparent over my stately home's rising costs. As a good steward of our heritage, I'm seeking all reasonable compromises in the pursuit of meeting them." He frowned. "Money isn't a dirty word. I could pretend it is, while one of England's architectural jewels crumbles about my ears. What purpose would that serve? Chances are, the government would acquire Ms Fairchild's extensive meadow at Ravensbrook via compulsory purchase and erect double the number of homes on it. Would you prefer that?"

Brandon moved in beside Julian, speaking under his breath. "Ease back on the threats and hand over to me so I can wrap up."

Twenty minutes later, Amanda lingered near a drinks table, sipping from a paper cup of orange juice. Julian pushed through a throng of discontented villagers.

"Amanda?"

Amanda tossed the empty receptacle into an open black bin bag. "Hello, Julian."

Julian squinted. "At least you're still talking to me."

Amanda studied his face with dispassionate eyes. "How did you expect the meeting to go?"

"This current descendant of Oakdene's onetime champion has slipped off the familial charger, it seems."

Amanda rolled her eyes at his smug reference to ancient history, waved under her nose yet again. "They might not be grubbing out my meadow, but I'll still have to look at that housing estate every time I open the front door."

"It won't be so bad once work has finished. Housing developments always stick out like a sore thumb when they're brand new. Give it a year and you won't notice the place."

"I wish I shared your optimism. What about the poor souls whose bones lie beneath that woodland?"

"The past is the past. People have to move on."

Amanda glowered. "I see. You shove the past under our noses, RE Oliver Asbury, whenever it suits you; but the moment history gets in your way, it doesn't matter anymore? Tell me if I'm reading that wrong?"

Julian flushed. "I don't want to fight. Any remains unearthed when the site is cleared, will be treated with the proper respect, I assure you." He reached into his jacket and pulled out a slip of paper. "Here's the cheque for your first painting of the manor."

"You haven't seen it yet. It's ready and waiting at my studio."

"Yes, I received your e-mail. Thank you. I've been preoccupied, as you can imagine." He handed the cheque to her, then whipped his hand away. "Tuck that out of sight, lest people think you're making a deal with the devil."

Amanda stuffed it into her pocket with reluctant acceptance. "Thank you, Julian."

"Are you still interested in producing more paintings?"

Amanda nodded. "Of course. I may not like this housing proposal, but I'm a professional artist. Your home is magnificent and worthy of immortalising in paint. When are you coming by to collect the picture?"

"Tomorrow morning?"

"That's fine."

Julian looked around. "Where did Peggy Greene disappear off to? I saw you sitting with her."

"A friend took her home. She's old and became more distraught than most." Amanda swirled her tongue. "That's saying something, too."

Julian rubbed his forehead. "I know. I'd best rescue my fellow presenters and try smoothing things over with the mob."

Amanda winced, then turned to leave, muttering under her breath. "Good luck with that one."

* * *

Abigail Webb had taken reasonable care of herself for a late-thirties, divorced single mother with a minimum wage job. Ever one to put her beloved son, Anton, before herself, she now struggled with the direction her second marriage was taking in regard to his safety. Abigail didn't consider herself pretty, which was a shame. She'd no chance of gracing the cover of glamour magazines; but from straight, straw blonde, shoulder length hair to a face she never made up - yet which glowed with natural beauty - she was a charming, shapely specimen of honest womanhood. This lack of self-regard made her an easy target for men who appeared inviting on the outside, but festered within like putrid tombs. Abigail married at twenty-five to a guy who'd fathered their only child, Anton, three years later. He ran off with another woman when Anton was five. Self-deprecating and honest, Abigail adored her son but lacked the fortitude to stand up to her abusive new husband.

As Paul turned the key in their front door with a face like thunder, Abigail adjusted her silken neck scarf on the step beside him.

Paul stepped inside and punched the hallway wall. "I can't believe how ungrateful those selfish, short-sighted pillocks behaved. Don't they have any idea the care I've taken in making the new house designs attractive?"

Abigail spoke with a soft voice, like a whispering wind. "It's a big change. Oakdene is such a pretty, traditional village. We've no modern buildings to speak of, except the school and community hall. They're over a hundred and fifty years old. Even the garage was converted from a shed. It's part of the local fabric."

Paul wheeled on her. "Are you joining their ranks?"

Abigail retreated against the wall. "Why does everything have to be about sides, Paul?"

He scowled and tossed a hand towards the front door. "Because that meeting was a festival of conviviality, wasn't it?" He gritted his teeth. "Did you hear what people said about my drawings?"

"They're upset. You wouldn't make them happy if the entire estate were built of traditional cob and thatch. Chopping down those woods will change the character of Oakdene beyond repair. Residents here like the familiar and traditional."

Paul hung up his jacket. "If they like the traditional, this should delight them. Traditionally there weren't trees on that spot, there were buildings. An entire village."

Gunshots blared from a television set in the living room. Paul thrust open the door, where Anton sat on a cushion watching a war film.

"What are you still doing up?" Paul growled at his stepson and tore the remote from his grasp. With a definitive flick, he switched off the set.

Anton fidgeted. "Mum said I could."

"Oh, did she?" Paul's eyes became pinpricks of light shining upon Abigail.

Abigail entered the room, walking on eggshells. "It's not late, Paul. Anyway, he's on holiday."

Anton stammered. "H-how was your meeting, Paul?"

Paul stared right through him, as though the child had committed an unforgivable sin and now bore no value as a human being. "Think that's funny, do you?"

"W-what? I was asking how-"

Paul gripped Anton's curly dark blond bangs and dragged him towards the kitchen. Anton cried out, limbs flailing.

Abigail grabbed Paul's tugging arm. His free hand whipped across her face with a resounding crack. She fell onto the sofa, clutching one cheek, with tears streaming from red eyes.

Paul snatched a feather duster with a cane handle from behind the kitchen door. "This jibing little runt will learn some respect if it's the last thing I do." He yanked Anton's t-shirt up, exposing the tender flesh of his young back.

Abigail staggered into the doorway. "No. Don't hurt my son."

"He's got to learn, Abigail. It's the only way we'll make a decent man out of him."

The words *'decent man'* on the lips of her hypocritical husband stung worse than the swelling welt on Abigail's face. She clutched the door frame and winced at every strike as the cane swished across Anton's tensed spine. The boy yelped and cried, begging to know what he'd done wrong.

Paul twisted one of Anton's arms to still him and continued administering his punishment beating. "Take it in silence, or I'll whip you twice as hard."

Anton sucked up the agony into a heaving bout of sobs, praying their volume wouldn't increase the vigour of Paul's strokes. He almost lost consciousness from the pain. Without warning, a final flick and associated burning sensation ended his torment. Paul opened the refrigerator and pulled out a six pack of cheap lager. The ring pull hissed on a can, followed by a rapid series of throat glugs while he downed the contents like a stranded desert survivor slaking impossible thirst. He crushed the empty in one powerful hand and tossed it at Anton's head, where the boy still hunched on the kitchen floor. "Go to bed, before I recover my energy and enthusiasm for another dose of discipline."

Anton sniffed and limped past his mother. He tore his arm from her grasp as she attempted to console him, before retreating to his room in solitary misery.

Upstairs in bed, Anton lay on his side, clutching the cold metal cross from Underwood against his body. His special treasure brought little comfort, other than the dream of one day selling it and moving away from Paul Gilbert and his temper. The wounds striping his back made resting in a face-up position too sore for sleep. Down in the living room, his mother's attempts to challenge Paul resulted in a familiar series of slaps and cries. Abundant tears followed, until Paul yelled at her to stop, accompanied by expletive laden threats regarding the consequences if she didn't. Anton pressed the cross tighter to his chest. "I hate him."

10
Burning Questions

Anton Webb made sure he was at the breakfast table early on Saturday morning for two reasons. First, he hoped to be finished and away before Paul came down ahead of his usual, shorter weekend working day. Second, if he took the opposite tack and laid in bed hoping for Paul to leave before rising, the risk of a laziness beating reared its ugly head. It wouldn't be the first time. Anton lived in a world of second guessing his stepfather to avoid offering flimsy excuses for punishment. The man loved to dish it out.

Abigail served her quiet lad an egg on toast as Paul's heavy footsteps hurried down the stairs. He entered the kitchen without a word, sat at the table, and flicked through pages of a feasibility study from the office. Abigail poured him a coffee and set down a bowl of cornflakes.

Paul's eyes scanned every line of text, his mind lost in the detail. He grunted at Anton. "Pour some milk on my cereals."

Abigail watched Anton lift a jug set in the table centre over Paul's bowl. Cold milk splashed against the generous pile of flakes before bouncing off and splattering the report.

"You stupid idiot." Paul grabbed a paper serviette and mopped the smudged print. "Can't you do anything right? How am I supposed to read this now?"

Anton drew back, holding tight to the jug with chilled hands matching its china white sheen.

Paul slammed the document down and lurched from his chair towards the door. "Where is the feather duster?"

Abigail watched Anton and her husband in guilty silence.

Paul sneered. "Oh, I see. Coddling the boy now, are you?" He grabbed Anton by the arm and dragged him from his chair, more milk slopping as he released the jug. "My hand works fine too, Abigail." He walloped Anton in a series of hefty slaps, while still regarding his wife. "If that duster hasn't reappeared when I get in from work, you'll find out for yourself."

When Anton shrivelled into a weeping pile, Paul wrenched open the back door and pushed him into the garden. "Get out of my sight." He slammed it shut, then downed his coffee in a single slug and ignored the cereals. "Don't forget I'll be home early."

Abigail hated herself in that moment, but spoke submissive words like an obedient slave. "Dinner will be ready and waiting."

Paul kissed her on the cheek and smiled as though Mr Hyde had transformed back into Dr Jekyll once more. "Love you. Have a good day." He winked, collected his papers, and then proceeded through the hallway to the front door. As his car engine started and the vehicle pulled away, Abigail held her head over the sink and wept.

* * *

"Don't you want any breakfast? Hey, stay away from the woods, Belle," Amanda called after Belinda, racing for the front door at Ravensbrook.

"I will," Belinda's voice accompanied birdsong from the opened portal. "I hope Mr Asbury likes the painting." She let the door swing free.

"Thanks. See you later." Amanda hung up a tea towel in time to catch an approaching V8 fanfare heralding Julian's Aston. She reached the doorstep as Belinda hurried across the meadow towards the woods. Amanda shook her head. *It's like talking to a brick wall, sometimes. She can't mean to visit Underwood again.*

Julian's car skidded to a halt. He hopped out and shielded his eyes from the sun, following Belinda's exit. "She won't be able to do that once site works commence."

"*If* site works commence," Amanda corrected.

Julian grinned. "An optimist? Aren't artists supposed to capture or interpret what's there? Are you a romantic painter?"

"I'm not a romantic anything; I draw and paint what I see. Things that leave an impression on me. Last night I saw a lot of opposition."

"Bah." Julian batted the comment aside like a troublesome wasp. "Initial shock. Once abundant new neighbours are saying hello, spending money in the shop and sending their kids to the village school, all this will blow over."

"There won't be any new neighbours if there aren't any new houses." Amanda focused on the front of Julian's hulking green sports car. "Is it my imagination or have you had the engine tuned? It sounded different."

Julian closed his driver's door. "No, but I can't fault your auditory observation skills. More than a mere artist's eye, it seems. There's a problem with it. Brian Taylor was inspecting the vehicle when his accident occurred. The authorities finally let me have the motor back, but now whatever was wrong has grown more serious. I'll book it in elsewhere before long. Brian's staff don't inspire confidence in me, I'm afraid. Not with a prestige motor like my Vantage."

Amanda shook her head in disbelief at his callousness. "How inconvenient for you."

Julian picked up on her annoyance and sarcasm. "I can't change the past. Brian was an excellent mechanic. It's a shame."

"So the world moves on like nothing happened? Pardon my bluntness, Julian, but for a man so caring and sentimental over his home and heritage, you extend those qualities to little else."

Julian stuffed his hands in the pockets of his smart trousers. "Have I been anything less than civil towards you, since our initial misunderstanding?"

"No."

"Was I a poor host during your visit at the manor?

Did I not pay you in advance yesterday, for a painting I haven't seen?"

Amanda winced. "You did. Sorry."

Julian huffed, then swept around the vehicle and placed a conciliatory arm on Amanda's reluctant shoulder. "You've absorbed bad vibes floating around Oakdene, that's all. Last week I was some benevolent gent up the hill, who left folk alone or invited them to the odd summer garden party. Now I'm the big, bad wolf, seeking to huff and puff and blow people's houses down - metaphorically speaking."

"How about converting the manor into apartments? Wouldn't that count towards the government's property development quota? How many rooms does one guy need?"

Julian's eyes almost popped out on stalks. "Heaven forbid. High Stanton has always belonged to the Asbury family and no-one else. Besides, I may find a nice young lady and raise a family. We'll never run out of space." His resting hand caressed Amanda. "Where's your studio?"

Amanda's skin crawled. She indicated the floor above, from the hallway entrance.

Julian fixed her with an inviting look. "Take me upstairs."

Amanda disentangled herself from his insistent grasp and stepped aside. "After you." She followed, trying not to clench her fists. *Take me upstairs? In your dreams, you suggestive, callous toff.*

"Which way?" Julian reached the landing.

"Straight on through the open doorway." Amanda

clung to the banister.

"Ah yes. Bright and filled with natural light." Julian scanned the other rooms nearby. "A pity the rest of your home is so dark and dismal."

"I'll get around to updating it, eventually. That takes time and money." She joined Julian in the studio. "I haven't wrapped your painting yet. It felt wrong before you'd examined it."

Julian positioned himself at Amanda's easel, where the picture rested beneath a white sheet. "A big unveiling? Marvellous. I feel like royalty. Should I give a speech?"

"Please don't. I hope you like it." Amanda grabbed the sheet in two places and eased it clear of the finished painting, placed back on the easel for presentation purposes.

Julian's keen anticipation fell into a fuming morass of facial negativity. "I'm not in any mood for games, Amanda."

Amanda shifted around the tabletop, where her mouth dropped open. That the painting was her original picture of High Stanton remained without question. She recognised her own work, plus the telltale corner signature. Now the manor glowed with tongues of searing flame, raging upward into a smoky sky. A shadowy figure held hands aloft in despair before an upstairs window, as though wracked with inconsolable agony. "I..." Words failed her.

Julian tapped his foot. "Where is the real painting?"

Amanda shook her head. "Something has happened to it."

"And you put this one on display as a joke?"

"No, I mean, this is the picture, but it's been altered. Julian, I swear when I set this up for you last night, the image showed a tranquil scene of the manor in sunlight. I was so proud of it."

"Do you expect me to believe that? What happened, did you sleepwalk and convert it into a raging inferno?" Julian pulled out his car keys, face crimson. "Don't bother trying to cash that cheque, Amanda. I'll cancel it this morning. I thought you were a professional artist, not some hip, Bristol political activist or green agitator. Well, I've no time for your sort. Good day." He stormed from the room and pounded downstairs. The front door opened and slammed, followed several seconds later by the Aston's engine roaring to life.

Amanda stood alone in her studio, face aghast at the acrylic scene of conflagration. She scanned the ceiling with terrified eyes. "What the hell is going on?"

Craig Symonds pulled up outside Ravensbrook an hour later. He slipped out of his battered Land Rover Defender while Amanda swept gravel with a broom, head bowed.

"Are you creating artificial molehills for a reason?" He raised an inquisitive eyebrow.

Amanda lifted her agitated face. "Levelling this out is tougher than I expected."

Craig opened the Landy's tailgate. "That's because you're using a broom." He pulled a rake from among his gardening tools. "The flat side of this will sort it out. What happened?"

"Julian Asbury's car." Amanda's response lacked any vital spark, much like her sullen appearance.

"Was he doing doughnuts outside your house?" Craig set to work, levelling the piles of gravel she'd gathered.

"No. He came to collect my first painting of High Stanton, but left without it in a rage."

Craig almost dropped his rake. "A rage? You're kidding. How could anyone not be satisfied with your work?" A cheeky light flashed across his countenance. "Didn't you make his house impressive enough to massage his over-inflated ego?"

Amanda rested on her broom. "Everything will become clear once you see it."

Craig whistled. "Ooh. Mysterious yet again."

Amanda watched him hard at work tidying the mess. "Thanks for coming over. I didn't cost you a job, did I?"

"Nope. I was enjoying a Saturday off."

Amanda bit her lip. "That almost makes it worse."

Craig snorted. "Don't be daft. When you phoned, I was nursing a cuppa and admiring your watercolour of Cosicott. It looks great on my wall. Anyway, we never discussed those revelations from Rachel Barnes you mentioned last night. Peggy was so unsettled I had to whisk her off home."

"I remember. How was she?"

"Still in a flap when we reached her cottage. She calmed down after I passed her that clay cat you made.

There's the power of positive memories for you."

Amanda sighed. "Good."

Craig addressed a new patch of disturbed gravel. "It was an excellent gift." He glanced up. "Are you going to tell me about Rachel, then?"

"Are you sure you want to hear?"

Craig rocked his head from side to side. "More freaky tales?"

"That night Belle went to play at their home, Rachel claims some kind of psychic phenomena took place in Laura's bedroom. It tossed papers around, winded Laura, and threw toys at Rachel when she ran to investigate. Belle was screaming and begging whatever it was not to hurt them, like she knew it."

This time Craig dropped his rake. "Shit. Rachel was serious?" He picked up the gardening implement again.

"I can't imagine why any adult would invent something like that. Least of all a responsible one who took Belle into her home before I arrived on the scene."

"Have you spoken with Belle about it?"

Amanda stared at the ground. "I don't know how. She becomes evasive whenever I push her over what happened. It's the same with any of the odd situations. She's more cryptic than Peggy. Either way, the Barnes family don't want Belle anywhere near their home or daughter."

"That's harsh."

"The thing is, Craig: I didn't detect any malice in Rachel's account of what happened. She seemed sad and conflicted about the whole situation."

"Do you think that disturbance could have been the mysterious Jonathan? How about a poltergeist?"

"I'm no parapsychologist, but Belle hasn't hit puberty yet. Don't they affect teenagers going through hormonal and emotional upheaval?"

"It's a popular theory. I'd argue Belle has suffered plenty of emotional upheaval, though."

"True."

"A straight-up, honest to goodness, old-fashioned ghost then?"

Amanda shivered and stared at the upstairs landing window. She recalled Craig's mention of a young man standing there during his first visit. "I hope not, but I'm coming around to that way of thinking. There's something else Rachel Barnes told me."

"There's more?"

"Belle was at the garage right before Brian Taylor died."

Craig finished levelling the gravel and walked over to her. "How does she know?"

"The short version is: Laura overheard some boys Belle was playing with, talking. They'd left her alone outside the garage on the day of Brian's accident. All these fatal tragedies Belle is associated with worried Rachel."

Craig scratched his short beard. "Does she think Belle unleashed a psychic storm that twisted metal and collapsed that ramp on top of Brian?"

"We didn't get into that, though I challenged her over it."

"Small wonder you've been distracted. What

happened with Julian and the painting?"

Amanda took his rake and set it alongside her broom against the wall beside the front door. "Come and see for yourself."

Craig followed her upstairs into the studio, where the altered painting still rested on Amanda's tabletop easel. He stood in open-mouthed horror at the devastating scene and dark, pained figure reaching towards a window from within. "Not your usual bucolic brilliance." His tone quietened upon catching Amanda's nervous expression. "You're going to tell me you didn't do that, aren't you?"

"Oh, I painted the manor all right; the manor in clear skies on a beautiful day. No fire, no smoke, no frantic silhouette in agony."

Craig leaned closer and examined the artwork. "A nine-year-old didn't do this."

"No, she didn't." Amanda swallowed hard.

Craig faced her. "Then who?"

Amanda shrugged.

Craig rubbed his brow. "Bugger me," he whispered his astonishment, then studied the painting again.

* * *

No guilt washed over Belinda at promising her aunt she'd avoid the woods, then plunging headlong into them. When a girl her own age appeared at the foot of her bed that morning, she was scared at first, then intrigued. Jonathan remained unseen and unheard, but the manner of this child's dress suggested a spectre of the same period. Her curling finger beckoned Belinda to follow, though she remained mute and solemn of face. Belinda dressed in a flash and was out the door in great haste as the mysterious girl's steps quickened. The whispering voices had left her alone overnight. Deep in her innermost heart, Belinda yearned to understand all she'd experienced. Now, with news the apparent source of her encounters may succumb to development, concrete answers were a necessity before literal concrete started flowing. Her pale, fleet lure cast a forlorn look behind, a brief smile teasing her wan face. It came as no surprise when the ruined church tower of Underwood appeared through the greenery ahead. Belinda shuddered at the memory of Sam Peebles' lifeless form laying with his throat sliced open. All the while warm gore had flowed over her face and body like a shower of unset strawberry jam, fresh from the cooking pan.

Ahead, the girl halted, facing the crumbling house of worship. Its solemn walls suffered the ever tightening embrace of strangling ivy, encouraged by the warmer weather.

Belinda stopped. She summoned enough courage to speak. "Hello?"

The girl still faced away. She extended a pale, pointing finger toward the church door.

Dark thunderheads obscured the brilliant sunshine out of nowhere. A resonant rumble tensed Belinda's muscles. The weeping of adults, both male and female, echoed from the church doorway. A cart pulled up outside the graveyard, stacked with the bodies of an entire family. Diggers stepped away from a pit set apart from the main church path, while a crowd of mourners assembled beside their minister. The man of God held a posy to his face, cheeks drawn and haggard from the apparent helplessness of his office. Jonathan stood beside him. Like the rest, he appeared oblivious to Belinda's presence.

Belinda searched the scene. Underwood's cottages stood almost solid again in her waking dream. A sombre man painted a large red cross on the door of one. Further weeping echoed behind it from another family sealed inside and condemned to die.

The girl from her bedroom whirled, face now swollen and spotted with a dark rash. She stumbled towards Belinda, who screamed and dived out of the way. Blood pooled beneath the girl's skin as she passed, staining her pallid flesh a horrid shade of purple. She clambered onto the cart, unseen by two men attending to the corpses with cloth tied about their faces. They raised an identical child's body off their conveyance. The beckoning girl became one with it and vanished. Her corpse swung through the air and fell into the open pit with a dull thud among her parents and siblings.

Belinda's head throbbed. She clutched it where she'd fallen and rolled over, crying out. "No. No, I can't take any more of this." The whispers came now, a deafening chorus of anger, bitterness and woe. Belinda screamed again until the tumult stilled quicker than it had arisen and engulfed her.

"Are you waiting to chop someone else up?" Anton

Webb stood in the empty church doorway, face ashen.

Belinda propped her back against a mossy tombstone and regained her composure. "What do you want, Anton?"

"You do realise you were fitting and screaming like a lunatic, Belle?" The content of his response hinted at the taunting she'd endured in the school playground, yet his body language lacked conviction.

Belinda hugged herself, desperate for comfort. "Have you put the cross back?"

"No. I came out for a walk and to think. It felt less threatening here today."

"What did you need to think about?"

Anton's eyes broke contact. "Stuff." He kicked a loose stone into the long grass beside her. "I'm sorry about what happened at school. I realise I apologised in Mrs Masters' office, but I didn't mean to act cruel. Honest."

Belinda noticed the sky had turned blue once more and birds now sang from lush, nodding branches. "Did you hear that thunder?"

Anton frowned. "What thunder? We've had clear skies all morning."

"Never mind."

Anton stepped forward and offered a hand to help her up. "You're weird sometimes, Belle."

Belinda accepted his assistance. "Aren't you playing with your friends today?"

"No. I wanted to be alone." He winced as Belinda's hand touched his back to steady herself on the way up.

Belinda gasped. "What's wrong?"

"Nothing."

"Pish to nothing; you're hurt. Show me."

Anton's defensive, emotional wall crumbled like the church tower behind them at the concern in her eyes. "My stepfather beats me."

Belinda's eyes watered. "Can I see?"

Anton rolled up his t-shirt, revealing a collection of cruel red lines running diagonally across his spine.

"Anton, this is terrible. You should tell someone. Does your mother hit you too?"

"No. She's more frightened of Paul than I am. Too afraid to do anything. I daren't speak about it."

Belinda squeezed his hand. "Have you put cream on those marks?"

Anton shook his head.

Belinda drew him towards the clearing edge, away from the church. "I know a damp patch where dock leaves grow. If they soothe nettle rash, they might cool your back. Shall we try?"

Anton eyed her with deeper regret over his recent behaviour. "Thank you, Belle."

Belinda tugged harder at his arm, a faint echo of the lively friend she'd once been. "Come on."

"Will you tell me what's going on?" Anton lay on his front while Belinda draped dock leaves across his stinging wounds.

"How do you mean?" Belinda reached for another plant.

"You know: why people keep dying around you;

why Laura is terrified you're a witch or possessed by evil spirits."

"I can't say, Anton. Everything started when you removed that cross from the old church."

Anton watched puffy clouds drift in a gentle summer sky; time rolling away with them as the day passed. "You don't half run on about that cross. I'm not putting it back, okay? The cross is mine."

Belinda wanted to compact the leaves she'd administered, but spite ran contrary to her nature. "How does that feel?"

"It's cooler. I'll die if Paul takes the cane of that feather duster to me again. Mum hid it this morning, but he threatened her."

Belinda stretched out beside him. "I'm sorry, Anton; I didn't realise. Everyone thinks you act strange sometimes, but nobody suspects this. Nobody who's spoken with me, anyway."

Anton rested his chin on folded hands. "I'll have to go soon. Paul works a short day on Saturdays. If I'm not in for dinner when he arrives…"

"I understand."

Anton stared into space. "I dread the approach of his car down that lane from the bridge. Even though I don't see it, I can imagine him drawing nearer. His face is full of anger."

"With you to take it out on?"

"Yes."

Belinda sat up and peeled the leaves away from Anton's back. "Put your t-shirt on and I'll walk with you to the edge of the woods."

"Thanks." Anton followed her instructions and stood up. "Belle?"

"Yes?"

"I've told you my secret. That helped a little. Won't you tell me yours?"

Belinda shook her head. "You can't help me any more than I can help you. Nobody can. I see and hear things others don't. Please don't ask me to describe them. I'm trying to shut it all out."

"Okay."

"I hope your back heals fast and your stepfather leaves you alone."

Anton set off with Belinda beside him. "If you change your mind… About talking, I mean…"

Belinda smiled. "Thanks."

"Belle?"

"Uh-huh?"

"Whatever happens once we go back to school, I promise I won't let people treat you mean." He extended his hand. "Friends?"

Belinda shook it. "Friends."

* * *

Paul Gilbert coasted through narrow country lanes on his way home from the office at Great Torrington. Villager reactions from the meeting on Friday night had cast shadows across his entire working day. He flicked on the car radio in his silver Ford Focus, hoping for soothing music to calm his fraying nerves. Instead, he picked up a local talk show of disgruntled Devon residents. Frustrated locals called in to voice concerns their beautiful county might disappear under a blanket of ugly concrete. Paul slammed a fist against the dashboard. "Bloody NIMBY wankers." He swerved to avoid an oncoming car, then downshifted as the arched stone bridge across the Torridge appeared around the bend.

The radio host's broad, West Country accent cut clear. "Next we'll hear from nine-year-old Howard Littlejohn in Winkleigh. Go ahead, Howard."

A cute boy's voice squeaked from the speakers. "Nan and Granddad told me all the new houses south of our village used to be fields. At school, Teacher said we should stop destroying the natural world. Aren't we supposed to care for the environment?"

The host chuckled under his breath. "Howard raises an excellent point. On one hand, the PM lectures us about boosting our green credentials; while on the other, he's overseeing the biggest destruction of green belt and grade-A agricultural land in our nation's history. Land on which development is supposed to be forbidden. Has this happened in your area? Call us to comment live on air."

Paul drove across the bridge, growling at the radio. "I'd call you, but you'd have to bleep out every other bloody word, you soap-dodging prick." The tender childish tones of the caller's voice switched Paul's mind to thoughts of Anton. *If that kid doesn't behave to perfection tonight, he won't sit down for a week.* The radio broadcast vanished under a cascade of static. "What the...?" Paul clicked its other preset buttons, discovering similar interruptions on all channels. "It's never done that here. I'll bet it's one of those new-wave cell phone masts messing up reception." He clicked the radio off, almost smashing his face into the steering wheel as the Focus lurched first one way and then the other. Two loud bangs beneath the bonnet, followed by a duet of rhythmic flapping, caused Paul to fight for control. The car pulled away from him again. Shredded rubber flew from both front wheel arches. Half in a skid, it overbalanced and careened across the verge, plunging towards the river on Oakdene's side. "Shit." Paul stomped on the brakes with zero effect, his voice rising in pitch to match the previous junior radio caller. His vehicle slammed into a solid tree trunk two feet from the waterway. Its airbag fired, obscuring his view of the mangled concertina bonnet metal and puffs of rising smoke from the engine bay.

Paul massaged his neck and pushed free of the bag. A young girl, around the same age as his stepson, stood on the overlooking bank. Cold, staring eyes peered at him from beneath locks of messy blonde hair. Paul pressed the seatbelt release without result. "Jammed. Great, I have nothing to cut it with."

The smoke thickened until glimmers of orange flame danced against shattered remnants of the broken windshield. Paul's nostrils flared, and he pulled the door handle. Warped tight into a twisted frame, it wouldn't budge. He shoved his shoulder against the door as waves of heat seeped over the dashboard. A sickening crack, like a long, drawn-out split, echoed from the tree trunk the car was wrapped around. "Oh

God, I need to get out of here." His eyes returned to the motionless girl watching him from the bank. An eerie mist - out of place on a clear summer afternoon - snaked about her ankles. While the windshield was history, his driver's power window remained in situ with no way to lower it. Paul hunched forward, eyes smarting at the blistering heat. He shouted to the entranced child. "Help. Call for help."

The entire front section of the car burst into flames. Paul shrieked and held up his hands to ward off burning agony. Fire overpowered the Ford's heat shield and filled the cabin. The petrol tank exploded a moment later, sending another crack and shudder through the swaying tree.

Belinda watched Paul's frantic torso flail to a slowing, blackened human twig that became one with the melting plastic and upholstery. His last scream faded beneath the roaring flames and a ground-shaking tremor. The tree toppled, flattening the burning car. One charred, semi-skeletal arm, dripping with melted flesh, protruded from beneath the tree trunk whose collapse had broken the driver's window and sandwiched the bodywork. Belinda rotated in a stupor and wandered back through the trees, neither heeding the noise and smoke behind her, nor able to comprehend what had occurred. Once again, the whispers that had risen to deafening heights in her mind, faded and vanished beneath the woodland floor.

* * *

"Do you see that?" Amanda stood on the doorstep at Ravensbrook and pointed.

Craig emerged behind her. After witnessing the altered painting for himself and Amanda's uneasy state of mind, he'd prolonged his visit and joined her for a bite to eat. Casual chit-chat transitioned into Amanda showing him the crumbling chimney mortar in the attic. Their joint inspection resulted in Craig's faithful promise to help correct it as soon as possible.

Now Craig followed the direction of her arm across the treetops, where a voluminous column of thick, black smoke rose beyond the village. "Someone must have started a fire down by the river. Kids playing with matches, no doubt."

A wailing chorus of emergency sirens carried on the air. Belinda emerged from the tree line and crossed the meadow. She dawdled; the picture of a carefree disposition or one lost in another world.

Amanda placed her hands on her hips. "Do you reckon Belle knows what's happening?"

Craig focused on the girl's approaching form. "She looks oblivious from here."

"It would make life easier for our developers if the woods went up in flames."

Craig snickered. "Why, Ms Fairchild, what a suspicious mind you have."

Amanda sniffed. "I never used to."

Craig unlocked his Land Rover. "Next thing you'll be wondering if Belle had something to do with it."

Amanda gasped, muscles taut. "Don't say that. I'm serious, Craig; that's not even funny."

"Mmm. I must dash. Say 'Hi' to Belle for me."

"I will. Thanks for everything."

"Sure. All I did was rake some gravel and bum a free lunch."

"I meant being willing to listen and get mixed up in all this."

Craig shrugged. "I'm no wiser about what *all this* is, but by heck is it odd. I'd say *'call if you're struggling,'* except after this morning you seem comfortable with that already."

Amanda touched her chin. He was right. "I'll never take the piss out of Essex boys again."

Craig grinned. "Don't do that; you might come up with a joke I haven't heard a hundred times." He climbed into the Landy, shut the door and rolled down the window. The engine started, and he poked his head out. "Later."

Amanda waved and watched him turn the car before rumbling off down the driveway towards the lane. She waved again when he honked before vanishing from view.

Belinda reached the other side of the meadow.

"How was your day?" Amanda asked.

"Okay. I ran into Anton from school."

Amanda clocked her dithering form and uneasy hands while she spoke. "Was he nasty to you?"

"No. We had a nice time."

"In the woods?" Amanda lowered her head to maintain diverting eye contact from her blushing niece.

"Sorry. Nothing terrible happened to anyone there today." Belinda chose her words with care. If the church vision she'd experienced was a replay of events from the 17th century, her statement proved true.

"Thank goodness. Do you know what's going on in the village? There's quite a commotion from the look and sound of things. A lot of smoke too."

Belinda didn't turn back to the distant, billowing skyward plume of car, tree and human ash. She remained silent.

Amanda studied her. "Have you eaten anything? Craig Symonds joined me for lunch. He says 'Hi,' by the way."

Belinda sniffed. "That's nice. No, I haven't eaten. I'm not hungry."

Amanda's face strained. "You must eat something, Belle. This isn't healthy; you're a growing girl."

"Can I decide later? I may want something then."

Amanda relaxed. "Okay." For an instant she considered mentioning the painting, but thought better of it. Belinda needed stability more than she did. Raising evidence of another inexplicable, creepy occurrence in their home wouldn't help.

Belinda wandered through the front door.

A heady stench of acrid smoke lingered at her passing, assaulting Amanda's nostrils. *Oh God, she reeks of it.* Amanda faced the now greying column once more and almost choked on a sudden, heartsick gulp.

11

A Hunger for Wealth

Brandon Beeching strutted up to the door of The Old Bothy, Gary Cripps at his side. Each man wore an immaculate suit. Gary clutched tight to a glossy, factory printed array of plans in a leather folder. Brandon pulled a ballpoint pen from a holder beside the clipboard in his hand. He checked a list of names and addresses acquired from the council's electoral roll.

"The Barnes family. Are you ready, Gary?"

"Don't you know people's names without reading that blasted list? You live in the same community."

"You can't expect me to remember everyone, even in a place this small. Besides, it never hurts to double-check. Imagine my embarrassment if I slipped up and addressed someone incorrectly. What would that do for our charm offensive? How would it look?"

Gary opened his folder. "Shoddy. Okay, here we go again." He adjusted his tie. "Do it."

Brandon drew his fat torso up to its full, lardy height and jangled the home's free-hanging brass bell.

Rachel Barnes released the door catch, still talking to her young daughter. "If you run into Anton outside, you can talk with him. But, you mustn't go round to his house right now, Laura. Abigail Webb will be distraught. She can't have you underfoot."

Brandon and Gary exchanged uncomfortable glances. Word of Paul Gilbert's death had spread through Oakdene quicker than the blaze that incinerated his screaming form. With cramped surroundings and awkward terrain, it took the fire service considerable effort to remove the toppled tree that pulverised his scorched remains. Two days later, Paul's co-conspirators stuck to their plan, already in possession of his architectural designs to complete the project.

Brandon put on a deep, fruity voice. "Good morning, Mrs Barnes. How are you today?"

Rachel's face fell at the sight of her visitors. Any semblance of civility vanished from her demeanour. "What do you two want?"

"Gary, the planning officer, and I are making household visits regarding the forthcoming housing development. Were you at the meeting on Friday?"

"Yes. As a result I've had to nag my husband about not swearing around the house, in case our girl picks up bad habits. I'm amazed anyone is still talking to you."

Laura appeared behind her mother, saucer eyes watching the smarmy duo.

Brandon coughed to clear the air, then noticed the child. "This must be the fine young lady in question." He leaned closer, addressing Laura. "Do you know, we're talking about erecting a large community playground at the centre of our expanded village? Swings, slides, roundabouts, a climbing frame; all manner of fun you don't get at school."

Laura looked past Brandon and Gary, her gaze drawn to Belinda Fairchild watching from across the lane. Belinda's longing eyes shone with happy memories of play as she pressed against the wall of a cottage opposite.

Rachel pulled Laura's head against her body, unaware of Belinda's presence. She stuck her nose in Brandon's face. "The only people you need to win over to your rotten scheme in this household, are the ones old enough to object. Both of them will, I assure you."

Brandon drew back. "Can't you see how this will bring greater investment and facilities into the village?"

Rachel stepped across her threshold and leaned around the corner. "Do you see that?" She pointed up the no-through road to the woods a short distance beyond. "At present, no traffic passes our home. Not except Julian Asbury's grounds keeper on occasional work visits. He won't be doing that anymore, God rest his soul." Her facial muscles tightened. "This will be the main access road into your eyesore. For months we'll have diggers, noise, mud and disruption. At the end, that tranquil scene bordering our freehold will be ruined by your modern, over-sized rabbit hutches. Plus, we'll have every vehicle belonging to the new homeowners driving past the cottage day and night."

Brandon fidgeted. "I can assure you disruption will be minimal. Other villages benefiting from new developments have seen property prices increase. Over at Chulmleigh with the sprinter line into Exeter connecting the Inter-city to Paddington, demand and subsequent house values are soaring."

Rachel shook her head. "We're on the Torridge, not the Taw or Little Dart. You can't commute from Oakdene. Nobody even wants to. That's why incomers move here. Talk to anyone who wasn't born in the village; I'll guarantee they chose Oakdene to escape modern developments. You can keep your greater investment and facilities, thank you."

Brandon motioned at Gary, who held up his open folder. "If you'll inspect the plans, I'm sure you'll realise none of your fears are justified."

Rachel backed into her home again. "Do you know what isn't justified, Brandon? You as a designated representative of this village. You were born and raised here and you're stabbing it in the back. Don't think for one minute people will forget. Or that they'll lie down and suffer this blot on the landscape without putting up a fight. Good day." She shut the door in their faces.

"Damn, that was pleasant." Brandon stepped away from the door.

Gary closed his folder. "We're on a hiding to nothing with these visits."

Brandon clapped him on the shoulder. "Have a little faith. Mrs Barnes was right about this road. It will be the only route in and out of the development. She's unlikely to hold a favourable view of our proposal."

"Will anyone?"

Brandon preened an eyebrow with idle fingers. "The

point is to reduce active opposition, not win hearts and minds. The fewer objections linked to the case file, the easier it will be to rubber stamp this without raising suspicions. You know the process as well as I."

Gary followed him along the lane. "What was all that about a playground? There are no recreation areas included in my plans."

"I said we were *'talking'* about erecting a playground. We don't have to build one."

Gary tucked the folder under his arm. "Try not to make it sound too much like a jolly theme park when you sell the idea next time. If someone asks to see it on the drawings, we'll appear total liars."

Brandon tutted. "It's an acceptable risk. Who cares? For all the threats of people putting up a fight, this project will go through in the end, regardless. They always do. Come on, next house."

Belinda watched them go, Brandon adopting a confident swagger. She'd overheard every word. Up the gentle ascent beside The Old Bothy, the woods beckoned to her with whispering voices. Belinda recoiled and ran in the opposite direction.

* * *

Brandon Beeching bid Gary Cripps goodbye later that afternoon. He waddled along the picture perfect streets of his home village, unsettled by the weight of passing angry stares. *I knew this development wouldn't be popular. At least the financial benefits are lucrative.* He stopped outside a smart, three-storey home with a tiled roof. Its expansive front garden, sporting immaculate borders, lay behind a brick and railing boundary. Gold lettering at the top of a stained wooden gate declared the property to be named '*Milford*.' A gentle snip of shears caught Brandon's ear. He pushed through the gate and found Craig Symonds edging the lawn in a pristine line.

"A polished job as usual, Craig," Brandon called.

Craig looked round. "How do." His greeting was polite without being effusive.

Brandon trudged across the grass and joined him. "Will you also threaten blood in the streets if I mention new housing?"

Craig snorted. "Is that the response you've had? I spotted you and Gary Cripps campaigning earlier."

Brandon sighed. "It might as well be the response."

Craig began clipping again. "If you're looking for a project cheerleader, I'm afraid you're knocking on the wrong door with me."

"As long as you don't poison my plants, I can live with that."

Craig didn't look away from his task. "Sabotage and dirty tricks aren't my style. I'll leave that to politicians."

Brandon frowned and paced towards the front door, amiability dissipating with every stride. "Tidy up around the acer before you go. It's a mess." Ten seconds later the home's smart, blue panelled front door slammed shut, followed by a kinetic rap from its disturbed brass knocker.

Craig paused, then felt eyes burrowing into the back

of his head. He pivoted to find Belinda staring at the house from across the front gate. "Hey, Belle."

Belinda mouthed a quiet, "Hello."

Craig picked up a can of WD40 and sprayed the shear blades in short, hissing sweeps. He set both items down on the path and joined his subdued witness. "What are you up to?"

Belinda remained still. "Nothing much."

Craig adopted a teasing grin. "Did you have an appointment with Councillor Beeching?"

If Belinda comprehended his joke, she didn't react. "That man is a liar."

Craig licked dry lips. "Far be it from me to encourage criticism of your elders, but I don't trust him either." He studied the house and stretched with a mild yawn. "His job is to provide a voice to residents and manage issues with the council. I suspect when Brandon's interests and Oakdene's differ, he'll always come down on the former side." He cleared his throat. "Don't tell your aunt I said that. She might not approve."

Belinda admired the flowerbeds. "He has a lovely garden."

"Yes he does."

"Thanks to you." She looked at him.

"It pays my bills. He didn't create it."

Belinda pointed to the far end. "Is that lavender?"

"It is. Buzzing with bumblebees. They love it."

"So do I. The colour and smell, I mean. I don't make honey."

Craig laughed, relieved to extract a semblance of

good humour and a fuller reply from the dreamy girl. He tugged the gate open. "Why don't you pop down for a closer look and a sniff? Brandon won't care, I'm sure."

"Thank you." Belinda made for an expansive patch of purple flowers swaying beneath one of the elegant home's broad windows.

Craig picked up a broom and began tidying. He cast an occasional glance in her direction. Belinda crouched and rubbed lavender between her fingers to bruise it before sniffing. Her eyes closed in ecstasy. Craig shook his head. *If that's a psychic murderer, I'm a four-leaf clover.* He continued sweeping.

Brandon pulled a handwritten note from beneath a bowl of fruit on his kitchen table, then lifted it high enough to read:

'Brandon,

I left for my reunion around nine. Back first thing in the morning. Supper is in the fridge.
A letter arrived for you with dreadful handwriting on the envelope. It's got a local postmark. I've put it in your study.

See you tomorrow,

Dorothy.

X.'

Brandon tossed the note in a pedal bin next to the Belfast sink, pulled a beer from the fridge and popped its crown cap. He sauntered into his impressive study, lined with floor to ceiling bookcases and a solid, antique mahogany desk.

Outside, Craig collected his tools and waited at the gate. Belinda still crouched near the lavender bushes.

"I'm off, Belle. Are you all right?"

Belinda rose and nodded.

Craig stepped down into the lane. "Don't linger too long; he's not in the best of moods today."

"Bye." Belinda waved, then edged closer to eager bees bouncing from flower to flower of the fragrant plant.

Craig strolled off, whistling to himself.

Inside the study, Brandon examined the letter mentioned in his wife's note. It lay on a Lincoln green ink blotter atop his desk, next to a brass inkwell and pen whose sole purpose was decorative. The handwritten address suggested a spider had wandered all over the paper at an odd angle; yet it remained clear enough for the Post Office to identify him as the recipient. He swiped a gold-plated letter opener from beside the inkwell and slit the rear flap. Inside, a folded note on plain paper bore similar scrawl in red Biro. He stood beside the window and held it up to the light for closer inspection.

'Beeching,

Traitors want to watch out. Oakdene was birthed in blood and blood will come again.

Row back your plans and you may yet live in peace.'

Brandon sneered. "Who do these prats think they're dealing with?" He pondered whether to retain the indirect threat - most likely written by someone with their opposite hand. *Why waste police time? If the best this loser can do is scribble vague intimidation and post it, we've already won.* He opened a cigar box, lit up a fragrant stogie, and allowed the thick, scented smoke to linger in his mouth. With a victorious smirk he lifted the poison pen letter and ignited it before dropping its curling, blackened paper into an ash tray. The envelope followed until he stubbed out the final remains of his relaxing cigar into nothing more than grey ash. He chuckled to himself. "Up yours."

His self-satisfied face alighted upon a row of heavy-bound leather volumes on a nearby bookcase. Brandon reached out and retrieved one before opening it on the now empty blotter. Pages of antique coins from around the world flashed by as he turned leaf after leaf of clear plastic wallets. Halfway through the book, he paused. "What? Who's touched my beauties?" Half a dozen leaves in the middle were empty, though each wallet still bore descriptive labels he'd added with great care and attention. Brandon grabbed another volume, then checked its contents with a forensic eye. More coins had disappeared.

A silhouette darted across the window. Brandon leapt out of his leather chair at the desk and stuck his nose against the glass. A young girl with a mop of wild blonde hair stood beside his lavender bushes. He banged on a pane and shouted. "Oi! What are you doing in my garden? This is private property, you scruffy little urchin."

The child watched him, unmoved and unmoving.

Brandon stormed into the hallway and tugged open his front door, still fuming and confused over the apparent theft from his proud collection. Outside, the girl was nowhere in sight. He huffed to himself, "Don't come back," then slammed the door and turned.

The same girl stood before him in unblinking silence at the base of the stairs.

Brandon went purple. "Thief. Come here, you. We'll see what the police have to say about a juvenile burglar in my home." He lunged forward with a stretching arm, then broke his own stride and almost toppled, face drained of blood. Clouds of swirling vapour blasted into the hallway. Each evidenced a will of its own, rather than adhering to one uniform direction a natural draught might induce. Brandon retreated into his study, stumbling over the doorsill as he backed towards the desk. The girl moved to fill the open portal while wreathing fingers of white cloud clawed around its frame. They entered and morphed into shadowy shapes of humanoid appearance. From each came a jingle, as of someone rattling metallic discs together. The flash of gold and silver caused Brandon to collapse into his chair.

Those indistinct shapes sharpened into figures of individual character. Their disfigured faces summoned a yelping scream from the fat councillor's tobacco darkened lungs. As the intruding vapours closed about him, violent movement and a muffled gargle were the only evidence to anyone outside of Brandon's horrors within. But, he lived in a posh house at the end of an extensive garden, removed from the villagers he looked down his nose at. Nobody saw or heard a thing. Nobody except the pale, frozen child lingering in his study doorway.

* * *

Amanda entered Oakdene with a spring in her step. An invitation to lunch at the pub from Craig wasn't a major life event, yet she enjoyed his company and hadn't sampled the village hostelry. She paused outside a posh residence called Milford. Two police cars rolled away from completing whatever business brought them to the village. She carried on up the lane, before stopping at The Royalist in its thatched glory. An earlier excursion with her camera had left Amanda with half a dozen possible compositions for a painting. She'd yet to proposition the pub's owners over commissions for bar artwork by a local artist, or the possibility of them displaying and selling other prints from her portfolio. She opened a low gate in a white picket fence surrounding the beer garden. Craig waved at her from inside, where he sat by an opened lattice window. Amanda acknowledged him and entered the bar.

Inside, broad, smoke-blackened beams clung to low ceilings like the gunnery deck of a Napoleonic era frigate. A polished metal post horn hung above the bar, where locals occupied every available stool. Behind the bar, a fat, balding, middle-aged publican pulled pints beneath a restored but deactivated flintlock Baker Rifle. The weapon's presence suggested a newcomer to the decor of a pub built more than a century prior to its genesis.

Amanda squeezed beside two male patrons engaged in animated discussion.

The first, a ginger-haired mid-fifties man with round glasses, slammed his hand down on a bar-top blue towel. "I've no idea who did it, but I'll tell you this for nothing: I'd have shoved every one of those coins down his treacherous gullet myself."

His companion, a narrow-eyed beefcake with a wheatsheaf tattoo on his left bicep and fraying white t-shirt, placed a finger to his lips. "I'd keep that to yourself until police catch the culprit. No sense landing in the muck on account of casual listeners." He eyed Amanda, standing perplexed close by.

The publican interrupted their awkward standoff. "What can I get you, love?"

Amanda reached into her handbag. "Pimms and lemonade, please."

"All the usual with that?"

"If you've got it," Amanda grinned.

"Ice, strawberry, cucumber and mint coming up.

Fancy a splash of gin? It's Thunderflower, a local dry one."

"Sure, why not? Thank you."

Amanda waited for her drink to arrive, paid, and then edged around busy tables towards Craig who stood waiting by a square one big enough for two. She flapped her spare hand towards the floor. "You can sit."

Craig took his seat beside a pint he'd kept company for fifteen minutes.

Amanda hung her bag on the chair back and joined him. "I've not been in here before. If every local in the country was this busy during weekday lunch service, our pub crisis could be averted."

Craig drew a finger across his lips. "It's not always like this, though it has been of late."

Amanda lifted her glass. "Whenever there's something juicy to discuss?"

Craig watched her. "You've heard then?"

"Heard what?" Amanda followed the question with a demure sip of her drink.

"Ah." Craig passed her a menu. "Perhaps we should order first? The lunchtime specials are worth a look."

"Really?" Amanda ran her eyes across the printed paper sheet, then peeped at what others were having. She paused upon noticing a man and woman dollop clotted cream on top of jam, smeared across two scones.

Craig followed her gaze and chuckled. "Tourists. I learnt quickly as an incomer that nobody much cares if you eat your cream tea the Cornish way around here."

Amanda wrinkled her nose. "True enough. Do it the Devon way in Cornwall though, and they'll string you up." She looked outside and inhaled fresh floral fragrances from a window box. "I saw two police cars shooting off from that posh place down the lane."

"Milford?"

"Yeah, that's the one," Amanda replied.

"Brandon Beeching's home."

"Is it? I didn't know."

Craig fixed her with a stare. "Brandon Beeching's *former* home."

"Is he moving? Can't say I'd blame him. He's become about the most unpopular man in the village. That architect, Paul Gilbert, was in the running. But, death absolved him. Wasn't that awful?" She fidgeted.

Craig noticed her discomfort. "What is it?"

Amanda shook her head. "It's silly. Belle arrived reeking of smoke after you left the other day. It made me think of your quip about her being involved."

Craig flinched. "Hmm. The entire village stunk after that fire, to be fair. Amanda, you haven't cottoned-on to what I'm saying yet, have you?"

"What's that?"

"Beeching isn't moving. Someone murdered him last night."

Amanda almost spilled her drink. "Murdered? How?"

"They force-fed him his own antique coin collection until he choked to death."

Amanda watched him in slack-jawed horror. "That's dreadful. Have they arrested anyone?"

"No."

"Do you reckon they suspect someone?"

"After the planning meeting? How about the entire village, if we're talking motive? The police questioned me first thing. They showed up on my doorstep before breakfast."

"Why you?"

"Because I worked in his garden yesterday and was one of the last people to see him alive. Dorothy Beeching, his wife, arrived home from a school reunion in Wiltshire this morning and found him dead in his study chair. I'm not under arrest, so must be off the hook for now."

Amanda wiped her brow. "Thank goodness."

Craig continued staring at her.

Amanda recoiled. "What?"

"I didn't mention that I saw Belle yesterday."

"Did you? She didn't tell me. Where was this?"

"At Milford."

Amanda froze.

Craig stroked the side of his pint glass with one finger. "We talked about Brandon before I cleared up. Belle liked the lavender in his garden, so I let her in for a closer look." He watched Amanda's throat muscles perform a hesitant swallow. "She was still there, enjoying the sights and smells when I left."

Amanda drew a sharp breath. "No." She looked at Craig with pleading eyes. "You don't think?"

"That Belle broke into his house and overpowered a forty-seven-year-old man weighing around twenty stone? No, of course not."

"Did you tell the police?"

"It must have slipped my mind." He winked.

Amanda gripped his hands. "Thank you."

"That doesn't mean nobody else saw her. But, I thought you should know."

Amanda cringed and crossed her legs underneath the table. She looked out the window again. "Why do I suspect they won't find fingerprints or DNA on his body?"

"The same thought occurred to me."

"What should I do with this information, Craig? Where do I turn?"

He shook his head. "I dunno. The coincidences continue stacking up, but I still don't believe Belle is involved. Not directly or consciously. Jesus, if you took it back to the start of this whole affair, that means she murdered her own parents. Assuming the incidents are linked, of course."

Amanda's eyes reddened and her voice cracked. "No, I can't accept that. Not about Jake and Karen."

"Me either. Let's hope someone ran Paul Gilbert off the road, choked Brandon Beeching, and that the law catches up with them soon. We'd both sleep easier if that happened, wouldn't we? The other deaths may yet be the simple tragedies they first appeared."

Amanda rubbed gooseflesh on her upper arms. "You're handling me, aren't you?"

"A little. I'm handling myself too. If something unnatural is swarming around Belle and causing this stuff to happen, no-one is safe. Tears won't flow over Brandon Beeching's demise, nor Paul Gilbert's - except for local sympathy directed at his wife and stepson. Nobody misses Sam Peebles. But Brian Taylor was loved. So were your brother and your sister-in-law. There's no rhyme or reason to this series of deaths. No obvious pattern."

Amanda placed her palms together in a prayer-like gesture before her mouth. "If they are all killings and without logic, how do we predict or stop them? What does any of it have to do with my nine-year-old niece?"

Craig bit his lip. "Sorry to hang a cloud over our lunch. I intended to return the favour for Saturday, before all this kicked off. Where's Belle now?"

"At home; or she was when I left. How can I help her? How do I ask her to explain the inexplicable, if she even realises what's happening?"

Craig sat back. "Be there for her. Earn her trust. Keep connecting. What else can you do? We don't even know what's going on. If she was present at every death, take comfort in the assumption she's not a target. The fact you live with her and remain unscathed is also a positive indicator. You're safe at home, other than from that freaky artistic spectre of yours."

"That's scary and annoying, but hardly in the same league as murder." She put her head in her hands.

12
Retribution Conducted

Amanda sat at the central table in her studio, organising images on her laptop. *I've taken so many shots since I moved down here. Thank goodness we don't use film these days, or I'd go broke on the back of development costs.* Dusk faded to grey, leaving her face in a pale halo of cold light from the computer screen. A deep, monotonous, intermittent tone made her sit up straight and listen. *Is that coming from downstairs?* She eased off a high stool and moved to the open doorway. *It's a ticking sound.* Amanda headed below, following the noise. In the hallway, the pendulum of an old grandfather clock moved in hypnotic, restful arcs. *That's odd. Belle said her parents bought this monstrosity from an antique fair, intending to repair it. The beast never worked before.* She examined the clock face. *One minute to midnight. Poignant. I'd better set the correct time.* As she reached out and opened the cover, the pendulum stilled. Amanda waited, half expecting the timepiece to start up again. When it didn't, she closed the cover and stepped back. *It must be moisture or atmospherics releasing latent tension in the spring.* She smiled at her own mental assessment. *Listen to you, Fairchild: a regular horologist.* She climbed the staircase once more, muttering aloud. "I've gotta stop watching those heirloom repair shows on TV."

Back in her studio, she sat on the high stool and continued paging through digital photographs. One of the stone bridge images appeared from the Sunday she'd picnicked with Belinda by the river. Amanda's attention swept over the arches, down towards the waterline, slipping beneath with a gentle current. The melancholy face of a young girl peered out of the water. "What?" Amanda overbalanced and toppled from the stool with a crash, slamming into the floor. *That wasn't there before; I know it wasn't.* She sat up to a burning sensation in her right forearm. *Crap, that hurt.* She winced and raised herself into a standing position.

"Are you all right?" Belinda stood in the doorway. Her sudden voice in the stillness caused Amanda to jump. At the same instant the laptop screen turned black, plunging them into darkness. The computer's power light winked out.

Amanda looked back to the door. Faint illumination through the landing window outlined Belinda's silhouette. Her faceless presentation, combined with the scare of finding that underwater girl in her digital photo, caused Amanda to grasp the table. She rummaged for a desk lamp and fumbled with its switch. A cone of yellow light splashed across the computer keyboard, from which a whiff like burnt solder emanated. Amanda pressed the power button without response. "That's all I need."

Belinda entered the room. "What happened?"

"My laptop is toast, by the looks of it." She sighed. "Another expense I could do without."

Belinda played with her straggly locks. "I have a little pocket money saved, if that helps?"

Amanda's eyes softened. "Thank you, sweetie. I'll manage; don't worry. You buy yourself something nice instead."

Belinda moved one foot in childish swirls against the floorboards. "Did you hear a ticking a while ago?"

"Yes. Your parents' grandfather clock started up for a few minutes. It's stopped again now."

Belinda frowned. "That's impossible."

"Don't worry, it happens. Old springs sometimes move. Air pressure, temperature changes and humidity all influence clockwork mechanisms."

"But it doesn't have a spring."

"Of course it does. The clock couldn't work without a spring."

Belinda shook her head. "No, I mean Daddy tried fixing it himself and the spring snapped into little pieces. He threw it away and left the clock alone."

"Oh." A sudden chill invaded Amanda's creative space. She gulped. "Ah well. One day, when the house is in better shape and I've sold more paintings, we'll have it repaired if you like?"

Belinda walked to the door and spoke without looking back. "Did you hear about Mr Beeching?"

Amanda's jaw tightened. She waited for several agonising heartbeats before delivering a monosyllabic answer. "Yes."

"Does that mean they won't build on top of the

woods now?"

"I wish it did, but I doubt it." Amanda tried some gentle fishing. "Craig told me you ran into him at Mr Beeching's house that evening."

"Craig let me smell the lavender."

"So he said. Did you stay long?"

"I can't remember." Belinda's speech grew laboured. "Was I late home?"

"No. We've not spoken about this yet, but if you saw anyone in his house, we should tell the police."

Belinda hung her head. "He shouted at me to leave his garden."

"And did you?"

Belinda's face turned sideways as she made to leave. "Once he stopped making a noise." She wandered back along the landing with meek steps.

Amanda fought back rising tension and rubbed her pained arm.

* * *

"What the heck do you want now?" Julian Asbury opened the main door to High Stanton in a foul temper.

Gary Cripps stood beneath a lantern over the entrance, his usually emotionless eyes teeming with fear. "We need to talk, Julian."

"We spoke on the phone." Julian stepped aside, then closed the door behind him.

Gary stammered. "I'm worried."

Julian went to move off, and then stopped in his

tracks. "What?"

"There's a madman on the loose targeting us." He grabbed the lapels of Julian's signature blazer.

Julian unhooked Gary's fingers and smoothed down the fabric. "Don't let your imagination run away with you."

"My imagination?" His hands dropped to his sides. "Brandon was murdered."

"But Paul wasn't. He crashed his car, and it caught fire." Julian escorted him into a comfortable lounge. "Why don't I pour you a drink?"

Gary slouched, voice subdued. "Okay."

Julian grabbed ice from a bucket with tongs and dropped it into two crystal tumblers. "Thirty-year-old scotch all right, old man?"

Gary nodded, finding no comfort in Julian's attempts to calm him with classic British reserve.

Julian unstopped a decanter and poured two double measures. He passed a glass to Gary. "Take a seat and savour that."

Gary accepted his hospitality without a word. He perched on the edge of a luxurious sofa before a cold, empty fireplace.

Julian sat in a matching armchair facing him. "Now what's this all about?"

Gary waved a hand while he spoke, as though it would better convey his emotions. "I got spooked when I heard about Brandon. I'd only said goodbye to him a short while before it happened."

"How did your campaign go in the village?"

"Most people gave us the cold shoulder. A few came

around after Brandon turned on the charm."

Julian frowned and jangled the ice in his glass. "Unfortunately, that fat fool told people we'd build a bloody adventure playground for the kids. I'm already getting questions from the village about it. What was he thinking?"

Gary sampled his scotch. "I told him to ease back on that."

"Well, he didn't ease back enough. Someone noticed there's no playground on the plans and complained to the council through other channels. We don't need scrutiny we can't control. Can you fix this?"

"It depends how high up the complaint has travelled. If we had alternate plans detailing Brandon's promised feature, that could extinguish the fire before it spreads."

Julian took a long belt of his drink. His eyes flared. "Do it. First thing in the morning, head over to the site and measure up a suitable spot, then submit revised drawings based on Paul's originals. You're still a qualified surveyor with access to equipment, aren't you?"

"Yes." Gary rubbed his eyes. "Okay."

Julian clenched a fist. "Nothing fancy. A slide or seesaw and some swings. You've gotta squeeze it in without reducing the number of properties. Be creative about plot sizes or whatever; I don't care. But, we're not taking a financial bath over Brandon running his big mouth off."

"What about his murderer or murderers?"

"What about them?"

"Aren't you worried they'll come after us, too?"

"Why? You're assuming some outraged villager or group has it in for us. Brandon stepped on countless toes to get to where he was. The man had more enemies than most people have hot dinners." He finished his drink and put the tumbler down with a pronounced bang. "Ah, that hits the spot. It wouldn't surprise me if his wife did it."

"Dorothy was attending a reunion."

"So she says. The woman doubtless has friends to back her up with a false alibi if need be. Can you imagine having a flabby, heart-attack-in-waiting like Brandon climbing and slobbering all over you at night? It must've felt like being mounted by a blue whale."

Gary set down his glass. "Must we speak ill of the dead?"

Julian laughed. "Why, are they coming back to get us? Crumbs, Gary, it's time to grow a backbone. And if courage isn't enough to carry the day, imagine what you'll do with all that extra money."

Gary gawped.

Julian gave an enthusiastic nod. "That's right. Once the development is built and the houses sold, you'll receive half of Paul and Brandon's cut, along with your own."

Gary stood and stretched a stiff neck. "Okay, I can do that."

Julian clapped him on the shoulder and they walked towards the door. "Good man. I thought a pay adjustment might bolster your resolve." They paused beneath the portrait of Oliver Asbury. "E-mail me the revised plans once you've concocted a suitable solution."

"I will."

"Take care." Julian let him out.

* * *

Next morning, Gary Cripps unlocked the woodland gate entrance west of Oakdene with a spare key Julian Asbury gave him at the start of their project. He parked, then lugged metal ranging poles from the rear of his blue Volvo estate and piled them with a clatter near the clearing by the overgrown church remains at Underwood. A total station electronic theodolite and EDM followed, along with its sturdy tripod.

Early sunshine diminished behind angry clouds, promising rain. A whiff of ozone in the charged air hinted at approaching storm relief after weeks of hot, dry weather. The coolness of a welcome draught teased fine hairs on Gary's forearms. He pinpointed a datum he'd used before, then set up the total station on its tripod mount. He opened black and white prints of the empty site with a film overlay of the housing proposal, then rested against a tree and considered his options. A bird launched from the canopy above in a flurry of wings and startled chirps. Gary watched the swaying leaves settle and sniffed. *I hope I don't get soaked.* A low, distant rumble of thunder rolled in from the horizon. *Great, that's all I need.* He secured the prints to a board and hurried back to the Volvo for a waterproof parka. No sooner had he donned the coat and zipped it, than heavy splashes of rain announced an imminent downpour amidst the swaying boughs. The breeze gusted into blustery stirrings, lifting the clipboard papers and flapping them as Gary reached the clearing again. *What miserable conditions to survey in. Should I wait in the car until the storm passes? It may circle the village and disappear.* A louder, pronounced outburst of thunder rippled across the leaden firmament. *On second thoughts, the sooner I take these measurements and give myself something to work with back at the office, the better.* He pulled an elastic band down across the clipboard to stop his plans from catching in the wind. *One of the bods in parks and recreation can help me with the details, but I know the basic footprint I'll need to earmark.* He peered into the total stations' viewfinder. A young girl lingered beside a ranging pole in the distance. Intense brown eyes watched him from beneath a fulsome mop of fine golden hair, flowing across her shoulders and lifting in the growing gale.

Gary pulled his face away from the measuring device and called to her. "Excuse me, young lady. I need you to move." An icy shower of rain came in sideways with a fresh belt of wind. Gary tugged his hood up and frowned at the motionless child. "Don't you have a jacket? You'll get soaked in this weather."

A vivid flash of light strobed the clearing, followed by a thunderclap resonating among the thick tree trunks like an array of tuning forks. Gary flinched. *Cripes, that storm covered several miles in no time.* He checked to see if the girl was also startled. Her former observation spot lay empty, with the ranging pole toppled from view. *It must have fallen amongst the ferns.* Gary stomped across the clearing, one hand fastened upon his hood to keep it from blowing down. He reached the spot and bent over, rummaging amidst the fragrant fronds. Another flash of lightning, followed by an immediate boom combined with needle-fine, chilled slanting rain, caused him to shiver. *Where can that pole have gone? Don't say the kid ran off with it.* He tore at the ferns with frustration-infused arms. *I'll have to fetch another from the car. Thank goodness I've a couple spare.* He pivoted and halted. Across the clearing behind his assembled kit, the girl once again stood motionless. This time she waited by the churchyard entrance. She remained mute and unblinking, wet clothes clinging to her pale body; sodden hair matted across her fixated visage.

Gary rubbed rainwater from his eyes. *She's a weird one.* He set off towards her. "Have you seen a metal pole that was standing back there?" He jerked a thumb across one shoulder. "It seems to have vanished without a trace." As he closed the distance between them to the halfway point, his body stiffened and his eyes went wide. Shadowy figures appeared in the churchyard, all about the girl. Gary's bottom lip wobbled. "What the hell?"

Anton Webb hurried from the village shop in Oakdene, clutching a white paper bag of penny sweets. His mother, Abigail, wasn't at work today. She'd managed a few afternoons here and there, with village volunteers filling in the gaps out of compassion over the loss of her second husband. Anton didn't understand why she cried so much. Paul Gilbert had made both their lives a misery ever since he wormed his way into Abigail's affections. The period after his fatal car accident near the bridge was the longest Anton could remember without enduring severe emotional, verbal, and physical abuse. Something inside told him it was wrong to celebrate Paul's death, but he'd never mourn his stepfather's loss. One upshot of the community outpouring of sympathy was special consideration among the populace. On this particular morning, that equated to an extra handful of sweets in his bag of goodies, at no additional charge. Small compensation for the burning scars that still stung his back, but better than nothing. His mind wandered to images of Belinda draping dock leaves across those fresh wounds to soothe them. *I wonder if she'd like some of my sweets as a thank you? I promised to stick by Belle. Things will be different between us than they used to.*

Dust whipping along the lane caused Anton to look up. Fierce clouds stained the azure heavens a dirty grey. Across the valley and beyond, towards Winkleigh, an inbound rumble of thunder disturbed Oakdene's breezy tranquillity.

I haven't seen Belle around the village this week. What if she's playing in the woods again? I'd best go that way and cut across their meadow to that creepy old dump she lives in. I'll run back along the lane from Ravensbrook before the rain gets bad, or stop there until it passes.

Anton's well-conceived musings were shot down in

short order. Spatters of precursor precipitation impacted his head while he hurried up the lane beside The Old Bothy, approaching the woods. He found the gate unlocked and open, with a Volvo estate parked further along the track. A deafening crack of thunder tensed his fingers around the bag of sweets he bore. *I'd better hurry.* He quickened his pace towards the clearing, hoping against hope Belinda would be there so he could hand over some sugary treats, then run home. Rain hammered down in stair rods.

Already drenched, Anton rounded Underwood's ivy-clad, tumbledown church tower in time to watch Gary Cripps set off in his general direction, pacing towards a bright orange surveying device on a tripod nearby. Gary called to someone across the space, enquiring about a lost metal pole. Anton followed his diverted gaze while circumnavigating the churchyard perimeter until his eyes fell upon Belinda. She stood in the entrance, as wet through as he.

Gary halted midway. His face distorted in terror, washed of colour that never returned after another flash of lightning dazzled everyone present.

Anton recovered from the reverberating boom of thunder, trembling his stomach muscles, then reacquired the scene. A mass of dark silhouettes stood all around Belinda in the churchyard. She appeared unfazed by their presence, as though in a trance. The shadows thickened and sharpened into figures clad in rough clothing, like something Anton had seen in school history books. Though he stood behind and to the side of them, horrible welts and pustules were still visible on their discoloured flesh. In a silent but definite march, the sickly throng surged either side of Belinda, making straight for the frozen planning officer. Anton's legs jellified, and he clutched a tree trunk to avoid collapsing into the saturated undergrowth. All he could do was watch in mesmerised fear.

Gary Cripps backed away and stumbled, still transfixed by the impossible assembly. Buboes from swollen, ruptured lymph nodes disfigured their bodies. Each face appeared as angry as the horrific open wounds distorting it. Interspersed between them, other figures lacking the same symptoms were marked only by cruel rope burns about their necks.

"What do you want with me?" Gary squeaked.

The furious apparitions stormed forwards on their hellish mission, disregarding his question.

Gary whirled, his limbs the beneficiary of a sudden adrenaline burst. He ran in the opposite direction to his otherworldly pursuers, unable to contain a wail of terror. Behind, the ardent nightmares closed the gap, arms reaching for their quarry. Grasping hands, blackened by congealed sub-dermal blood, tore at his parka, taking hold. Gary fought against their clammy touch, desperate to break free. He pushed a low-hanging branch aside to reveal his missing ranging pole. It had been wedged at a forty-five-degree angle into the spongy spoil, its tip pointing straight at him as though by premeditated design. Gary yanked open the parka's zipper and allowed the coat to pull free of his arms, gaining a moment's liberty from the wrestling hands. He staggered into a half turn, eyes stinging from fierce rain filling their sockets. The silent dead gripped both his bare forearms and dragged him towards the angled pole. Gary whimpered and struggled. His frantic stare drifted beyond those closing, horrific faces to fall upon that girl across the clearing. A boy around the same age clutched tight to a tree trunk, thirty feet away on her right. The captors' rubber-like fingers tightened around Gary's arms and his attackers broke into a vigorous charge, bringing him along for the ride.

Blood spurted in a fountain around the metal ranging pole as it ruptured Gary's spine and burst through the front of his skyward facing chest cavity. Trickles of the same crimson life fluid ran from his gargling mouth, washed into bouncing pink spray by the relentless rain. His silent executioners stepped aside, forming a circle. Gary's arms and legs flailed in spasms, bringing zero relief to his impaled torso. An immediate, blinding flash of lightning arced into a fork that connected with the metal pole, conducting over 100 million volts to earth. A shower of sparks lurched from the tip and the ranging pole glowed orange. Steam rose around Gary's cavernous chest wound. His hair ignited like dry grass, despite dripping with copious moisture. His mouth stretched into a soundless scream, head sagging backwards. Flames licked his melting flesh, rising into thick, black clouds of vapour-laden smoke. Both eyeballs collapsed inward at the same moment. His limbs stilled in a face-up spread-eagle, like a pagan human sacrifice lost in worship of vengeful, long-forgotten deities.

Anton watched from his tucked away position. The smoke dissipated, and with it the grotesque assailants. Gary Cripps' lifeless, charred form hung suspended; a hideous parody of a pinned butterfly in a presentation case. While the storm passed overhead, the blackened corpse kebab slid down the angled pole in a ponderous descent. It broke apart into gobs of stinking human flesh and offal.

During the penetrating downpour, Anton's paper bag of sweets turned to mush, dumping its contents amidst surrounding ferns. He stared at the last fragments in his clutching hand, then let them fall. Final raindrops trickled from his curly blond bangs. A different flow spread around his groin, still pressed for comfort against the tree. He pulled back, revealing a dark stain from the inside out around the crotch of his shorts. Its warm accumulations dripped down his leg, while pockets of blue opened in the clearing heavens.

Belinda turned to him. Her empty eyes blinked back to life, registering his presence. The horror distorting his countenance caused her to locate the smouldering remnants of Gary Cripps, wafting a fetid fragrance in her direction. Belinda's cheeks reddened. She faced Anton again in time to see him break into a run along the track eastwards, back towards Oakdene.

"Belle?" Amanda called down the stairs after the solid front door at Ravensbrook banged shut. When no reply followed, she descended and found her sodden niece in the hallway wearing a pathetic expression. "Look at you," Amanda sighed. "When that storm broke I was worried you'd get caught out in it. Stay there, I'll run up and fetch a towel. We can't have you dripping all over the house, even if it's still in a state." Her nose wrinkled, and she held two fingers beneath it. "Poo. Were you near someone's barbecue? You smell like burnt sausages." She smiled. "Typical for a warm spell to vanish the moment people try cooking outdoors."

Belinda watched her run upstairs and then return with a clean, fluffy towel.

Amanda wrung out Belinda's waterlogged locks. "You'd best jump in the bath and change your clothes. Summer or not, you'll catch a chill if you remain like that."

* * *

Anton Webb woke with a start, pyjamas damp from a night sweat. The first light of dawn glimmered around his bedroom curtains. He'd awoken four times, each the result of graphic replays from events at Underwood the day before. In the last dream, those discoloured and disfigured attackers rotated to face him. Each wore a sickening and self-satisfied grin. A discordant tumult of whispering voices danced through his head, repeating the same phrase over and over: *'You enabled this.'*

Anton sipped water from a glass by his bed, then slipped out from beneath the covers. He knelt on the carpet and opened a wooden cupboard door set into the bed frame beneath his mattress. Assorted action figures and models were pushed aside until he withdrew something wrapped in a threadbare tea towel his mother thought she'd thrown out. Anton laid it on the bed and opened the folds of cloth. Inside, the tarnished brass cross stared at him like an exposed, guilty secret. Anton touched it with trembling fingers, half expecting angry ghosts or rotten corpses to burst from his wardrobe and claw him to pieces. When no discernible change in the room's atmosphere or occupants followed, he stood and drew back from the antique symbol of faith. *I must get rid of this. Belle was right, after all. But I can't put it back. No way am I going near Underwood after yesterday. I won't visit Ravensbrook, either.* He wracked his brain for a solution. *I'll post it to Belle. If she's so set on the cross returning to where I found it, she can take it there herself. Will all this scary stuff stop once that happens?* He pondered Belinda's involvement as a motionless witness during yesterday's incident; the dreamy aspect to her face, and her startled realisation after the fatal drama reached its conclusion. *Is she in league with those things? Does she control them or do they control her?* Anton remembered Belinda's kindness again and his promise to be a friend. *Belle didn't want to talk about it before, so I'll leave her alone. We'll still be friends, but I'll give her space and stay away from the woods. That's the best idea.* He covered the cross and returned it to his under-bed cupboard. In his heart of hearts, he knew this was a coward's option. It paid lip service to his former resolve over Belinda, without actually supporting her.

"There's fresh milk in the fridge." Abigail Webb stared out of the kitchen window in the same stupor that had hung about her like a permanent fog since Paul's death.

Anton retrieved a jug and poured cool milk across a bowl of cereals at the breakfast table. After he put it back and sat down, he paused, spoon in hand, while watching his mother. "Mum?"

Abigail didn't look round. "Uh-huh."

"Do you have a large padded envelope about this big?" He stretched out his hands to approximate the dimensions of the cross.

Her son's visual demonstration forced Abigail to turn. She wiped a red, runny nose on a tissue and sniffed. "Try the cupboard in Paul's study. He used to keep assorted packaging in there. Why do you need one?"

"I want to send somebody a package."

Abigail lifted a half-finished cup of tea from the draining board and sat down opposite. "I didn't realise you knew anyone outside the village?"

Anton spooned cereal into his mouth to avoid answering.

Abigail let the question evaporate into the unusually calm kitchen. Everything about the house felt quiet without Paul there. His death provided her an escape from relationship tyranny she'd never believed possible. Yet, despite that, Abigail found herself once again raising a boy alone on a meagre salary with no prospects for love. Back to square one, like the days following her divorce. "Do you have enough money for postage?"

Anton nodded while he chewed.

Abigail touched her forehead. "I'm sorry, I haven't given you any pocket money this week. How much was it again?"

Anton watched her dazed face before swallowing to answer. "Don't worry, Mum. I can go without for a while. You need money for more important things."

Abigail looked away and wiped a silent tear as it fell, moved beyond words at her nine-year-old boy's consideration and surprising maturity. In that moment she made herself a promise: *No matter how tough things get, I'll never stay with another man who lifts a hand against me or my son.*

After breakfast, Anton approached Paul's downstairs study door with trepidation. Even looking at the room - let alone entering it - was enough to warrant a beating from Paul in times past. He couldn't remember when he'd last stood inside. Tucked together on the bottom shelf of a tall, slender cupboard next to a desk holding a laptop computer, Anton found Jiffy bags of various dimensions. He estimated the largest to offer sufficient capacity for his package. On the way upstairs - padded envelope in hand - Anton listened while his mother spoke on the hallway phone with considerable energy.

"You're kidding? Gary Cripps, too? Was it murder, like Brandon Beeching? No. At Underwood? The same place Julian Asbury's grounds keeper killed himself. What happened?" Abigail drew a sharp breath while the caller relayed juicy details. "Oh, my gosh. Impaled and struck by lightning. Did he stumble onto the pole? I see. He fell backwards. You're right, it's a horrible accident." Abigail felt herself well up again as the person speaking in her ear backpedalled. They'd realised the association of a *'horrible accident'* with her late second husband. "It's okay, Kate. I would've found out one way or another. What's going on in Oakdene these days?"

Anton shivered at the memory of Gary's final ordeal, then hurried up to his room.

"Ravensbrook?" Kate Miller the postmistress held up Anton's package, one eyebrow raised so high it almost vanished beneath her low fringe. "Why don't you save yourself some money and trot down the lane to deliver it in person?"

Anton had anticipated a response like this on his way to the village shop. "It's a surprise for someone."

Kate read out the address he'd written in blue marker pen. "Belinda Fairchild?" Abigail's colleague, Kate, was also the woman who'd phoned about the 'accident.' The last thing Anton needed was more awkward questions, despite his mother's lack of interrogation tenacity in her present state of mind. It wouldn't do for Kate to share the details of this transaction.

"Don't tell anyone, or you'll ruin the secret."

Kate smirked. "Got a soft spot for the Fairchild girl, have you?" She chuckled to herself. "Ah, those were the days." She applied stamps to the padded envelope while Anton counted out some change. "Don't worry. Your secret is safe with me. The Post Office is not unlike the priesthood in that regard."

Anton scratched his head.

Kate pursed her lips, amused by the confusion in his young eyes. "I won't tell a soul."

13

The Conduit

Belinda peered through her bedroom window as Stuart Neat drew up in his red Post Office van. Undisturbed sunshine had returned to Oakdene, with only a few broken tree branches supplying evidence of the storm two days before. Three tiles had dislodged from the roof at Ravensbrook. They shattered on the driveway with nobody present to suffer injury. Amanda opened the door. Stuart passed her a large padded envelope, then engaged in the latest gossip. Word of Gary Cripps' demise had yet to disturb their isolated home. At first Belinda wondered if Craig Symonds would call. He'd become something of a familiar feature in their lives since her aunt arrived from Bristol.

Five minutes of chitchat later, Amanda bid the postie farewell. Belinda listened to her ascend the staircase, followed by the creak of landing floorboards outside her closed bedroom door. A soft knock followed.

"Come in." Belinda moved away from the window and sat at a small dressing table.

Amanda opened the door. "Hey." A package in her hand bore an address in blue marker pen, written by a child's hand. "Stuart delivered a parcel for you."

Belinda remained seated. "Who's it from?"

"I thought you might tell me. Could Laura have sent you a present? Maybe it's a peace offering or returned item. Had you loaned her anything?"

"No."

Amanda crossed the room, steps hesitant and face streaked with worry. She stopped three feet from Belinda. "Stuart also told me some sad news."

Belinda said nothing.

Amanda licked her lips. "Gary Cripps, the local planning officer died during that storm you were out in the other day."

Still no response.

Amanda closed the remaining distance and set the parcel down on the dressing table. "They found him at Underwood, fused to one of his metal poles. It was struck by lightning."

Belinda trembled and looked at the floor.

Amanda went on, hesitant about the horrors she was describing, yet desperate for answers. "That lightning strike set the poor man on fire." She counted to three before finishing her emerging line of thought. "His body must have stunk like burnt sausages."

Belinda darted off the chair and threw herself face-down on her bed. She tugged a pillow over her head and sobbed. "I didn't do it. It's not me. I didn't want to hurt that man. I don't even know him."

Amanda perched on the mattress beside her. She touched Belinda on the back with tender fingers. "You saw what happened?"

Belinda pulled the pillow tighter. "Everything is a blur. First, I heard the whispers like I always do. Then it was like walking through a dream. Sometimes I have horrible nightmares about things I don't remember seeing."

"But you were at Underwood during the storm, weren't you?"

Belinda tossed the pillow aside, rolled off the bed, and curled into a tight ball in a nearby corner. She yanked at her own hair and screamed over and over. "It wasn't me. I didn't do it."

"Shh." Amanda dropped into a crouch before her, fighting to soothe Belinda's anguish, yet worried about what would happen if she touched her again. "Nobody thinks you've done anything bad."

Belinda buried her face in folded arms around her knees. "You do. I've seen the way you look at me whenever someone dies." She spat out a tearful accusation. "You think I murdered Mummy and Daddy, don't you?"

A stab of emotional turmoil caught in Amanda's throat. "No, darling; of course I don't."

Belinda screamed again, voice hysterical. "It was the villagers."

"The villagers killed Gary Cripps?"

No response.

Amanda gulped. "Did the villagers kill your parents?"

Belinda sobbed, voice calm and soft now. "I don't know. Even Jonathan won't tell me."

Amanda rocked on her haunches. "Your friend

Jonathan? The one you said is buried at All Saints?"

Belinda shot a distraught stare towards an empty corner of the room opposite. She barked a hoarse rebuke. "Why won't you tell me? I thought you cared."

Amanda glanced to the empty spot, muscles tensing. "Can you see Jonathan now?"

Belinda sniffed. "He just walked out."

Amanda sighed. "Belle? Did you ever see or hear things others couldn't, before Mummy and Daddy died?"

Belinda's eyes glazed over. "Not until the day before."

"When you experienced that scary vision at Underwood?"

"Yes."

"I'll ask again: did Underwood's villagers kill Gary Cripps?"

Belinda gave a silent nod.

"Assuming that's possible, why would they do such a thing?"

"They're restless and angry over the way they were treated."

"How do you mean?" Amanda leaned closer. "What could our local planning officer have done to upset people who died during the 17th century?"

Belinda shrugged. "Something bad happened. It still touches people today. They bear the mark."

"Those who've died lately?"

Amanda screwed her eyes shut a moment while she spoke. "I hear angry whispers in my head and feel awful when I'm around certain people in the village."

"Do the whispers originate from the woods?"

"Always." Belinda hugged herself.

Amanda forced a weak smile and opened her arms. "Have you kept one of those for your aunt?"

Belinda flung herself into Amanda's embrace. They swayed together while Amanda kissed her crown. She groomed Belinda's wild hair between soothing fingers. "Is Jonathan a part of those whispers? He lived during the same period, if he's the teenager buried in Oakdene."

"No. Ravensbrook was Jonathan's home. He remembers the bad things that happened, but isn't part of the other voices. He hasn't attacked anyone."

"Has he told you much about the events at Underwood from his lifetime?"

"No. He says he wants to protect me."

Amanda cocked her head. "That's one positive, I suppose. Your story reminds me of something I heard from an old lady in the village."

Belinda tried changing subjects. "Amanda?"

"Yes, sweetheart?"

"Teacher gave us a project for the summer holidays. But, I don't know where to begin."

"Why didn't you say something earlier?" Amanda couldn't disguise the relief in her voice at switching gears to the normal topics one would discuss with a girl at primary school. She'd taken the supernatural talk about as far as it would go. Solutions remained fleeting, and a distraction proved welcome. "What does she want you to do?"

Belinda stretched towards her schoolbag, resting

beside the dressing table. Amanda slackened her affectionate grip enough for the child to withdraw a printed slip and hand it over.

Amanda held the note up and read aloud. *"Summer Project: Reach out to someone less fortunate than yourself, then write about your experiences in not less than 500 words."* She put the slip down beside them. "That's a good assignment. Let's see." She blinked. "I know, I'll take you to meet Peggy Greene. She was the old lady I mentioned."

Belinda fidgeted in her grasp. "Is she less fortunate than me because she's old?"

Amanda laughed. "Some might say that. No, Peggy lost her sight to a sickness called diabetes, twenty years ago. Her husband died. Someone gave her a cat which she adored. That died too. She's had a rough time."

Belinda lifted her chin. "She's the one you made that clay model for?"

"That's right. Peggy could be considered less fortunate than you, though she'd not appreciate anyone pitying her. She doesn't mince her words. But she'd enjoy meeting you, I'm sure. Then you'd have something to write about for your project."

"Does this blind lady know about the bad things that happened at Underwood?"

"Not in any detail. Peggy senses things others don't. I won't have her upsetting you, so we'd best avoid talk of Underwood, ghosts and whispers. You'll like her garden; it's beautiful. If you tell her how much, that'll lift her spirits. Afterwards I'll help you compose your essay for school. Sound good?"

Belinda nodded.

Amanda indicated the padded envelope on the dressing table. "Are you going to open that?"

"Can I do it later? It might be a secret."

"It's your parcel. You can open it whenever you like - alone or with me. You're too young for it to be something illegal, so I'm not worried."

"Like drugs?" Belinda sat up straight.

Amanda grinned and stood up. "Or whatever. I've artwork to take care of. Are you okay?"

"Yes."

"Promise me you'll stay close to the house today?"

Belinda clambered to her feet. "Okay. I don't feel like walking far, anyway."

"Good." Amanda reached the door, turned back, and focused on the padded envelope. "It could be a box of chocolates from a boy who likes you." She winked.

Belinda screwed up her face in disgust. "Ew."

Amanda stepped onto the landing with a bounce in her step. "One day you might not mind so much."

"Like you and Craig?"

Amanda bit her lip. "He's a nice man. We're friends."

"Does he need to send you a box of chocolates if he wants to change that?"

Amanda walked out of sight towards her studio, head shaking in mild amusement.

An hour passed before Belinda plucked up sufficient courage to open her parcel. She closed the bedroom door and sat at her dressing table. Once the flap tore asunder, she reached an arm inside. Cloth from a worn tea towel met her fingers, wrapped around the contents. She withdrew the item and laid it atop the packet before unfolding the linen surround.

"Anton." Her classmate's name sounded under Belinda's breath in a worried whisper. The emerging cross emitted a dull glint from sunlight slanting through the bedroom window. Her thoughts drifted back to Anton watching her in the churchyard as Gary Cripps' remains smoldered around his blackened ranging pole. *This must go back.* She covered the cross in the tea towel again and clutched it to her chest. *I promised Amanda I wouldn't visit the woods today, but this is important. What if more people die because I didn't return the cross in time?* Convinced of the importance and moral rectitude of breaking her word, Belinda crept along the landing. Amanda sat hunched over her tabletop easel beyond the open, light-washed studio doorway, lost in creativity. Belinda winced as a floorboard creaked beneath her attempt at catlike stealth. She held still, scanning for movement in the room ahead. Amanda didn't register or respond to the disturbance, so Belinda kept moving in short, breathless steps. She eased around the newel post and slipped downstairs, staying close to the wall and hoping to lessen further structural groans from the wood underfoot. She twisted the front door's chunky handle and pulled it wide enough to squeeze through before pulling it shut behind. Outside, she caught her breath a moment, then broke into a run across the meadow, still clutching the wrapped cross. *The sooner I get rid of this and return home, the better. If I'm quick, Amanda may never know I left.* As the dip in the meadow sloped back up towards the waving, broad-leafed tree line on the horizon, Belinda redoubled her efforts. Its shallow gradient climbed over a sufficient distance to tire her pounding young ankles. She panted, desperate to reach Underwood and end the horrors plaguing them all.

Five minutes later, she plunged into lush, heavy undergrowth. Every bough fought for precious sunlight and an expansive place at table in nature's photosynthesis feast. Down below, greenery receiving crumbs of sunlight falling from that same table swayed amidst a dappled emerald gloom enveloping Belinda on her way to the old church. The soft woodland floor seemed to vibrate beneath her feet. Negative thoughts disturbed the single-mindedness of her pursuit: *'Turn back.' 'There's no hope.' 'It's too late.'*

Whence this dissuading diatribe of discouragement arose, she couldn't say. A patch of charred undergrowth and a ring of ashes on the clearing's edge brought her up short. Belinda's chest heaved, the wrapped cross rising and falling as her horrified eyes examined the spot where Gary Cripps died; the place from which his remains were extracted. Underwood's derelict church became visible on the other side now, peaceful in its leafy setting. Belinda edged around the powdery reminder of another life lost in her overwhelmed presence. She didn't look back, but ran straight towards the churchyard entrance. The temperature in the clearing plummeted. Belinda hurried through the decaying porch into the roofless chancel. Shafts of sunlight illuminated the sanctuary like fingers from heaven, yet produced no warmth on this occasion. *Where did Anton remove the cross from?* Her eyes fell upon the altar. *That must be the spot.* She approached with determined steps that met an unseen resistance, like wading through invisible treacle. Its power grew the nearer Belinda came to her goal. Now the whispers rose from beneath the ground again. A throbbing buffeted her shoulders, knocking her off course. She fought against a trill in her voice and called out. "This has to stop. How many more?" At the rear of the altar, a patch of freshly disturbed masonry mingled with older rubble. Belinda spied the altar's hollow interior and remembered Anton's triumphant assertions of being a treasure hunter. *Of course. The cross must have been stored inside.* She laid her burden on the dirty altar and unravelled its cloth. The whispers rose to a chorus of shrill laughter. All resistance against her body ceased. Belinda lifted the cross and crouched beside the widened gap; the place Anton had dug to retrieve his trophy. Meanwhile, on that same afternoon, she'd experienced her first vision of the tortured souls who now overshadowed her daily existence. She placed the cross inside and waited for magic to happen. The laughter grew louder and more confident. Belinda murmured to herself. "Those bad thoughts were right: it's too late. How do we stop it?" She scanned the open sky before watching the useless lump of tarnished brass in its dark tomb for the duration of a hurried mental discourse. *I can't leave it exposed for anyone to take. What if there's something else we have to do? Are there special words to say?* She reached inside and swiped the cross up, rose to her feet, then re-wrapped it. Seconds later, she hurried from the church across the clearing. Every tree and leaf echoed the first word spoken to her by one of Underwood's stranded spirits: *'Vengeance.'*

Puffing from the effort, Belinda tripped and stumbled over treacherous roots. In her mind's eye, they rose in malicious spite to punish her attempts at thwarting a long overdue reckoning. Pulse racing, she broke free of the woods and ran downhill at full tilt into the meadow. *For now, the cross must remain safe at Ravensbrook.* Would Jonathan say something of it to her? Did he know what had to be done? What about the blind lady she'd visit with Amanda?

* * *

"Who is it?" Peggy Greene's reddened eye sockets appeared around a gap in her semi-opened front door.

"Hi, Peggy. It's Amanda Fairchild. I've brought my niece for a visit. Is that okay?"

Peggy opened the door wide, cracking a vague smile. "Of course. Welcome, Amanda." She pulled her lavender shawl closer. "I'm staying in the living room today. The weather is warm, but I'm not feeling the benefit this week."

"I'm sure that'll be fine." Amanda stepped inside, followed by Belinda. "I baked a coffee walnut cake.

You mentioned liking them."

Peggy waved her cane about. "In that case: welcome twice over, my dear." She paused, sightless eyes sweeping the hallway. "And you've brought young Belinda. I'm pleased to meet you, child."

"Pleased to meet you," Belinda replied in a shy voice.

"Everyone calls her 'Belle,' Peggy," Amanda said.

Peggy grunted. "Some around here have called her less pleasant things."

Amanda looked from one to the other.

Peggy reached a frail hand in Belinda's general direction until she found her arm. "For a blind old bird, I still hear all the village twittering. You mustn't mind me, Belle. Come into the living room, so I can gauge how well you live up to your nickname."

Amanda read the confusion on Belinda's face. She touched her own cheeks with both hands and mouthed the words: *'she wants to feel you,'* in silence. She'd already covered Peggy's penchant for building mental pictures of her guests during their walk over. Amanda cleared her throat and tapped the box in her hand. "I'll cut some slices of this and fix tea, shall I?"

Peggy led Belinda into another room, calling behind. "Please. I've just boiled the kettle. You know where everything is."

"Yep. It's becoming my second home."

Peggy sat on a floral, two-seater sofa next to a rustic inglenook with copper hood and a freestanding rack of iron implements. Her clay cat model rested in pride of place on a table to the left.

Belinda followed her lead and sat alongside. She broke the awkward silence. "You have a beautiful garden, Mrs Greene."

Peggy emitted a rattling cough. "Now, now, none of that. I appreciate your manners, but you must call me Peggy. Everyone else does."

Belinda corrected herself. "You have a beautiful garden, Peggy."

"Thank you. It was my pride and joy when I could still see. I only hope my gardener maintains it the way I remember."

"It's the best in Oakdene."

"Flatterer," Peggy flicked a dismissive hand in front of her face. "Now then, how are you enjoying your summer holidays? Eight weeks off school?"

"Yes." Belinda didn't elaborate.

"You don't sound too enthusiastic. Make the most of them. The time will come when you'd give anything for the halcyon days of your childhood. How old are you?"

"Nine."

Peggy cackled under her breath. "Another seventy-eight years and you could look like this." She stuck her face forward with a silly grin.

Belinda didn't know whether to laugh or recoil in horror.

Peggy patted her arm. "If that doesn't inspire you to make the most of your youth, I don't know what will. So, 'Belle,' is it? Let's have a better look." She lifted her hands, and Belinda leaned forward without further prompting. Peggy's arthritic, bony fingers found the cascading locks of free-flowing hair first.

Amanda entered, bearing a tray of tea and cake.

Peggy twisted on the sofa towards the sound. "Like strands of fine silk. What colour are they, Amanda?"

"She has beautiful golden hair. Difficult to tame, sometimes."

Peggy slid her hands beneath Belinda's chin, pressing against bone and muscle structure. "She's a beauty indeed. Hearts will break over this one; mark my words."

Amanda sat down and passed round slices of cake on a coffee table. "Consider them marked. The tea is drawing."

Peggy's fingers stopped upon reaching Belinda's brow. Her face froze, mouth open in a silent gasp.

"Is everything all right, Peggy?" Amanda asked.

Peggy dropped her hands and clasped Belinda's shoulders. Vacant eyes stared into the big brown ones of her young guest with curious emotion. She spoke in a reverent whisper to Belinda. "You've seen them, haven't you? They call to you from beneath the trees."

Belinda sat speechless.

Amanda settled in a chair opposite, face taut with alarm. "What makes you say that, Peggy?"

Peggy licked cracked lips. "They called to me once, long ago. Their voices were distant then." She addressed Belinda again. "It isn't that way with you." Her fingers trembled. "Have you disturbed something at Underwood?"

Amanda leaned closer and poured out the tea, keen to downplay Peggy's escalating theatrics with a firm interruption. "Here's a cuppa. What sort of something, Peggy?"

Peggy didn't turn her face. "An item of some sort?"

Belinda flushed. "Yes."

Amanda blinked. "What?"

Belinda stared into the blank countenance fixed upon her. "We unearthed an old metal cross inside the overgrown church."

"Who? You never mentioned this before," Amanda said.

"One of my school friends found it and took it away."

"Was it Laura?"

Belinda shook her head. She decided against disclosing the contents of her recent parcel. If Amanda failed to make the connection, so much the better for now.

"You shouldn't take things that don't belong to you." Amanda sat stern and upright once more.

Belinda's face fell. "That's what I said. I wanted it put back."

Peggy shook her head in disagreement with such force it threatened to roll off her shoulders. "Too late. That won't help now. You've uncorked the wine of retribution. It won't go back inside the bottle after fermenting for over three centuries."

Belinda whimpered. "We didn't do it on purpose." Her body shook in a rising spasm.

Amanda stood. The clay cat model beside her exploded in a shower of tiny fragments, littering the table and carpet beneath. She sidestepped, hand to her mouth.

Belinda shook free of Peggy's grasp and ran into the hallway. The front door opened and then slammed behind her.

Amanda sank back into the chair, head in one hand. "Oh no. This visit was all my idea, too."

Soft tears glistened amidst the dry fissures of Peggy's wan cheeks. "I didn't mean to frighten her. I'm sorry, Amanda. When the images come, I must speak them. Forgive me. You'd best run after the child."

Amanda grunted. "No. She'll want to be alone. If I had to guess, I'd say she's gone to All Saints. Belle claims the ghost of a young man who talks to her is buried in the churchyard."

Peggy picked up her cane and set it before her like a biblical prophet with their staff, intent on speaking words of power. "She's sensitive. I don't mean easy to hurt or overwhelm, though that's a side effect of her disposition."

"You mean she's sensitive to the kinds of things you are? Like psychic phenomena?"

"More sensitive, although she's not a psychic. Whatever the children unleashed at Underwood senses Belle's nature and latent ability. She's a conduit for their manifested rage; neither able to control nor stop it."

Amanda picked up a cup and saucer to stop herself from shaking. Instead it rattled, announcing rising fear to her sightless host. "Now you're scaring me."

Peggy hung her head. "She's not safe, Amanda. I wish I could tell you what to do. When the final die is cast, I fear for your beautiful niece."

* * *

Julian Asbury paced the halls of High Stanton, desperate to escape a mental prison of concerns encircling his financially vital development project. After the death of Gary Cripps, he'd become the last remaining conspirator. A courtesy e-mail from someone called Philip Thompson introduced himself as *'acting RED officer for the are*a.' It described how he'd be in touch soon to progress the planning application at Oakdene. How well had Gary covered his tracks? What loose ends needed to be tied, before a council rubber stamp would allow him to place the late Paul Gilbert's architectural plans in the hands of a commissioned builder? A mobile phone warbled to life inside his blazer pocket. Julian noted the caller ID as *'Gary Cripps - Office.'* The irony of someone calling on that landline didn't escape him. He wished it were Gary calling from beyond the grave. That way he'd extract the intelligence to counter anyone with morals or integrity at Torridge District Council torpedoing their project. He connected the call.

"Julian Asbury."

"Good evening, Mr Asbury. Philip Thompson. Did you receive my e-mail?"

"I did. You're standing in until Gary's post is filled by a permanent new employee."

"That's correct. We're all shocked about his tragic accident. But, as I mentioned in my e-mail, the council are keen to keep applicants' proposals on track. Some delays are inevitable, though we'd like to minimise their effect."

Julian released a gentle sigh of relief, watching the estate's peacocks strut across the lawn through a tall window. "Then we're of a similar mind. I realise the phrase *'time is money'* gets overused in such circumstances, but here it's the literal truth."

Any warmth and sociability evaporated from Philip's voice. "Yeah, about that: I've given Gary's plans and your supporting documentation the once over, and I'm astounded."

"It's a splendid development. Our local architect knew the village well, you see."

"Err, no, that's not what I meant."

"Oh?"

"I'm astounded any planning officer for Rural Economic Development would give such an outrageous proposal the time of day."

Julian's eyes twinkled. "It's received council support at the highest level, to date. Brandon Beeching championed the project."

"Hmm. Well, I don't know about that. However, doubling the size of Oakdene - a traditional Devon village of predominantly Grade 2 listed buildings - with a modern development right on top, won't fly with me."

Julian growled. "Aren't you making decisions above your pay grade, if local councillors are on board?"

"Not at all. That anyone even tabled this idea, beggars belief. It's a media storm waiting to happen. I can't imagine it'll pass consultation."

"Councillor Beeching disagreed."

The line went quiet for a moment. "Councillor Beeching danced to his own tune on more than one occasion."

"Do you have a superior I can speak to? You're doing my head in."

"My superiors will be in touch, no doubt. When they look at this development proposal in the light of day, the air will turn blue around here."

Julian's lip curled over his teeth. "Now you listen to me. I've invested considerable time and effort into this project. My financiers are waiting to advance significant funds, covering initial building costs. Windows for those funds, along with the availability of approved, large-scale building contractors, are limited."

"I'd tell your financiers and builders this won't happen, if I were you."

Julian gripped the mobile phone so tight in his sweaty hand, it almost zipped out like a bar of soap in the bath. He hammered his other in a fist against the tall window. Its juddering impact scattered the peacocks into a startled frenzy.

"Mr Asbury?"

"I'm still here."

"I realise this is disappointing news. If you were misled by Councillor Beeching or my predecessor, I can only apologise. We're keen on transparency, and this project has been kept in the shadows. Hushed up - so to speak - from those staff I've interviewed on its periphery. That raises major concerns."

Julian took a breath, calming his nerves. "What would it take to make those concerns vanish?"

"I'm sorry?"

"This is a profitable venture. Or it will be, if it goes ahead. Someone with the right connections or authority and an eye on their future, could do well out of it. New houses are a fact of life, after all. A discrete pragmatist embraces the inevitable in a manner which builds them up." He grinned. "If you'll pardon the pun."

A stony silence reigned.

"Philip?"

"I don't think I've anything further to say to you, Mr Asbury. It seems my concerns were justified."

"Wait... I..."

"My superiors will be in touch, like I said. Good evening." He hung up.

Julian threw his phone against the wall, causing its screen to crack. "Shit." Scarlet of face, he stormed along the corridor and kicked open the door of an impressive, wood-panelled study. A decanter of cognac found its way into his hands within seconds, the contents one quarter depleted to fill a snifter near overflowing. He gulped down a mouthful and tugged open the top desk drawer. Inside, a pile of red-inked bank statements and utility bills - some stamped '*Final Demand*' - greeted him like regretted flings with disreputable lovers. He slumped into a leather office chair and knocked back another belt of the expensive XO. Beyond the study window, his Aston Martin glimmered in the dwindling light. Julian leered at it, wits dulled by the speed and liquid volume of his intoxicating beverage consumption. *You're on borrowed time, like everything else around here.* He banged his head against the desk blotter and sat still.

The study lay in darkness when Julian came to, three hours after emptying the decanter. He thrashed about for the switch of a green-shaded banker's lamp, knocking the crystal drinks holder to the floor, which shattered on impact.

"Bloody hell," he shouted, fingers clicking the lamp into action at last. Its meagre yellow light didn't travel further than the desk, leaving the rest of the study swallowed up in velvet folds of gloom.

A faint noise arose from the hallway outside. Julian staggered aloft, then zigzagged towards light beyond, outlining the door frame. Its brass knob twisted in his hands and he stuck his head into the corridor. An anguished murmur, redolent of some weeping, bereaved husband or father, came from nowhere, yet everywhere at once.

Julian rubbed his eyes and clutched his head. "I've gotta quit drinking so much." He shook himself and listened again. This time the sound evidenced a definitive direction. Julian worked his way along the wall for support, unsteady on his feet. The crying intensified as he neared the main hallway. "Hello?" The reverberating boom from his voice made his head regret the verbal inquiry. He lowered his voice a fraction. "Who's there?"

With a surge of effort, Julian pounced into the hallway, half-expecting to catch someone on the front door mat who'd gained access without permission. Had he left the door unsecured while lost in his mental turmoil? Instead, the expansive area remained empty. A flicker of movement caught his eye from a painting on the wall.

"What would you do in my shoes, Oliver?" he slurred, while drawing nearer to the antique portrait.

Two tracks of fresh, fine red paint - suggestive of blood - ran from the cavalier's eyes. Julian stood for a moment in disbelief, then collapsed in an unconscious heap on the cold hallway floor.

14

Carrick's Lament

"A conduit for manifested rage?" Craig Symonds squatted, positioning an electric lamp towards the chimney in Ravensbrook's attic. "That's a wild one, even for Peggy."

Amanda plugged in a second unit on the landing below and carried it up to join him, unravelling the power cable with each step. "I haven't mentioned her comment to Belle. She'd already run off before Peggy uttered it."

Craig took the second lamp from her and set it on the opposite side. "This should provide sufficient light for the job in hand." He read the discomfort in Amanda's body language. While that wasn't new after everything they'd experienced in recent weeks, she'd never looked so tense. "Uncorked the wine of retribution? Another priceless statement." He scratched his beard. "If I wanna be a 'glass half full' guy, that allays our fears over Belle causing this spate of sudden deaths. She was present, of course. But, we never believed her guilty of direct involvement…" He gave up mid-sentence as Amanda slouched. "I'm not helping, am I?"

"You're trying."

"So Belle ran off to All Saints, while Peggy scared you half to death with fears for her safety. Where is the little lady, by the way?"

"In her room. She had an early tea and retired sharp."

"Of her own volition during the summer holidays?"

"Yeah. It bothered me too. At least she's home safe and not roaming the woods."

Craig ran his fingers across loose mortar in the chimney brickwork. "Or following another potential victim. How many can there be, before these spirits are satisfied?"

"I don't know. After Peggy's assertions about the final die being cast and what it means for Belle, I'm not eager to find out."

"What was Belle doing in the churchyard?"

"Sitting beside Jonathan's grave. Somehow, I knew she would be."

"Have you found any more altered paintings?"

"No."

Craig frowned. A crumbling lump of dried mortar burst in his fingers. He reached down for a torch Amanda had brought up with them, then shone it through the exposed gap. "It amazes me the crap you find stuffed behind dodgy brickwork sometimes. What's that?" He reached an arm through up to the elbow. "Look at this space." A loose corner brick dropped onto his foot from above. "Ouch. It's a good job you didn't leave the chimney much longer. The entire stack could collapse, if it's like this all the way through." He withdrew his arm in a cloud of dust.

Amanda put a hand in front of her mouth and coughed. "What have you found?"

"I'm not sure." Craig held a rectangular object, two hands high, wrapped in a dirty rag. He squatted next to the first lamp he'd positioned and freed the item from its protective covering. A compact, leather-bound book rolled into his opposite palm. He grinned. "Is it someone's forgotten shopping list, or a collection of their steamy romantic secrets?"

Amanda crouched beside him. "Open it."

Craig eased back the cover. "I thought this looked old."

Amanda leaned over and read aloud from immaculate, handwritten script. *"Journal of Reverend James Carrick - 1666."* She thought for a moment. "I've heard that name before. Yes. That's right, Julie Clement mentioned him as the first vicar of All Saints. He was also minister at Underwood during its demise."

Craig lifted a fabric bookmark attached to the spine. "Someone stopped reading at a certain spot. Either that or it indicates a special entry. Hey, this dust is getting down my throat. Do you fancy a glass of water in the kitchen? We'll inspect the book before rolling up our sleeves and diving in here."

"Okay." She rose and descended to the landing.

Craig followed. "Did James Carrick live in this house?"

"I don't know. Carrick isn't the same family name as Jonathan's. Belle insists he claims Ravensbrook was his home."

They slipped down the main stairs, filled two glasses with water, and sat at the table.

Craig opened the book at its marker. "Shall we start here?"

"Why not."

He took a breath and began. *"Wednesday 5th September 1666. My heart is heavy to breaking. Even as word reaches us of a great fire sweeping through the city of London, a fiercer conflagration scorches my soul. Oliver Asbury arrived from his estate at High Stanton, burdened with the most horrid revelations which the sanctity of my office forbid me to share aloud. He sought prayer for a troubled heart, though it required every ounce of God's grace within me to accede to his request. How blind a shepherd have I been to miss such deceit and wickedness at work within my parish? Weighed down by grief and love for my bereaved flock, I failed to grasp the events in which our whole community was embroiled. God forgive me, I know not where to turn."*

Amanda sipped some water. "Not quite the idyllic life of your average country parson."

"Quite." Craig turned the page. *"Thursday 6th September 1666. Sleep fled from me yestereve, like Jonah's flight from his calling at Nineveh. Unable to disclose that which I received in confidence from Oakdene's founding benefactor, I wrestled with my conscience throughout the night watches. After prayerful consideration at first light, for my peace of mind, I have decided to record Oliver Asbury's confession in writing. No soul may share it during our lifetimes. But, posterity should record the true fate which befell my beloved parishioners at Underwood. Perchance their troubled souls find peace in the arms of our Saviour once their story is known."*

Amanda mashed fingers together in front of her pouting mouth.

Craig slaked his thirst in a hearty gulp. "Why is none of this surprising me?" He held up the next entry. *"Friday 7th September 1666. Herein I will endeavour to relay the despicable sins for which Oliver Asbury sought forgiveness and prayer. So heinous are the actions of Oliver and his conspirators, my faith struggled in accepting the precious blood of Christ could absolve them. Will my departed flock honour his supposed penitence in the world beyond, or the realm between - a place I fear they linger? Even now, people steer clear of the old village. It has become a troubled site of restless souls, held back from their heavenly inheritance. And so, to the truth: For two years prior to the arrival of The Great Plague in Underwood, Oliver Asbury cajoled its populace to sell their homes. Resting on a level patch of ground beneath High Stanton's hillside woods, most understood the village offered a perfect opportunity to expand his lumber fortune. But, home is home. Nobody took up his offer to rebuild on land he'd purchased further east, beside the river. Land he offered in freehold for those who'd accept. Much changed in little time, once the plague struck last year. I'd jested with Oliver that tasking his men to deliver a cart of wrapped cloth parcels from London as gifts for the community, would fail to change their minds. How wrong I was, but in a manner I never suspected."*

Amanda gasped. "Belle mentioned a dream where cloth was given to the villagers, right before they fell sick. She claimed they were happy then."

Craig read on. *"Oliver obtained his 'tainted chalice' of fabric in the full knowledge it lay infested with rat fleas. Those self-same miniature devils spread the plague throughout London and beyond. If Oliver could not buy Underwood's people out, he'd wipe them out. Village children were first to experience troublesome flea bites. Soon after, the swelling, fever, skin discolouration and bleeding began. I fell prostrate before the altar and wept for the Lord's mercy as we sealed the infected in their homes, that others might be spared. One evening, a party of men set off from the village, climbing the hill. They bore torches and farming implements, faces angry as the spitting flames held aloft to light their way. When I enquired of the healthy what was afoot, they informed me someone had accused our local landowner of causing the plague. Even then I protested his innocence and gave chase to dissuade them from hasty action based on fear, grief or wild speculation. I was too late. Were it not for Judge Gawdrey and the visiting militia at High Stanton, that magnificent house would have succumbed to flame and my flock been guilty of murder. Instead, Gawdrey ordered those responsible be strung up from the roof trusses of their own homes, as punishment and a warning to others."*

"Oh, my goodness." Amanda's face fell.

"Sick bastards," Craig spat. "Do you want me to go on?"

"Please."

"Okay, where was I? Oh yes." He shook his head. *"So much pain and suffering haunted what remained of the village. When Oliver extended a branch of forgiveness and friendship to help build anew on the spot he'd originally offered, nobody was minded to stay put. I know not how little he paid for Underwood's parcel of land. We buried the last victims in a plague pit at the old church. Burdened by grief for our brothers and sisters, I sought to fire the heartbroken and downcast who remained with victorious, uplifting tales from scripture of moving into a Promised Land. We christened our settlement Oakdene, in reference to both tree and valley. Insufficient people and skills existed for the village to flourish, so Oliver Asbury sent word far and wide of his ongoing, generous offer. He tore down the old homes and part of the church to re-purpose their stone. Saplings planted on the site obscured what remained. More people arrived afterwards. In the short time since, our new home has flourished. Several of those in our founder's circle of influence received generous assistance with their accommodation. At the time I thought little of it. Only after Oliver confessed to me in secret did I realise every man bore a portion of the guilt from his plan. None have yet come to me in person, but I will name them here:*

Charles Peebles
Seth Beeching
Isaiah Cripps
Eamon Gilbert
Gabriel Taylor
Morgan Trehane

I confess as a minister of grace, I would find little encouragement in hearing each conspirator detail his sins. Once was enough for my tortured spirit to endure. Now I fear another man of the cloth may suffer similar agony. A sickness of the lungs I have endured these past three months grows fiercer by the day. May God have mercy on my soul." Craig indicated some faded brown splotches on the page. "That looks like blood."

"Julie Clement said James Carrick died of consumption."

Craig held up the journal with his finger pressed against the list of conspirators. "You do realise the significance of those names: *Peebles, Beeching, Cripps, Gilbert, Taylor*? This is Old Testament type stuff: the sins of the forefathers visited on future generations. That sucks for a lovely guy like Brian Taylor. The wine of retribution is blood guilt. Underwood's restless, deceased villagers are punishing the descendants of their murderers. All except someone called Trehane. I don't know anyone by that name. The family must have died out or moved away." He rested the book down.

One silent tear rolled down Amanda's right cheek. "My sister-in-law's maiden name was Karen Trehane."

Craig's eyes widened. "Are any of those other bloodlines in the Fairchild family?"

"Not that I'm aware."

"Could Jake's death have been collateral damage? I mean: wrong place at the wrong time, standing beside Karen in front of that wall we fixed up?"

Amanda wiped her nose. "If Peggy is right about those angry ghosts piggy-backing Belle to manifest their wrath, that means she *was* here when Jake and Karen died."

Craig groaned. "Poor mite. There're a few more

entries."

Amanda sniffed. "Let's hear them."

"*Saturday 8th September 1666. Young Emily Crawford visited in a dreadful state. She suffers most terribly from hearing the angry whispers of her departed friends, ever since walking among Underwood's ruins. Day and night they accost her with horrific dreams and visions. I prayed for the child, but couldn't bring myself to cast out the devil. How could I rebuke our adversary, when Emily named the source of her affliction as those whom we hold most dear in our hearts? I am undone; my faith in tatters.*" Craig nodded at the ceiling. "She sounds like Belle's forerunner, or someone with a similar gift."

"I wouldn't call it a gift." Amanda ground her teeth.

"You know what I mean." Craig turned over another page. "*Sunday 9th September 1666. The joy of Sabbath service failed to penetrate my being today. This knowledge of Underwood's true fate is a terrible thing. Oliver Asbury continues in his prosperous life, along with the guilty accomplices who share his blessings. Is there no justice? When I consider myself a sinner saved by grace - as are we all - I realise judgement of my fellow man is not mine to apportion or dispense. Yet it galls me to tend those still burdened by loss, while others responsible for their anguish skip through life without consequence. God forgive me, I almost hope they use His liberty as an occasion to the flesh, like the good book says in Galatians. For in such they may experience the Lord's displeasure. Emily Crawford was not in attendance at church. Later, someone from the village found her drowned beneath the bridge. No-one spoke of suicide and I'll not utter it, lest she be denied burial in our new churchyard at All Saints. Yet in my heart of hearts, I know those disembodied voices caused such torment she threw away God's greatest gift to ease her own suffering."*

"The girl in my painting?" Amanda asked.

"It's a fair bet. Now you have a name to go with her: Emily Crawford."

"Belle saw her on a Sunday."

"I remember you saying." Craig lifted the book again. *"Monday 10th September 1666. Another restless night. I awoke with determination to aid my deceased brethren at Underwood in their quest for peace. That, or to ease their haunted affliction upon the struggling mortals of Oakdene. When we departed our former place of worship, I brought with me a brass altar cross once set in a stand. For three hours after sunrise I petitioned heaven with prayer and supplication for the restless dead, blessing the cross upon each Amen. This afternoon I sealed it inside the altar at Underwood, which still stands whilst so much else has already vanished into memory and legend. If our worshipful emblem doesn't aid each soul's passing to their deserved destination, I pray God its presence will soothe or placate the furious blood which cries out to the heavens from those cold tombs beneath the trees."*

Craig clicked the knuckles of one hand. "Damn, Peggy scares me when she's that accurate. He's writing about the cross Belle and her friends uncovered. It has to be. The item Peggy asked about being disturbed."

Amanda turned ashen. "That's right. On the day before Jake and Karen died, and this mess started." She shifted in her seat. "Belle claimed she wanted to put it back, but Peggy said it's too late now."

"Without James Carrick and his prayers? Small wonder."

"Is there any more?"

"One last entry." Craig drew a breath. "*Tuesday 11th September 1666. God help me, I'm not long for this world. I cough blood throughout the day and my energy fades like dwindling sunlight at dusk. This journal cannot be discovered now, were the Lord to take me without further warning. Tomorrow I will make a short walk south and leave it in the safekeeping of my sister, Rebecca Dowland, at Ravensbrook Farm. I thank God for the good man she married, and that the isolation of their home spared them the horrors of The Great Plague at Underwood. Even so, they witnessed many a tragic funeral during those dreadful days. I fear for the future of their happiness. Rebecca is no longer of birthing age. Their only son, Jonathan, evidences similar symptoms to my own.*"

Craig and Amanda exchanged stunned glances.

Craig continued. "*It is a double shame as the lad - despite being an able-bodied farmer - also displays considerable artistic abilities and strong leanings towards the ministry. He has read for me in church with great spirit and emotion, and stood by my side in support at each graveside committal throughout the last year. How long until both of us rest beneath the greensward at All Saints? How long before our human remains reside forever in this new spiritual home, which grows and improves in appearance with each passing week? Who first will stand before the judgement seat of God? I always felt my nephew dwelt under a calling he was yet to fulfil; some ministry still to serve. It seems I suffered an idle fancy. How typical of a loving uncle! I draw strength from knowing we shall sojourn together in paradise, though I grieve for the loss my sister and her husband will endure. It is one small mercy neither he nor I will go down to the grave beneath the hand of man's greed. We have been more blessed than others we once knew as friends. Pray for us. Pray for Oakdene. Pray for Underwood. In His service and by the grace of Almighty God - Reverend James Carrick."*

Craig closed the book. "That's it."

Amanda shook back rising emotion. "Jonathan Dowland is the teenage boy's name inscribed on that gravestone Belle visits. He died the following year in 1667."

"I imagine James Carrick went first, from his description of the illness and how far advanced it was." Craig's eyes sparkled. "Jonathan displayed artistic abilities, hey?"

"I caught that. My resident shadow painter? Ravensbrook was his home after all."

"Ravensbrook Farm, in the journal."

"That's right. It was a farm, long ago. Why didn't his spirit move on? He sounds like a young man of faith, at peace with everything around him."

Craig blinked. "You got all that from the text?"

"Didn't you?"

"When you consider what's going on with that housing development, some of the recently murdered descendants are a chip off the generational block. I exclude your sister-in-law and Brian Taylor from that, of course. Sam Peebles, too, even though he was an awkward git. I doubt he knew much of what Julian

Asbury and his goons were planning."

"Yeah. Oliver Asbury and the original conspirators screwed an entire village over, then bought its land to make a profit from easy access to logging. Julian Asbury and his chums are screwing the present village over by selling that same land to make a profit from building homes once again. Or those still alive are, anyway."

"And so everything goes full circle, after a fashion. Not quite how Julian Asbury described at the consultation meeting, though. Thank goodness we're not in the middle of a bubonic plague outbreak." Craig sat back in his seat. "I wouldn't put him past pulling a similar stunt to his ancestor. Smug, self-righteous little prick."

Amanda sat bolt upright and froze.

"What is it?" Craig asked.

"Blood guilt."

"Yes?"

"How about if one life isn't enough? What if Underwood's villagers are gunning for entire bloodlines?"

"So no descendant of the guilty may enjoy a peaceful life? Creepy, but possible. To the best of my knowledge, none of the deceased had siblings or offspring. I'm unsure about other living relatives, but if so they don't live near Oakdene."

Amanda squinted. "None of the deceased? You don't get it, do you?"

"Get what?"

"Belle is Karen's daughter. Trehane blood runs in her

veins too."

Craig puffed out his cheeks, assessing the validity of her supposition. "How could I have forgotten that? Wouldn't the ghosts have swooped on her right off the bat? She remains untouched. Uninjured, anyway."

"What if they need her? If she's this conduit Peggy suggests, what happens when all the other bloodlines have ended?"

"If I'm right about siblings and offspring, there's one more target still unharmed, aside from your niece: Julian Asbury himself."

"And if he dies? If the restless spirits of Underwood don't require Belle anymore?"

Craig drummed his fingers on the table. "I don't know."

Amanda gripped his arm. "Remember the last thing I told you Peggy said to me: *She's not safe. I wish I could tell you what to do. When the final die is cast, I fear for your beautiful niece.*" Amanda turned her head towards the ceiling beneath Belinda's bedroom. "I need to check on her."

"Okay." He examined his watch. "Once you're happy, we'd better get cracking on that chimney stack in the attic. Time is pressing on."

Amanda hurried upstairs and along the corridor.

Craig deposited their empty glasses in the sink. Hairs rose on the back of his neck at a shrill tone of distress in Amanda's voice as she called over the banister.

"Belle isn't in her room."

* * *

Belinda had tried to sleep for an age. Craig Symonds arrived two hours after she'd excused herself and retired. Amanda's lingering expression of concern followed her up the stairs. Outside her room, muffled sounds of industry arose from two adults carrying items up to the attic. Minutes later, Craig's rich voice - faint but loud enough for her to grasp - spoke to Amanda.

"This should provide sufficient light for the job in hand."

Any follow-on verbal exchange vanished amidst floating whispers seeping through her window from across the meadow. Belinda rolled onto her stomach and pulled the pillow over her head in what had become something of a habit. A familiar, wispy hand touched her shoulder blade, causing Belinda to jolt from its unexpected presence.

"Go away, Jonathan. I want my normal life back; the one I had before ghosts took over. I want Mummy and Daddy."

The whispers grew louder, their sound transitioning into visible shapes of a shadowy crowd filling the bedroom.

Something snatched Jonathan's hand away. Belinda lifted the pillow and turned over in time to see him crowded out of her chamber. His hands reached in desperation, face strained with a pleading concern that made her sit up. She pressed herself against the headboard before addressing the amassed group of dark figures. "Leave him alone. I thought Jonathan was your friend."

The spectral silhouettes drew closer to her bed, their essence wrapping around Belinda's tensed limbs.

"No, I won't go with you. You'll hurt someone else and I don't want to watch." Belinda shook her distraught face with a quivering bottom lip. "Why do you need me? Why can't you do this alone?" She shut her eyes and thrust all her weight down into the mattress. A numbness spread throughout her body, which gave way to an insistent drive, impossible for Belinda to resist. Her thoughts grew fuzzy, and she swung her legs off the mattress as though sleepwalking. Out on the landing, faint sounds from the attic continued as Belinda wandered in a soundless trance downstairs to the hallway. She slipped through the front door. It swung to a silent close behind her, moved by unseen hands.

A warm breeze blew the white fabric of Belinda's nightdress in gentle ripples. Her bare feet pressed into the lush meadow underfoot. Daisies nodded and parted in the moonlight as she swept through them at a funereal pace. No life spark danced in her now-open, mournful brown eyes. A juvenile executioner in a reluctant occupation; she didn't even register the strands of fine golden hair fluttering across her face. The woods drew nearer, dark and foreboding. Their sinister approach washed over Belinda with the same lack of response all else in her immediate environment induced. From tree to tree, human-shaped shadows darted hither and thither. Outlines of men, women and children comprised the throng. Their uncoordinated frolic spoke of excitement and anticipation, as of those on the cusp of a long desired event. Belinda pressed on. Silvery light illuminated her form when she stepped into the clearing near Underwood's church. The same silvery light fell across dreamy outlines of former residences, resurrected in semi-transparent imagery that hung on the night air like a heavy mist. Ghostly hands emerged beneath the churchyard turf. Beside its boundary, an abundance of glowing figures climbed out of a communal burial pit. They stood in a line like soldiers awaiting inspection while Belinda passed by, her face frozen in a deadpan, emotionless gaze. Without a word, they fell-in behind.

The effort of climbing the steep, wooded slope north didn't tire Belinda's calf muscles during her steady ascent. A chill aura danced and crackled across the fine hairs of her skin. She crested the rise and stepped through a gap in an elegant stretch of box hedge into the well-manicured grounds of High Stanton. Anyone inspecting its horticultural adornments up close might notice a lacklustre presentation suggesting tender loving care was now required. Since the death of Sam Peebles, Julian Asbury had other things on his mind and little time (or money) to consider hiring a replacement grounds keeper.

Belinda halted two hundred yards from the imposing, elegant manor house. Lights in half a dozen windows suggested the owner was home. Yet no such clues were required for the driving forces behind her mission. They knew with absolute certainty that the descendant of their betrayer and arch conspirator dwelt within. Belinda followed the gravel drive. Its sharp stones indenting her tender, unclad feet still elicited no response. The procession of spiritual figures compressed into the single form of that lost-looking nine-year-old, wandering at night with definite purpose down the driveway of an English stately home. At last she reached the sweeping path lined by intricate topiary. High Stanton's sturdy oak and iron studded front door loomed large above her slender, solitary form. Inside her clouded mind, Belinda wrestled with images of angry men tossing lit torches through the windows, long ago. Meanwhile, others in ancient military garb raced around with buckets of water to extinguish a spreading blaze. In the end, every agitator was rounded up on their knees before the house, while a cavalier and a stern-looking man in a grey wig strutted before them.

Belinda shook her head, but remained unable to dislodge or deny the forces willing her hand to reach up and grab a stiff bell cord.

From somewhere deep inside, a sharp jangle sounded. The impatient clip of approaching determined feet suggested a brusque gait. A heavy bolt slid back. The door opened, first a crack, and then wide in the hands of Julian Asbury.

He blinked and then scowled at the young, barefoot girl on his doorstep wearing her nightdress. "What do you want?"

15

For Whom Belle Tolls

Craig Symonds took the main stairs at Ravensbrook two at a time after hearing Amanda's sudden, anguished announcement.

"Are you sure?"

Amanda stood in Belinda's bedroom doorway. "Of course I'm sure; her bed is empty. See for yourself."

Craig entered the room, then dropped to the floor and scanned beneath the bed frame.

Amanda tapped an impatient foot. "She's not playing hide and seek." She tried not to snap at Craig, but needed some kind of outlet for her emotional upheaval.

"I realise that. Frightened people - especially children - do strange things sometimes."

Amanda leaned against the door frame. "Sorry."

"Forget it. Okay, calm heads. We've been reading a powerful and horrific account of tragic events, on top of Peggy's latest and most worrying set of predictions. Let's take a breath and consider the logical possibilities first. Did we wake her with our noise? Might she have gone to the bathroom, or for a mooch around your studio? Is there somewhere else in the house she likes to spend time? Could curiosity have drawn her to investigate the attic, while we were downstairs?"

Amanda composed herself and gave a semi-confident nod. "Excellent suggestions, all. I'll check the bathroom and my studio. Will you conduct a sweep of the attic?"

Craig snapped her a mock salute. "Yes, General."

Amanda frowned.

He patted her shoulder as he passed. "It was the way you said *'conduct a sweep,'* that's all. Will we require a pincer movement or an approach from the flank?"

Amanda folded her arms. "I'm glad you're enjoying yourself."

Craig cleared his throat and gave up on defusing the tension bomb with attempts at humour. "I'll check the attic."

"Good. We'll go room to room afterwards, working our way back downstairs."

"Gotcha." Craig thundered up the smaller second staircase into the roof space. He collected the torch he'd used to peer into the chimney cavity, then checked every beam and crevice of the dusty space. *I hope Amanda has better luck below. She'll be in a state if Belle has gone walkabout at night.* Satisfied the only person roaming around the wonky wooden supports was himself, Craig tucked the torch into his belt and descended to the landing. *I'd best keep this handy, in case we need to check outside in the dark.* He found Amanda clinging to the newel post as though hugging her niece. "No luck?"

She shook her head.

Craig placed a hand in the small of her back. "Okay, down we go. I'll check the rooms on the right-hand side of the hall, while you search the others."

Amanda stopped halfway down and turned, eyes panicked. "What if she's not there?"

"Why don't we tackle that subject once we're sure it's true? She could've fallen asleep on the sofa, for all you know."

"I suppose. Oh, dear God, let it be so." Amanda moved again at a rapid pace. "Belle?"

Craig wasn't sure whether calling her name was for Belinda's benefit or Amanda's, but took part in the action, regardless. "Belle? Are you there, honey? Amanda and I want to speak with you." His examination of each nook and cranny drew a blank.

Amanda appeared in the kitchen doorway. "She's not asleep on the sofa or in any of the other rooms. I checked the back door, too. It's locked from the inside."

"Then either she's vanished or exited through the front." Craig tugged open the main door.

Amanda joined him on the doorstep. "We'd have noticed her pass, if she'd left while we were reading James Carrick's journal."

"I know. Were you downstairs the whole time before I arrived?"

"Yes."

"Then it happened while we were in the attic together. Not too long ago."

Amanda swallowed hard. "Long enough."

A loud bang struck the floorboards of Belinda's

room, causing them both to whirl.

Amanda almost tripped over herself, scrabbling up the stairs again.

Craig followed. "We didn't search her wardrobe. Maybe she was hiding in there?"

Amanda froze at the entrance to Belinda's room. Sure enough, the wardrobe door hung open, but no child sprawled on the floor. Instead, a tarnished brass cross lay amidst an old rag it had rolled out of while toppling from its hiding place.

Craig squeezed past and checked the wardrobe. "No way that thing launched out of here unaided. It wouldn't have travelled so far across the room under its own steam." He parted Belinda's clothing but found no-one inside. "It was thrown." He squatted beside the religious emblem. "I realise I'm stating the bloomin' obvious, but this must be the cross Belle and her chums unearthed at Underwood. Presumably the same one Carrick sealed inside the old altar to hold restless souls from the village in check." He left the cross where it lay and straightened. "Didn't Belle say she'd urged her friends to put it back, despite Peggy telling you it was too late?"

"That's what she told me." Amanda gasped and slapped her forehead. "I'm so stupid."

"What?"

"Belle received a package the other day. It was postmarked from Oakdene and addressed in a child's hand. I teased her about having a secret admirer in the village, because she asked to open it alone. This would be the right size." Amanda groaned. "Ugh. She didn't have a beau sending chocolates; it was the cross. But why?"

Craig shrugged. "Right after Gary Cripps kicked the bucket by lightning, fire and impalement? If you were nine and heard stories about your pal being responsible for a spate of mysterious deaths - all the while insisting the cross you'd swiped and kept hold of should be returned - wouldn't you get spooked? Whoever kept this before, mailed it back to her because they're too scared to deliver it in person, or worried about being discovered."

"That makes sense."

"Do you reckon your resident ghost threw it onto the floor?"

Amanda looked about. "I have no idea. If he did, for what reason? It can't do anything. Belle reckons she sometimes hears him while away from the house."

"I'd suggest he's not with her now." Craig studied the dull metal symbol again. "Is it a clue to Belle's whereabouts?"

"If she'd run off to the church at Underwood, wouldn't she have taken the cross with her?" Amanda picked the metallic object up and laid it on Belinda's mattress. Leaving it on the floor felt disrespectful.

"It's a shame you can't talk with Jonathan the way Belle claims to. You could ask him a straight question."

Amanda stroked a matted and well-loved teddy bear sitting on Belinda's dressing table. "What's next? This hasn't helped at all."

Craig withdrew the torch from his belt. "Have you got your front door key? We'll check the immediate house perimeter and grounds."

Amanda tapped a bulge in her trouser pocket. "Yeah."

"Good. Close the house up. If we miss Belle and she doubles back without realising we're on the hunt, we'll find her waiting outside the front door, unable to get in."

"Right. That'll work." Amanda and Craig hurried back down to the hall. Amanda pulled the door shut behind them and checked the lock.

Craig switched on the torch. "Not that I mind flitting about on a summer's night like a blue-arsed fly, but I'm also keen to find Belle safe and sound."

"Thanks." Amanda followed him around the base of Ravensbrook's principal structure, eyes following every movement of the torch beam in hopes of it reflecting Belinda's sweet face. Once they'd made it to the front again, Amanda ran a trembling hand down one cheek and followed the horizon with a vain squint.

Craig extinguished the torch. "What about Jonathan's grave? You've found her there a couple of times after she was upset."

"I don't have any better ideas." Amanda tapped another trouser pocket. "My car keys are inside the house."

Craig pulled out his own and unlocked the Land Rover. "Jump in."

Amanda climbed into the front passenger seat while Craig fired up the engine. The Defender's knobbly tyres bit into gravel and gained purchase. It lurched in a circle before roaring northward up the drive, across the brook and along the lane into Oakdene.

The village remained quiet at the best of times, with the barest minimum of occasional traffic. Several patrons spilled out of The Royalist, despite it being a pint or two before last orders. Craig swerved to avoid someone he knew, not paying attention as they stepped into the lane. The Land Rover squealed to a halt near the churchyard entrance. Amanda was out and running before Craig had switched off the headlights and engine. She cast one soulful glance at Jake and Karen's burial plot on her way around the church. Its older collection of graves on the other side huddled beneath dark trees wrapped in a concealing cloak of night.

Craig sprinted up behind her six seconds later. He shone the torch across a modest stone marker inscription in front of Amanda and read it aloud. *"Jonathan Dowland, 1648 - 1667.* I see what you mean. The poor guy never made twenty." He turned both ways and flashed the light about. "No sign of her?"

"None."

"Crap. Surely she can't have gone to Underwood? Not at this time of night."

"I don't know. It's the last place I want to search, but the way I feel right now, no angry spirit would dare mess with me."

Craig winced. "Shall we call the police?"

"If we don't find her within the hour, then yes. Where else could she be?"

Craig twisted. "Peggy is a night owl. She should still be up. Do we have anything to lose by knocking on her door?"

"I suppose not. After you."

Craig led the way back past his vehicle. He crossed the square and walked the few strides leading to Peggy Greene's cottage.

"Who is it, disturbing a body after dark?" Peggy's tone rang short with a faint hint of worry as the door opened a crack.

"Peggy, it's Craig and Amanda. Young Belle has vanished from her bedroom at Ravensbrook. Amanda is beside herself with worry. We've checked the house and the churchyard, but to no avail. Sorry for blurting all that out, but we thoug-"

Peggy gripped the door tighter and stopped him mid-flow. "Which churchyard?"

Amanda licked her lips. "All Saints."

Peggy shook her head, causing the short white hair with dark grey roots to flop across her unseeing eyes. "Wrong one."

Amanda wanted to shake the old woman, but took a hold of herself inside. "You mean she's at Underwood?"

Peggy stuck her nose out into the night air and cocked her head. "Can't you hear them?"

"Hear who?" Craig asked.

"The voices on the wind. They are euphoric; drunk on the blood of vengeance. Never has their call carried so far and with such power." Her hands shook. "Tonight is the night; I feel it in my bones. The last two lives upon whom they seek judgement will end by their empowered hands." She drew back inside with a mournful whisper. "Empowered by Belle; executioner and condemned."

Amanda's shoes hammered on the path in a rapid retreat.

"Amanda?" Craig shouted as his companion tore down the lane on foot at full tilt. His voice dropped to a monologue. "I'd better fetch the Landy." He squeezed Peggy's wrist. "Get yourself inside, Peggy. We're sorry to have troubled you."

Peggy caught hold of him as he attempted to pull away. "Go to them, Craig. Go to Amanda and Belle. Stand by their side, though your heart fails in your breast at the hopelessness of this situation. The villagers of Underwood have forgotten what it means to be human. Forgotten what love and joy or forgiveness look like. So consumed are they by a need for justice, they won't stop until justice is satisfied in their eyes. I've dreamt it every night for the last week. Do you think me mad?"

Craig unfastened her claw-like, bony grip and kissed the arthritic fingers. "No, Peggy. I don't think you're mad. Stay safe." He ran back up the lane to his Defender. *How far has Amanda gone now?* He jumped into the driver's seat and turned the ignition key. The starter motor whined but failed to crank the engine into life. "Not now. Oh God, not now." He tried again with the same result. "Shit. Shit. Shit." He let the car door bang shut and pounded down the lane in the opposite direction on foot. The torch worked its way out of his belt to clatter and roll around in the gutter beside a row of quiet homes. Craig wheeled and retrieved it, then bore right at The Old Bothy and tore up the incline towards the woodland gate.

Amanda had already made the moon-washed clearing by the time Craig reached her. Its ruined church tower stood silent and at peace. The noise of his panting approach cut through the stillness and made her turn. "She's not here."

Craig indicated the open-roofed structure. "Have you checked inside?"

"Yes. No sign of her. If Jonathan threw that cross out of Belle's wardrobe, it must have had some other meaning."

Craig clutched a stitch in his side from running too hard. "Not necessarily. He may have pointed us in the right direction. I've never known Peggy to be wrong." He caught his breath. "On that note, Belle would have passed through on her way."

"On her way where?"

"To visit the penultimate victim. The one before Underwood's villagers turn on Belle herself for their final satisfaction, if we're right."

Amanda spun, her attention sweeping the steep wooded hill. "Julian Asbury."

"The same. It's a fair bet she - or rather *they* - are paying him a terminal visit at High Stanton."

"Is your car by the gate?"

"Do I look that out of shape? It's still parked at the church. The starter motor fried. Sorry."

Amanda looked south towards denser patches of woodland that led onto the far side of the meadow at Ravensbrook. "There's no time to backtrack and fetch mine." She set her face towards the hill. "I hope you're up for another run."

* * *

Julian Asbury was partway through a spare decanter of cognac when the front doorbell jangled. With no visible way to escape the claustrophobic walls of his impossible financial maze, knocking back stores of premium booze now provided daily relief. Or rather, it distracted his troubled mind under a cloud of intoxication. Not yet half cut, he'd once again detected that anguished masculine wail echoing along High Stanton's elegant corridors. When he'd awoken from his previous collapse in the hallway, the first time it happened, Oliver Asbury's portrait appeared no different from usual. Gone were the tears of blood streaming down his face. Julian had categorised the inexplicable event as hallucinations induced by a combination of stress and alcohol. As the hair-raising noise commenced once more, he had no such excuse to fall back on. The ringing front door bell disturbed wild ideas about disgruntled villagers from Oakdene moaning to induce a fright. He shook his head and left the study, impatient feet echoing a tense rhythm on the cold stone floors. *Desperate fools. Like ghosts or superstitious nonsense could run me out of my home. If I can't counteract Gary's replacement at the council,*

Oakdene's plebs will get their way over the housing development, regardless. Then this place will go to the dogs.

The sight of a young girl standing in her nightdress on his doorstep took Julian by surprise. Ever the devious schemer, his next thought featured manufactured accusations of child grooming to get him out of the way. Was someone crouched in the bushes with a camera, waiting for him to bring the girl inside? No doubt that arty activist, Amanda Fairchild, looking for payback.

He blinked and then scowled at the barefoot girl. "What do you want?"

She regarded him with soporific eyes akin to one under narcotic influence. A bluish aura spread outward from beneath her flesh to manifest in crackling, dancing lights.

Julian backed away from the door. "What the hell is going on? What do you people think you're playing at? I'm calling the police." He fumbled beneath his blazer and withdrew a replacement smartphone, sourced the day after his rage broke its predecessor. With a single swipe he illuminated the screen. His usual photographic wallpaper of High Stanton's impressive facade (ready to show off while answering a call in public) had been replaced. Now it displayed Amanda's painting of the house on fire, with a tortured figure beside one window. Julian let the unit drop to the floor in shock. Its impact launched the text messaging app with a winking cursor. Writhing dark figures rushed out of the young girl's body on either side, like shadowy imps intent on mischief.

Julian shook his head. "This isn't possible. Why are you doing this? Where are you from?"

The wispy shapes solidified into human figures of either sex, encompassing the entire gamut of human age ranges. Man, woman and child stood in solemn assembly, some covered in cruel swellings and discoloured skin, others - all men - marked by fierce rope burns about their necks. The winking cursor on Julian's phone typed a single word in a rapid series of clicks:

'Underwood.'

Colour vanished from Julian's cheeks. He took another backward step, almost losing control of bowel and bladder at the hideous visitors from another time, crowding the hallway of his ancestral home. "What do you want with me?" His voice grew shrill. "My forebear gave your relatives a new home." He thrust one wavering finger at Oliver Asbury's portrait. "He was the hero of Underwood and founder of Oakdene. I'm his direct descendant. You should feel gratitude in my presence."

The moaning Julian heard before rose now to a deafening volume and ear-whistling pitch. The cavalier portrait's face twisted into a scream before his eyes, skin bursting with swellings, bruises and disfigurements to match the silent assembly crowded beneath.

Julian repeated part of his previous statement in a subdued tone, lacking conviction. "He was the hero of

Underwood and founder of Oak…" The apparitions turned their faces from the screaming portrait back upon him, stealing his final word. A handful of villagers moved off, leaving through the open door into the night.

Julian's voice shook to match his gesturing hands. "That's good. Some among you still understand gratitude and propriety."

The rest watched him, silent and unmoving, like the curious, nightdress-clad girl among them with dazed expression and unblemished skin.

From the grounds close by, impacts of splintering wood and breaking metal carried on the night air.

Julian took half a step forward. Sudden disabling fear at approaching the motionless dead halted the advance, born of concern for his country estate's wellbeing.

One of the tall windows shattered in the expansive dining hall to Julian's right. A heavy, clanging, metallic object smashed into the floor. He recognised the now dented orange container as a liquid gas cannister retrieved from a concealed external rack. Another pane of expensive, leaded light glass fragmented into a myriad shower of glistening shards. A second gas cannister, hurled with unimaginable force, clattered against the flagstones. Tongues of flame appeared outside, sputtering from ignited rags soaked in fuel. A sudden explosion shook the front of High Stanton. All remaining glass in the three storey, stone mullioned banqueting window blew inward. Tall curtains on either side caught fire in a savage roar, flapping as though in agony. The missing villagers reappeared on the doorstep, some clutching makeshift torches, the others axes, shears, forks and other gardening or maintenance implements purloined as tools of retribution.

"My home," Julian half-shouted in anger, half screamed in terror.

Two of the torchbearers sidled into the dining hall, their sputtering burdens igniting tapestries and rugs as they went. When they reappeared close to Julian, it wasn't their presence that made him stagger backwards in terror; nor was it the grim determination and anger writ-large on every ancient countenance. The nightdress girl took a step forward, gaze still fixed on him, yet lost. Whoever she was, something about her controlled or worked with these terrifying apparitions. To see her innocent face on a normal day, one would find nothing of consequence to trouble the heart. Watching her emotionless visage draw near like a conductor leading some infernal orchestra of murderous, troubled souls stole every ounce of courage he possessed. The front door slammed shut, its bolts sliding home without a visible hand to move them.

Julian turned with a loud, frightened whimper and ran for his life.

* * *

"I never realised how steep this hill is." Craig puffed and grabbed the root of a gnarled elm to keep from losing his footing. Halfway up the wooded slope, his energy levels flagged and threatened to evaporate. A long day of physical work in the gardens of Oakdene, followed by the busy and emotional events of the evening with Amanda, left his reserve needle close to the metaphorical empty mark.

Amanda reached out a hand to help him. "I can't lose her, Craig."

Craig blasted air from determined nostrils and squeezed her pale grip in reassurance. "I know. If she's there, we'll find her. Don't worry."

"Belle is the only family I have left. Jake and Karen entrusted her to me."

Craig took a breath and soldiered on. "You haven't lost her yet."

Amanda slid on a loose patch of dislodged soil. She scrabbled at it, seeking purchase. Rich, red Devon dirt clogged beneath her fingernails. Its fragrant, earthy aroma did little to calm fraying nerves within an ace of their breaking point.

Now it was Craig's turn to offer a hand. Together they scaled the steeper last section and broke through swaying ferns at the wooded escarpment's summit. Both companions bent double, gasping for air and muttering silent prayers for enough strength to keep moving.

A deafening blast parted tree canopies above, dropping green leaves in a whirling flurry of succulent life cut short. The pair hit the ground on instinct.

Craig rubbed his sweat-stained forehead with dirty fingers. "What the heck was that?"

Amanda released her pent-up fears in a single word. "Belle." She stumbled up, pushed through the trees and staggered between the abundant bastions of box hedge skirting the estate.

Along the driveway, High Stanton's impressive dining hall windows stood devoid of glass. On either side, tall flames from burning fabric illuminated the holes like broken teeth.

Amanda clasped both hands to her mouth. "No. It's catching fire. The whole place could burn down."

Craig reached her side. "Like your painting and Carrick's account of the night an angry mob went after Oliver Asbury."

Amanda broke into a straight run down the drive towards the topiary-lined path. Craig followed two strides behind. When they reached the front door, it stood shut. Amidst the crackling flames spreading throughout the dining hall to one side, a terrified male outcry faded from someone fleeing in horror.

Craig tried the door. "It's locked." He slammed one shoulder against its iron studded woodwork with considerable vigour, then regretted his action and rubbed the spreading pain. "We won't get in this way."

"How about the dining hall? Can you give me a boost?" Amanda darted left.

A wall of heat wafted over their heads as they approached. Craig stepped back and peered towards the empty holes aglow with flickering amber light. "That's suicide, Amanda. It would be like tossing you into a furnace. We need another way inside."

"Where?" Amanda threw up her hands, pacing with

a hopeless expression.

Craig peered across the lawn. "That looks like a tool shed. Let's see if we can find an axe. A giant home like this must have other, weaker doors. I'll break one down if I have to. The flames haven't spread too far yet."

They sprinted the distance in a heartbeat, both slowing when dancing firelight from the manor illuminated the shed. Its padlock lay smashed in two amidst door panels splintered like matchwood. Craig flicked on the torch and scanned its interior. "Someone beat us to it. There's not much left." He swiped a spade from the rear. "This will have to do. I hope the handle is solid, or it'll fold like a house of cards the moment I wallop something."

Amanda fixed on the manor. "We've got to hurry. Belle is in there; I know she is."

Craig grunted. "Unless Asbury is pulling an insurance job on the joint, I'd say that's a given. Let's check around the side."

They darted from wall to wall, Amanda taking charge of the torch in their quest for another entry point. "Here. An arched door," Amanda called.

"Stand back so I can take a decent swing." Craig steeled himself and readied the spade. His muscles tensed and he battered the door. Its impact jarred his hands through the gardening implement, but the portal stood firm. "Come on, you bastard." Craig swung the spade again. A sharp splintering ran the length of the handle and it sundered like a galleon's mast on a storm-tossed sea. Its metal blade dropped to the earth with a dull thud. "No." Craig discarded the flaking wood still left in his hands and retrieved the blade. "What if I wrench the door open with this?" He examined the frame, but found no crack wide enough to insert his would-be lever. "It's as solid as the front. We'd better keep looking."

They continued around the rear of the property. Amanda's torch beam fell on a pair of exterior angled doors set in a stone base inches above ground level. "What's that?"

"A wine cellar, I reckon. Back in the day they'd have brought the stuff in by barrel, not individual bottles or small cases."

"Can we get through?"

Craig crouched beside the access doors. "Shine that light here again."

Amanda complied, illuminating a rusty padlock securing the handles together.

Craig held the detached metal blade in both hands above the lock. "Let's hope that rust isn't superficial, surface corrosion." He shut his eyes. "Come on, my beauty. Be a good lock and give up the ghost." He struck metal against metal, slicing one of his hands. Blood dripped from an angry tear in two fingers. He winced, dropped the blade, and clutched the wounded appendage to his shirt.

Amanda rested her torch on the stone surround, picked up the blade between lithe fingers and repeated his action. The padlock cracked into three corroded remnants of its former self, freeing the handles. Amanda shot Craig a sidelong glance. "Are you okay?"

Craig tore a section of his shirt off and wrapped it around the bleeding fingers. "It looks worse than it feels. I'm more worried about blood poisoning." He gave a frustrated laugh at Amanda swinging open the freed doors with ease. "Plus my ego took a bruising when you did that."

Amanda recovered her torch. "Don't be a twit. Your blow did most of the work."

Craig stood still for a moment, eyes twinkling in admiration at the courage and tenacity on display before him. "This might not be the time, but..." He reached a hand across and pulled Amanda close for a brief, intimate kiss. She didn't resist, eyes welling up at the explosive cocktail of emotions pulsating through her soul. Tears ran unrestrained when she withdrew.

"What was that for?"

"Luck. And because whatever happens inside, I had to show you how I feel."

Amanda sniffed. "Belle and I need you, Craig. We can't do this alone."

Whether her words referred to the moment in hand or their onward lives - should they survive to lead them - Craig didn't know. All he knew was Peggy's charge rang true. He would stand by their side until the bitter end, even if that redoubt took place at the very gates of hell.

Amanda pointed the torch ahead. "There're steps leading into the cellar. Let's hurry."

"Take care that the wood isn't rotten. I'm right behind you."

Amanda glanced at him across her shoulder as they

descended, eyes still moist. "I know."

16

The Last Rites

Julian Asbury tore through the building with no intended course or plan of action; his mind wiped clean by fear. For now, all he knew was a need to keep his pursuers at bay and not find himself at a dead end, with nowhere left to run. He skidded into an adjoining hall, feet sliding out from under him. Desperate arms reached for anything to stabilise his flight and avoid lying down before the approaching terror. A large blue and white bone china vase wobbled in his grasp, then toppled from a polished mahogany table and shattered on the floor. *What do they want with me?* Based on appearances and the message typed on his abandoned phone, questions over their identity seemed irrelevant. All bar that of the catatonic child on a rigid death march of which she appeared unaware.

Julian slammed into the corridor wall opposite. Orange light appeared, followed by twisted, near inhuman snarls of fury barrelling down the route he'd run. Soon they'd be in sight and fall upon him to punish whatever imagined offence he'd given. *Are they looking for Oliver? Why now?* He pushed away from the wall and stumbled onward, reaching for the old staff backstairs outside High Stanton's enormous kitchen. A narrow, straight and utilitarian staircase of bland stone steps, the backstairs railing gave Julian enough extra leverage to propel himself upward. The clamouring din drew nearer, reaching the broken vase. *Can I hide somewhere?* He snorted. *Don't be a fool, Asbury. If those apparitions have risen from the grave, is there anywhere they won't find you?* That final thought stole adrenaline-fuelled drive from his muscles. If the statement proved true, how pointless was it to run? Where could he flee to? Julian rounded a bend in the stairs and launched up the next flight. *Can I fight back? How do you defeat something that isn't alive, yet able to attack? What use is physical force against angry ghosts?* Rational sense, reason and sanity defied the existence of that which sought to end his own. Yet it was no less real for that. He thundered on, reaching a narrow wooden door at the top. In a flash, he ripped it open and pulled it shut behind him. High on an abandoned, vertigo-inducing servant's walkway above the main stairs, Julian sought some way to secure the door. *Can those beings drift through walls the way they emerged from that child? They appear solid now.* His eyes fell upon redundant staff accommodation from ages past through a half-open doorway. Inside, moonlight filling the grand stairwell atrium through a skylight, and the rising glow of spreading fire from far below outlined a modest chair. Julian dashed into the room, grabbed the chair, and dragged it to the backstairs entrance. He jammed it beneath the door's brass handle, then wedged its legs at an angle against the walkway railing. Not a man of faith, Julian still found his subconscious conjuring a silent prayer to the ceiling. A supplication that some physical laws still applied in a reality now turned on its head. When you didn't know the rules of the game afoot, all bets were off and you could only try.

Amanda reached the wine cellar floor without incident. Craig's heavier frame snapped the last wooden step, making him stagger but without suffering further injury. Amanda scanned the torch across a low, vaulted ceiling of chambers. Several still contained old barrels, long since empty and forgotten. Assorted crates and bric-a-brac lay strewn with dirt and thick, dust-laden cobwebs. "There must be an internal door here somewhere."

They followed the only route of travel available from the steps until it branched at an underground crossroads.

Craig scratched his chin. "Which way now?"

Amanda squatted on her haunches and washed the floor with a cone of light. "Over there."

"What makes you so sure?"

"The dust has been disturbed by footprints ahead."

Craig patted her back. "Never knock an artist's observation skills." He set off in the direction indicated.

Overhead, a rising noise from the spreading conflagration rumbled through the structure.

"There's the door." Amanda's bobbing torch beam fell upon a rough portal with a wrought iron ring handle, set above three stone steps at the corridor's end.

"I hope Asbury doesn't bar it from the other side, or we've had it." Craig tested the handle with a deft touch, checking for heat. "Still cold." He twisted it and the door juddered open, swollen with moisture from the damp underground space. "If we hit smoke, try to keep below it. Breathe too much of that in…"

"I know." Amanda barged past.

Craig joined her and found himself in a cramped hallway adjoining an old butler's pantry. This staging space between the kitchen and one of High Stanton's more intimate formal dining rooms, also connected with the downstairs corridors.

Amanda ran towards the noise of fire. She and Craig reached the foot of a sweeping, grand staircase filling a large atrium. A pounding as of fists or tools against wood caused them to crane their necks upward.

After the momentary relief of securing the backstairs door, Julian realised he'd also blocked his only way of escape. Impossible, resurrected bodies and assorted tools from his grounds keeper's shed hammered on the vibrating barrier. The chair held fast, but it was only a matter of time before the door shattered. He gripped the railing and gritted his teeth, peering down the precipitous drop to the atrium floor at the base of the main staircase. *I must make it below to the family floors. What about doubling back to the front door? Could I unbar it, or do those things stand guard?* His mind recalled the exploding dining hall windows. *If I can reach the minstrel gallery on the bedroom level, I'll drop into Oliver's old banqueting space and climb out through the windows; as long as the fire isn't too fierce.* He swung one leg across the walkway railing and fought not to close his eyes. *A single foot wrong here, and they'll peel what's left of me from the atrium floor.* His other leg crossed the railing and he shimmied down, supporting his body weight from two whitening hands, feet kicking at the air. *How far is that drop to the family bedrooms? I'd better swing under or I'll fall straight down.* He risked a peek between his kicking feet. A man and woman stood on the ground floor, staring up at him while the jammed door continued to bang and shudder.

Julian frowned and spoke to himself aloud. "That's Amanda Fairchild."

Amanda ran for the posh stairs. "We've got to help him."

Craig gave chase. "What about Belle?"

"If she's on the other side of the door up there with the killers and Julian dies…"

Craig puffed. "Gotcha."

When the main staircase ended at the family landing, they realised accessing the staff floor above was impossible here. Julian's feet continued to dangle. He swung his legs over the family landing banister but failed to let go in fear. Fragments of splintered wood tumbled over the staff walkway railing, dropping past to land on the ground floor. Frantic, bruised, and discoloured arms burst through the disintegrating backstairs door above. A scratching of fingernails dug into the soft, work-shy flesh of Julian's weakening hands. He glanced upward into the gleeful, furious eyes of a small brother and sister tearing at his grip. A rising squeal of panic and desperation escaped his open mouth.

Amanda and Craig reached over the drop and grabbed Julian's ankles.

Craig shouted above the din. "Let go. We've got you."

Julian's resistance and distrust mattered little, as the combination of scratching children and vanishing strength caused his fingers to un-clamp from the railing without conscious mental instruction. His upper torso toppled backwards, head down over the remaining drop. Amanda wrapped her leg around the banister uprights for added support, desperate not to tumble with him. Craig reached across, gripped Julian's shirt, and tugged him level enough to slide his body back onto the landing. Above them, angry hisses faded through the shattered door. A broken chair leg followed remaining debris in a clattering shower onto the cold, hard floor below.

Julian caught his breath. "What are you two doing here? Are you behind this?"

Craig set his jaw. "Yeah, because we always summon an army of angry dead people to attack those we don't like."

Amanda helped Craig up, eyes narrowing upon Julian. "And then save their lives."

Julian stammered in a state of near hysteria. "There's a girl with them. Mortal, like you and I. She controls them somehow."

"That's my niece. They're using her to rain down judgement upon your ruthless ancestor and his conspirators."

"Conspirators?" Julian pulled himself up against the banister on shaky pins.

Amanda got right up in his face. "Oliver Asbury and his pals deliberately infected Underwood with bubonic plague, after the villagers refused to sell up and line his pockets. He bought their land for his lumber empire, then established Oakdene under a philanthropic pretence." If looks could kill, she'd have done the executioners' job for them. "The apple doesn't fall far from the tree, does it, Julian?"

"But I haven't killed anyone. Why do they want me? If what you say is true, Oliver was the guilty party."

Craig grimaced and gripped Julian's shoulder in an unfriendly pinch. "It looks like they'll settle for the next best thing. After all, why care who suffers as long as they get 'paid,' right? You know all about that sentiment, don't you?"

The cacophony of snarling, shrieking voices approached from the downstairs hallway.

Julian tore free of Craig's grip. "They're here. We've got to move."

A swarming army of angry souls - still solid of form - reached the atrium floor. In their midst, a glassy-eyed Belinda lifted her head towards the three figures on the landing above.

Amanda choked back overwrought distress. "Belle." She reached for Craig. "What can we do? How do we stop them?"

Craig shook his head, at a loss.

Julian thundered down a side passage and disappeared through a polished door. He slammed it shut and slid a solid bolt behind.

Craig's blood boiled. "Bastard."

Furious pursuers flooded up the staircase.

Craig tugged Amanda away from the banister and followed Julian's escape route. "All the while he's alive, they'll surround Belle and use her power to attack him. I'm betting the moment he's history, this conduit nonsense will end. We've got to stay with Julian until that time. Afterwards… Well, let's get the hell out of here and hope it ends there. Even if it doesn't, we can't stay in this burning building with that mob."

They reached the bolted door. Wafts of smoke snaked between subtle gaps in its warped frame.

Craig backed up a pace. "If I'm reading our position right, that great hall must be on the other side. It's a bloody inferno."

Belinda stepped onto the landing at the far end of the corridor. She processed towards them with almost bridal poise, surrounded by the pathetic, seething manifestations of those who'd haunted her waking and sleeping with little respite.

Amanda released an anguished shriek and ran for her niece. "Leave her alone." A pustule-infested woman and throat-scarred man grabbed an arm each and dragged Amanda away from her.

Craig observed a definite physicality infusing their grip. He tried a test swing at the man with a clenched fist. That courage-stealing figure stumbled backward from the blow, only to be replaced by three others who threw Craig against the barred door. His back protested, burning with a surge of pain to match the conflagration within. The men hauled Craig aside, then took an axe to the obstruction. They were halfway through it when Amanda crawled along the wall and reached her injured companion.

"Craig? Can you move?"

Craig winced. "My back is killing me." He twisted his neck to watch the axe blows. "They're not here for us, or we'd be dead already."

The door broke apart and the crowd pressed through, followed by Belinda.

Energetic flames leapt high from ignited panelling, wooden structural beams and furniture in the dining hall. Most smoke vented through the broken, sixteen foot windows, yet heat levels inside surged with blistering intensity. Julian stood at the far end of his minstrel gallery, beaten back from climbing over its edge by flames rising from a long, blazing table below. Amidst the roar of fire, he caught the door's final crack.

"Stay away from me." He pressed his back against the far wall, hands raised in a vain, defensive gesture.

Belinda stopped halfway along the gallery. Her head swivelled and took in a heavy iron chandelier suspended over the primary space. A rope secured it to a hook on the gallery wall nearby. Underwood's villagers grabbed Julian by his upper arms and forced him forward onto his knees. Two of the women untied the rope from its hook, taking an impossible weight from the chandelier in their stride; one which would have challenged six men. The forlorn young brother and sister stood before Julian. With a single motion, they touched his face. A trickle of swirling, discoloured blood beneath their skin flowed into Julian's body as though through twin syringes. His frame quaked and convulsed. Buboes formed around his groin, armpits and neck. His skin darkened and grew rough as sandpaper. An instantaneous belly heave in response, vomited a shower of blood. It sprayed the unmoved siblings' faces. Swollen areas of flesh burst and bled, while Julian threw his head back in a throaty gargle. His captors lowered the chandelier's rope - now knotted into a noose - over his neck.

Amanda and Craig stood motionless in the empty doorway, eyes like glass.

Both women who'd unfastened the rope released their restraining grip. The chandelier plummeted from the high ceiling as the villagers stepped aside. With a sudden yank and whiplash snap, Julian flew diagonally sideways into the air. The iron chandelier shattered the burning table on impact, leaving Julian Asbury dangling from the ceiling where it once hung. His feet jerked in a furious dance, emptying assorted items from his pockets onto the dining hall floor far below. Every head turned towards the fitting landowner in his final death throes. After his body went limp, Belinda clutched her head and then recoiled from a wall of heat rising around the minstrel gallery. Her face registered the figures she'd seen in countless visions, standing clear as day in that fiery space. Without a word, their eyes fell upon her, burning with vicious hatred.

"Belle." Amanda burst from the doorway and pulled her backwards in a shielding embrace.

Belinda cried.

The corridor ceiling behind Craig collapsed in a deafening hail of timber, plaster and rising smoke, cutting off any hope of retreat.

Craig peeped across the minstrel gallery railing to where the fallen chandelier had split the table and doused its flames. The bisected furniture's far end stood at a raised angle, reaching the lowest stone mullion. He tapped Amanda's shoulder. "Get her over the edge and make a break for the windows."

"What about you?"

The villagers assembled before them. They closed the distance with accusing faces locked on Belinda's sobbing form.

"Now," Craig shouted. He grabbed a lump of broken door wood and hurled it at the axe-wielding villager. Its impact caused him to release his implement, which never made the floor before Craig seized it. With a hiss of metal slicing hot air, he whirled, brought it around and took the head clean off another man rushing to intercept. The body folded and dissociated into white smoke, before its escaped, seething essence encircled him like a spiritual coiling python without physical purchase.

Amanda dragged Belinda to the railing's edge. At this end, the split table lay raised towards them. "I'm going to drop you over, darling. Try to stay clear of the fire. I'll be right behind."

Belinda's lips quivered.

Amanda hugged her tight and kissed her cheek. "I love you." She lowered Belinda by her hands, then let go once her arms would reach no further.

Belinda dropped onto the table and slid towards the fallen chandelier.

Meanwhile, Craig backed up to Amanda, swinging the axe in defensive arcs with his final ounces of remaining strength. "Get down there with her." His face screwed up from a fresh flurry of spinal pain.

Amanda slid across the railing, clung for a second, then released her grip and followed Belinda's descent. She rolled onto her chest, away from the flames.

Belinda ran over, then craned her neck towards the ugly throng charging Craig on the gallery platform above. He flung himself over the railing and crashed onto the table, twisting an ankle. "Ugh." He clutched the fresh injury, yet struggled to his feet. Remaining still was a death sentence in that blaze and he knew it, regardless of any wall of pain he had to push through. Belinda reached his side and propped him up with the scant support her young frame and limited strength could supply.

Amanda pushed her upper body away from the floor, eyes smarting at the heat. Through the haze she noticed the glitter of metallic objects nearby; items that had dropped from Julian's pockets during his frantic last moments. Amidst the loose change, something larger sharpened from a blur into clearer focus: a single key attached to a fob bearing a set of white wings emblazoned with two words of uppercase text. Amid their hopeless plight, that text caused her to reach out and snatch it in an act of desperate faith: '*ASTON MARTIN.*' She found her feet in an instant and darted back towards Craig and Belinda. One finger pointed to the opposite raised end of the table, beyond the broken central chandelier. "Jump through the window, Belle. Roll when you hit the ground. It's a tall drop; taller than you."

Belinda handed Craig's arm she'd supported to her aunt, then ran the ascending length of the divided table between snapping tongues of fire licking at her ankles.

Stiff hands pulled clawing villagers over the gallery railing, spitting in fury.

Craig hobbled beside Amanda, his spine and ankle surging with fresh agony.

"You can do it." Amanda helped him between the stone mullions until he dropped into the grass below. She cast a furtive glance behind.

Underwood's villagers tore through gaps in the flames without reaction, as though nothing slowed their pursuit.

Amanda jumped down and rolled on the soft ground. Belinda already stood, supporting Craig on the path.

Craig caught the cries of rage above flames outlining High Stanton's empty windows. "I can't run; you'll have to leave me. They'll be on us in seconds."

Amanda pressed a button on the key fob. Thirty yards behind Craig, an artificial orange light - not born of fire - snapped his head around. Hazard lights winked on the parked Aston, signifying its readiness for action.

Craig wiped away sweat dripping into his eyes. Sudden relief flooded over him like a temporary, natural painkiller. "Clever girl."

Amanda ran ahead, opened the passenger door, and slid its seat back to the full extent of travel. "You'll have to sit Belle on your lap. There'll be enough room." She eased Craig into the seat, then positioned Belinda in his arms. "Hold tight."

Humanoid figures wearing drab rags dropped from the dining hall windows as Amanda swung into the driver's seat and shut her door. The moment she inserted the key, folding electric mirrors whirred open and the dash lit up with the words *'POWER,'* *'BEAUTY,'* *'SOUL,'* and *'SYSTEM CHECK.'* A warning tone bleeped, but nothing happened.

Amanda's eyes bulged. "There's no ignition. How do I start it?"

Dark silhouettes swarmed across the grass towards them in the rear-view mirrors.

Craig peeked forward around Belinda's shoulder, his eyes drawn to a circular button labelled *'ENGINE START'* below the dashboard vents. "Try that."

Amanda pressed it once without result, then pressed it several more times in rapid succession to make sure. "It's not working."

Craig shut his eyes a moment, remembering a car

magazine article he'd once read in the waiting room of a doctor's surgery. "Depress the clutch."

Amanda complied and the button lit up with a red surrounding ring. She needed no further instruction. One further finger press elicited a hearty roar from the V8. Amanda tugged her seatbelt round and clipped it home, then selected first gear, released the brake and buried the accelerator pedal. The Vantage fishtailed away in a shower of dirt, spraying frantic, otherworldly scratching hands grasping for its rear bumper. The hand-built prestige motor's exhaust note drowned out their frustrated cries. Amanda corrected course and lifted her foot to avoid ploughing straight through the box hedge. Translating all those petroleum-powered horses from the engine bay into tarmac traction during a frenzied escape, proved harder than she'd imagined. The Aston lurched left and powered between tall brick gateposts marking the driveway's end. Amanda put its sleek back out again on a tight, downhill, right-hand hairpin.

Craig swallowed hard. The steep hillside vanished in a sheer drop on his side of the road they'd almost left.

Amanda fought against rising hyperventilation. "Where do we go, now?"

Belinda reached a desperate hand towards the windshield. "Jonathan."

"No, honey. We can't go home; it's too close. We'll be no safer there."

The Aston lurched again, this time of its own accord. An unhealthy grinding replaced the sweet music of its pistons.

Craig clutched Belinda in one hand and the door in the other for added stability. "We don't have a choice, if we even make it that far."

Amanda skidded right at the base of the hill, leaving twin ribbons of rubber imprinted on the road's surface. Flashing blue strobes of a fire engine on the lane behind them lit up the trees. Amanda drove on as fast as she dared, the car developing a stronger will of its own with each passing second. A dark navy night sky above the hilltop grew in luminosity, highlighted by a flickering halo.

Craig twisted for a better look. "Someone's noticed the fire at last and called for help."

They flew through the village, kicking up dust. Its quiet homes flashed by, followed by more trees. Engine and oil warning lights winked to life on the Aston's instrument panel, preceding a mighty bang. Smoke wafted into the cabin. Amanda coughed and brought the vehicle to a juddering halt at an angle in a soft roadside depression. The trio decamped close to where the wooded lane opened onto the meadow at Ravensbrook, and the road became its driveway.

Craig limped away from the wrecked car and pushed up against a tree. "Take Belle and run, Amanda."

Amanda grabbed his arm with a determined yank and slipped it across her shoulders. "We started this together; that's how we'll finish it." The pair staggered on, with Belinda three steps ahead.

A familiar, terrifying tumult of voices swarmed among the trees.

Belinda faced the lip of the meadow. Blood-crazed, manifested souls tore into the open, baying for grim justice. She twisted round to where Amanda struggled with Craig. "It's me they want." Without another word, she broke into a run towards the farmhouse.

"God keep her safe," Craig grunted between slant-eyed spasms of pain.

Amanda watched her flee and then gasped. She patted one of her pockets. "Belle doesn't have a house key. I've still got it."

Belinda reached the turning area outside Ravensbrook, then arrived at the same realisation regarding entry into her home. She pivoted close to the doorstep and watched the throng of ghostly tormentors blasting between her favourite daisies on a furious quest to take her life. Her will gave out and she sank to the ground, hair blowing in a soft breeze as her nightdress settled.

Amanda and Craig were almost at the turning area. No matter how hard they pushed, both knew they'd never reach Belinda before the villagers.

Craig pointed a trembling finger at the house. "That can't be one of them."

The front door of Ravensbrook swung open with slow purpose.

Clean-limbed with a shaggy mop of straw-blond hair, a male figure walked out onto the doorstep. He possessed a pleasant, oval head with deep-set walnut eyes and buoyant facial muscles, suggesting someone of perpetual, good-natured mischief. Tall, slender yet toned from hard manual labour, a certain sadness lingered behind his playful stare. In his arms he cradled the brass cross from Underwood, now polished to a high sheen. Belinda looked over her shoulder. She reached for him, then clutched and buried her face in his leg while he stood above her. One gentle hand lowered and stroked her hair. With the other, he held the cross high, causing the approaching villagers to halt before them.

Amanda's eyes brimmed. "That must be Jonathan." She set Craig down in the grass nearby, her own strength flagging in the same moment. With an exhausted grunt, she collapsed beside him.

Jonathan waved the cross in a slow, demonstrative motion for all to see. With a tone of authority beyond the years of his former mortal lifespan, he spoke across the crowd in a resonant boom. "My friends, my neighbours, brothers and sisters in Christ; what are you about? Do you remember nothing of what James Carrick taught us, nor the blessed words of Holy Scripture? *For it is written, Vengeance is mine; I will repay, saith the Lord.* It is not for you to dole out judgement and retribution." His eyes filled with tears, and his voice cracked. "I watched Underwood fall. Reverend Carrick and I stood side by side at each of your funerals. We wept for your loss. The true magnitude and evil of Oliver Asbury's deeds were only revealed to me in death." He let his words ride on the night air for a moment before continuing. "I know Uncle James sought for your eternal rest on his knees with a heavy heart. Also, that he felt a strong call of God upon my life. Neither of us realised his prayers birthed in me a final ministry of love to you all: that I should remain behind in the world between, until you walked free of your restless, entombed slumber. Remain until I brought you to the light, like a true shepherd of souls." He shook his head, face pleading. "Be not consumed by wrath and unforgiveness. Release your suffering and embrace peace by absolving this innocent child from the guilt you hold to her account. My friends, over three-and-a-half centuries have passed since you went down to the grave, waiting for a moment to rise and seek recompense. Already you've tormented Belle beyond anything your own children suffered." His face grew stern. "There can be no peace without forgiveness. You killed Belle's parents. Now the offence you charge against her for the deeds of others, lays at your own feet. She needs to release you, as much as you need to release her." His sad eyes fell upon Belinda. "Can you forgive them, Belle? So grievous is your hurt; yet within you lies the power to escape the trap that ensnared the folk assembled here."

Belinda's dreamy gaze moved from face to face, her heart weighed down with loss. She gave a slow nod.

Amanda clutched onto Craig and wept.

Jonathan held the cross in both hands and kissed it. "It's time we went home. Not to a forgotten village beneath the trees, but an eternal home where other loved ones await. Free this child as she has freed you. Free yourselves, and allow me to complete the ministry to which God has entrusted my eternal soul." He stood still, watching his former peers' lost faces. "If you take her life, there will be no further chance of salvation. She is the last heir of the final bloodline. Whatever you choose, your fates rest with Belle."

The villagers stood still for a silent minute. A strange aura of calm replaced the angry terror of each visage. As one, they filed forward in a single line. Belinda flinched.

Jonathan stayed her with a tender hand. "Fear not. They're coming to make their peace. I feel it in my spirit."

The children approached first. Both siblings Belinda witnessed in her initial vision at Underwood reached out and hugged her. Their bodies vanished in a cool breeze reminiscent of chilled vapour from an opened freezer door. One by one, every villager touched Belinda and followed their peers to eternal rest. The last man extended a hand toward Jonathan, who shook it.

Jonathan nodded at him. "Tell Uncle James I'll be along soon."

A subtle smile warmed the dead man's face. He squeezed Belinda's shoulder and vanished.

Amanda and Craig stood and drew near with great effort and stiffness.

Belinda wobbled to her feet and met Jonathan's affectionate stare.

Amanda coughed, a tremor in her voice upon addressing the now visible ghost of Ravensbrook. She could only compose one simple icebreaker in her flustered state. "I like your paintings. Well, what you did with my paintings anyway."

Jonathan smiled. A haunting light in his departed eyes reached into Amanda's soul; yet he didn't scare her. "And I yours." He indicated the semi-renovated home. "This is a fine house. I hope you'll enjoy many happy years here." A sudden frown creased his forehead. He turned northward towards the horizon. In the distance, across the village, a single light like a shooting star in reverse, flew upward into the heavens. His face relaxed, and he touched Belinda. "You won't be seeing that girl under the bridge anymore, either. Now she's gone, our journey in this world is complete; its tragedy passed." With a soft sigh, he bent forward. "I love you, Belle. Be at peace and live a good life." He kissed her on the cheek. Without another word, his body faded into a dimming vapour. The brass cross dropped onto the gravel drive and remained still.

Craig limped over and sat on the doorstep. "James Carrick was right about his nephew having a calling after all."

Amanda sat beside him. "And death was his ordination." She opened her arms.

Belinda melted into them, rocking from side to side while Amanda nuzzled and kissed her crown.

17

Home

EXCERPT FROM 'THE TWO RIVERS METEOR' NEWSPAPER.

Further investigations into unscrupulous planning procedures at Torridge District Council have brought no fresh evidence to light. Speaking to the Meteor, Councillor Mike Abrams stated, 'After the debacle at Oakdene, we initiated a thorough retrospective analysis on all development documentation going back a full eighteen months. We hoped to detect any other issues our internal processes fell short on. I am relieved to announce that following scrutiny by an independent auditor, no recent major development was found lacking. Due diligence has been observed in every case. Minor concerns raised relating to the behaviour and unprofessional conduct of certain staff were noted. We deem it in the public interest to clarify those employees no longer work for our organisation.'

Councillor Abrams refused to be drawn on whether those staff were among the deceased in the terminal storm that has plagued the picturesque village of Oakdene during recent weeks. Devon & Cornwall Police report no new developments or suspects in their ongoing investigation over

Councillor Brandon Beeching's violent murder.

A recent, tragic fire that destroyed the nearby country estate of High Stanton left parcels of land available for public sale. The newly founded 'Oakdene Community Trust' has raised sufficient funds from villagers to purchase a plot; the one earmarked for that controversial housing development Torridge District Council halted. Local vicar, Reverend Julie Clement, had the following to add:

'Oakdene was a village created from the displacement of an older community almost wiped out during The Great Plague. While that's not unusual in England, the idea of a modern housing estate appearing on the bones of our predecessor didn't sit well with my parishioners. When the land went up for sale, donations came in so fast we secured the site without issue. Our community trust has opted to leave the wooded area alone; free in perpetuity as a place of recreation, remembrance and reflection for the village. A brief ceremony of blessing and dedication will be held next week, in what still stands of its former church.'

Accident investigators at High Stanton concluded its owner, Julian Asbury, started the fire deliberately. It appears an act of attempted insurance fraud to stave off bankruptcy. When malpractice over the Oakdene development scheduled for land under his freehold came to light, he is believed to have grown desperate. Police stated Mr Asbury's remains were found in the ruins, and his top marque Aston Martin discovered burnt out nearby. Whether he sunk into depression leading to a last minute, unplanned suicide or was overcome after the fire spread out of control is unclear.

Also unclear is involvement by other parties or opportunists relating to his fate and the presumed vehicle theft. Connections between Mr Asbury's death and the murder of Councillor Beeching remain in the realm of speculation.

* * *

"Have you locked up?" Amanda took Peggy Greene by the arm.

Peggy rested her cane against the front wall of her cottage and gave its door a hearty tug. "Safe as houses." She broke into a toothy grin.

Amanda shot a searching glance across the garden. Craig knelt in the grass, digging a weed out from between rose bushes with his bare hands. "We can't take you anywhere, can we? It's not a work day."

Craig grinned. He rose and deposited the offending plant in a nearby bin before brushing his hands together. "This isn't my Sunday best." He waved an open hand across a frayed, open-necked shirt and dirty trousers. "Besides, by the time I've bricked up and rendered the rear of that altar, I'll look worse."

Peggy collected her cane and sniffed the air. "It's a glorious day. Do you hear that?"

Amanda listened, worried eyes narrowing from efforts to detect anything unusual. Birds chirped in the treetops whose lush canopies swayed in a whispering ripple of leaves. "I hear nothing."

Peggy banged her cane tip on the garden path. "Exactly. No voices on the wind. No phantom sounds of pain, anger, or betrayal drifting across the treetops.

All is as it should be; as it always should have been."

Amanda walked behind Peggy down the path. "Well, if you put it that way, I never heard the voices myself. Not until I encountered the people they belonged to."

Peggy was almost the only person in Oakdene who'd ever learn the true events from the night High Stanton burned. Her discretion was unquestionable. Not that anyone would believe such a fanciful story, were the blind pensioner's character or sanity to suffer alteration on account of failing health. Then she'd be written off as a senile old biddy.

Amanda continued. "Belle was the one who always heard them, right from the beginning."

"Where is she?"

"Near the old church at Underwood. We left her there with the vicar and some of her school friends. More people are arriving all the time."

Peggy stopped near her garden gate while Craig opened it. "What of the cross they found?"

"We left it in Julie Clement's safekeeping, along with Reverend Carrick's journal. It seemed proper that she become custodian of his writings, even if she never discloses their contents."

"Did you tell her everything?"

Amanda cleared her throat and smirked at Craig's amused expression. "No. The bare minimum. We said we'd found the journal at Ravensbrook and believed she should have it. Adding that Belle confessed to one of her friends removing the cross from Underwood, came easier on the back of it. After she'd read Carrick's journal, Julie understood its significance from a historical and religious point of view. It delighted her to receive it as well. This dedication ceremony was her idea when the village acquired the land. She loved Craig's suggestion of sealing the cross inside the altar again during the service. In her eyes, we're honouring James Carrick's wishes and memory, and respecting those whose bodies still lie beneath the woodland clearing."

Peggy nodded her approval. "Congratulations."

"Huh?" Amanda asked.

"You left out the most important part of the story without lying to the minister."

Craig snorted. "I suppose we did. She's a pleasant lady. Clement by name, clement by nature. When was the last time you visited the woods, Peggy?"

"Far too many years ago. But I'm not sorry."

"Because of what you felt?" Amanda stepped down into the lane.

"In part. And because now I can visit without hearing those voices or absorbing such horrid, disembodied emotions. In truth, I prefer my garden. A new peace has settled upon the village; the old one and the new."

Craig shut the gate. "I've noticed. Oakdene has always been a haven of tranquillity for me." He smiled to himself. "Or it was until Amanda rocked up."

Amanda gave his shoulder a playful punch.

Craig continued. "But even I can detect a fresh calmness. Someone even commented on it at the pub the other day, though they'd no explanation for its cause."

Amanda wandered at a relaxed pace. "I imagine most will pin it on relief that the housing estate is history. That development plan caused so much upset and agitation."

"Yeah." Craig wiped dirt from his hands, still struggling with a minor limp and aching back.

Amanda looked both ways and crossed to the uphill, no-through road beside The Old Bothy. "It's had a dramatic effect on the Barnes family. I couldn't believe it when Rachel and her husband underwent a change of heart over Laura playing with Belle. Rachel claimed they'd overreacted before and decided whatever happened at their house wasn't Belle's fault. They were willing to give her another chance if she'd agree. Amazing." She screwed up her face. "Okay, I wanted to tell them where to shove it, but I wasn't about to spoil things for Belle."

Craig shook his head. "It was an upsetting incident for them. But, a lot else has happened since." He jerked his head back in a northerly direction. "Water under the bridge, so to speak."

Amanda hummed. "That and I believe their daughter drove them mad, begging. Belle's other friends, like Anton and Jane, swallowed their fears and have reached out to her again. Laura watching from afar while her former bestie played with them, must have impacted the child."

Peggy blasted out a rattling cough. "Children are sensitive to spiritual things, even if they can't describe how they feel. This new atmosphere in Oakdene, guilt at abandoning one of their own and Belle's sudden release from supernatural turmoil won't have escaped them."

Craig sighed. "Ever the sage, Peggy." He shortened his stride up the incline towards the woods, then winked at Amanda. "So, can I call you Mandy now?" His face twisted in agony as Amanda kicked his injured ankle. "Ow! What was that for?"

Amanda shrugged. "I told you what happens to people who call me Mandy. If you ever try a rendition of that song, I'll smack your other ankle."

Peggy chuckled under her breath. "Your squabbles make life interesting. They bring happiness to my weary bones."

Craig paused, bent over, and massaged his lower leg. "Okay, Amanda. I thought it would be easier, you know?"

"Easier?" Amanda frowned.

"Yeah. What with Aman*da* and Belin*da*..."

"You have trouble distinguishing between two completely different names, because they both end in *da*? What are you, some kind of idiot? Anyway, we call my niece Belle, in case you'd forgotten."

Craig straightened and threw up both hands in surrender. "I promise I'll never raise the subject again." He struggled to conceal his amusement. Amanda wasn't cross with him, and he knew it. He cherished her feisty nature and enjoyed their sparring. Ever since the night Underwood's restless souls found peace, Craig had given her and Belinda emotional space to reconnect and form a stronger bond. Without the terrifying experiences that once hung over the child's head like the sword of Damocles, she was more her old self - albeit grieving the recent loss of her parents. But Craig always kept his hand in with quick, regular visits for random, made-up reasons. Amanda was her own woman and knew what she wanted. If that included more of him in her life, he mused she'd leave him in little doubt over her intentions.

When they reached the woodland gate - now forever unlocked - Craig opened the latch and swung it clear. His repaired Land Rover stood nearby. The trio filtered through, catching sight of a busy assembly of villagers further down the track.

At the woodland clearing, Julie Clement stood outside Underwood's open-roofed, semi-ruined church. All about its ivy and moss laden graveyard, Oakdene's residents of all ages assembled.

Julie clocked the last arrivals out of one eye and took a deep breath. "Ladies and Gentlemen." A warm smile melted onto her face. "And our younger residents, of course." A general titter of laughter drifted upward through sighing, laden boughs. "We are gathered here today to re-dedicate this site as a place of peace. No soul remains on this earth who ever met the villagers buried beneath our feet, in person."

Amanda and Craig shot each other knowing side glances across Peggy's head.

Julie proceeded. "Yet it warms my heart that without prompting, you felt an urge to reach into your own pockets and purchase this land. Not only purchase it, but ensure it remains untouched for future generations." She rocked with pride. "I may look for the best in people, but I like to think such generosity wasn't only about preserving the aesthetics and isolation of our community from a modern invasion."

Another round of subdued, polite laughter chased through the crowd.

"Words can't convey the genuine pain and anguish which created these ruins." Her voice wobbled with an emotion few understood. "I recently read a personal account of how Oakdene's first minister sealed a cross inside Underwood's altar, in hopes it would bring his departed flock peace." She smiled at Belinda, standing nearby. In her hands the child held the polished brass cross, while Anton Webb, Jane Perkins and Laura Barnes waited behind. "It is providential that as we purchased the land, that same old cross - once forgotten through time and decay - came to light once more. Now the children who discovered this symbol of faith and love, will lay it to rest in the proper place."

Amanda wiped one eye with her finger and whispered. "Bless her heart. She's glossing over the embarrassing specifics of its disappearance for the kids' sake."

Craig nodded.

Julie opened her hands to the crowd. "In a few moments we'll file inside and observe this sacred duty in honour of our dead forebears. Local gardener, Craig Symonds, has prepared some bricks and mortar to seal and render the altar afterwards. First, if you would, please bow your heads in prayer."

The attendees complied with her request.

Julie followed suit. "Oh Lord, we come before You, the grateful populace of a village born during turmoil and unimaginable sorrow. With one heart we lift up the deceased residents of Underwood and commend them to Your eternal keeping. May the love and prayers of my predecessor, Reverend James Carrick, forever rise before Your throne like fragrant incense. In his memory and that of his beloved flock, we re-dedicate this land as a site of peace; a memorial to the dead and a source of blessing to those on their present journey towards eternal glory. Fused with nature's beauty, may Underwood bring gentle moments of pause and tangible encouragement to all who visit. In Your blessed name we ask it. Amen."

The crowd mumbled a joint, "Amen."

Julie beamed and clasped her hands together. "Now if you'll follow the children and myself inside. Take care around the walls. They're sturdy enough, but I can't rule out falling masonry from the upper portions." She signalled for Craig.

"Excuse me, ladies." Craig moved away from Amanda and Peggy.

Amanda patted Peggy's hands, resting atop her cane. "We'll be along in a moment."

Inside the church, Oakdene's villagers filled every available space. Belinda, Anton, Jane and Laura joined Julie Clement behind the altar while Helen Masters, the primary school head, looked on with warm contentment. To one side lay a board containing various shaped bricks, bags of sand and cement, plus a large plastic container of water. Craig shovelled a 3:1 mortar mix together. He'd already chiselled crumbling bricks away from the former altar hidey hole prior to collecting Peggy. He paused when Julie held up a hand and invited the assembly to join her in The Lord's Prayer by way of accompaniment. As voices of the living lifted in faith rose through the broken roof, the four children knelt and laid the cross together in the spot from which Anton had unearthed it.

Amanda recited the famous words of supplication from memory. Words she grew up with that now took on new meaning. Jonathan Dowland and his sad afterlife ministry filled her thoughts at the lines, *'Thy kingdom come. Thy will be be done, On earth as it is in heaven.'* They drifted to the tragic souls of Underwood, whose pain in limbo manifested spiritual power through Belinda's sensitivity in a thirst for mortal justice. At the end, their chosen conduit and ultimate target of rage provided a path to peace once they released her, and vice versa. Amanda swallowed and spoke the final relevant phrases with hearty enthusiasm. "*And forgive us our trespasses, As we forgive those who trespass against us. And lead us not into temptation, But deliver us from evil. For thine is the kingdom, and the power, and the glory, for ever and ever.* Amen."

Julie Clement stepped aside with the children and allowed Craig to set about his task. While he worked, the crowd milled about under the trees outside, exchanging pleasantries.

Laura caught Belinda's arm between loose fingers,

her eyes sheepish and sad. "Have all your bad dreams ended now, Belle?"

Belinda nodded. "I still wake up missing my parents. But, the pictures of them I see in my mind are happy ones."

"Has your aunt settled at Ravensbrook?"

"Yes. You should visit us and see her studio. She's a wonderful artist."

Laura threaded her hair between meek hands. "I'd like that."

Anton called after them, with Jane Perkins at his side. "Come on, you two. We're going to play hide and seek."

The girls ran after them into the bushes, laughing and squealing with excitement.

"How are you getting on?" Amanda leaned over the altar, back inside the church.

Craig mortared another brick in place. "Fine. It'll take a while. Once this lot are fixed solid, I'll slip a gentle cement render over the top. Where's Peggy?"

"Outside in the clearing."

"You might as well take her home. I've enough spare materials here to sort out your chimney. How about I pick you up at Peggy's, then take care of that wobbly stack before it collapses?"

"If you wouldn't mind." She fidgeted. "Craig?"

Craig poked his head above the altar. "Yeah?"

"I still haven't thanked you."

"For a little sand and cement? Forget it."

Amanda flushed. "You know what I mean."

Craig ran a trowel between bricks. "I figured you two needed space without me bringing up that night again. But if you ever need to talk about it, I'm around."

"You risked everything to save Belle."

Craig shrugged. "What was I gonna do? She's a good kid. Nobody deserves what that girl suffered; not even some little shitbag. Belle is an absolute darling. You should be proud of her."

"I am."

"Glad to hear it. That's one brave nine-year-old."

"It might be nice if we saw a little more of you." Amanda pulled at her blouse. "If you'd like."

Craig's eyes glinted, but he didn't offer a direct response. "Ravensbrook still needs a ton of work. Don't even get me started on its non-existent garden. Helping you make the place respectable could take, ooh…"

"How long?" A smile crept up one side of Amanda's face.

Craig paused from his labours. "As long as necessary until we're both happy with the result."

Amanda leaned over and delivered a brief, soft kiss on his mouth. "That sounds perfect. I'll see you back at Peggy's."

"Good." Craig watched Amanda glance back as she left the church, then smiled to himself and resumed his task.

"See you later, Peggy," Amanda called along the

hallway, then shut Peggy's cottage door.

Craig sauntered back down the path to where his Land Rover sat parked in the lane.

Amanda climbed into its passenger seat and examined his clothing. "You didn't get too messy."

Craig started the engine. "A few hours in your attic should fix that." He pulled away.

"How is the altar?"

"Solid as a rock; that cross isn't going anywhere. A moot point after... Well, you know."

"The Landy sounds healthier than before."

"Andy Mears and Greg Hansard did more than fix the starter motor; they tuned the beast to perfection. They're carrying on Brian Taylor's thoroughness."

"It's a wonderful legacy." Amanda watched the village pass. It transitioned into woodland near the burnt spot they'd abandoned Julian Asbury's deceased car, then opened up beside the meadow in front of Ravensbrook. "I've a new painting to show you."

"I'm glad you haven't been too distracted for work."

"This one isn't for sale. It's a unique, private piece."

Craig drove across the brook and pulled around in front of the old farmhouse. "Is it up in your studio?"

"Nope. Hanging over the living room fireplace."

"Framed already? You have been busy."

Amanda swirled her tongue behind one cheek. "Come and see."

Craig got out and followed her across the threshold.

Over a broad-beamed inglenook fireplace with a spacious, intricate grate hung an acrylic picture of Ravensbrook. The scene depicted the house in its current state, set against a stunning red, pink and orange sunset.

Craig admired her work from afar. "Turner would appreciate that sky."

Amanda tilted her head. "Something of a closet art aficionado, are we?"

"No." He smirked. "I love spectacular skies, so I remember they were his trademark. You know, most people would wait until the house was renovated before painting and hanging a picture of it."

"True."

Craig drew nearer to the fireplace. "You've captured an emotive moment in time. A scene from recent history none of us will ever forget. It's beautiful. Wait, is that?" He poked his head closer to the main structure. At the upstairs landing window, wistful eyes stared from beneath a shaggy mop of straw blond hair. "It's Jonathan. This reminds me of the evening I glimpsed him there, when I came to look at your downstairs wall."

"So you did see a young man upstairs, after all?"

"Uh-huh." Craig blinked. "Wait a second, did this…?"

Amanda laughed. "Don't worry, *I* painted it; all of it - Jonathan included."

"Phew. What does Belle think of the picture?"

"She adores it. I came down this morning and found her staring at the scene with faraway eyes."

"Lost in a trance?"

Amanda pivoted as the front door opened. "Not like before. A happy one."

Belinda hurried into the hallway, flushed from fun and exercise in the great outdoors. She ran and flung her arms around Amanda.

Amanda hugged her. "Did you have a good time with your friends?"

Belinda nodded and then smiled at Craig. "Do you like the new painting?"

"It's magnificent," Craig replied.

"Now we'll always have Jonathan with us."

Craig pursed his lips. "He'd like that, I think."

"Are you staying to tea?" Belinda looked from Craig to Amanda, no guile hiding behind her gentle countenance.

"If I'm invited. But, after I help Amanda with a chimney problem in the attic."

Belinda let go of her aunt and flopped down on the sofa. "More crumbling bricks?"

Craig struggled to skirt the issue without resurrecting images of Jake and Karen Fairchild's fate in her mind. "We need to make it safe, so that fabulous painting stays put down here."

Belinda jumped up, still full of beans. "Can I help?"

Amanda and Craig gawped at each other.

Craig puffed. "You'll have to ask your mo... I mean, your aunt."

Belinda turned to Amanda, unfazed by his slip of the tongue. "Can I?"

"If you like, darling." Amanda qualified her approval with a wagging finger. "But not in that dress."

Belinda thundered out into the hallway and hurried

up the stairs. "I'll be back as soon as I've changed. Don't start without me."

Craig slipped his hands around Amanda's waist.

She melted into his embrace and rested her head against his left shoulder. "That child has found a new lease of life."

Craig took a long breath. "She always had an extra dose, I'd say. Maybe that's one quality that made her such an attractive proposition to Underwood's villagers. They needed her zest and energy, as well as her perception and spiritual receptivity."

"I never thought of it that way. At last she can live life to the full."

When Belinda returned downstairs, she found the front door open and hurried outside. Amanda helped Craig unload materials and tools from his vehicle. With a spring in her step, Belinda joined them.

Behind Ravensbrook, a breathtaking sky similar to Amanda's new painting blazed with chromatic brilliance. At the upstairs landing window, no figure lingered. Yet from somewhere in the glorious heavens above, an artistic young Devon farmer with a heart full of grace looked down in love and smiled.

ABOUT THE AUTHOR

Devon De'Ath was born in the county of Kent, 'The Garden of England.' Raised a Roman Catholic in a small, ancient country market community famously documented as 'the most haunted TOWN in England,' he grew up in an atmosphere replete with spiritual, psychic, and supernatural energy. Hauntings were commonplace and you couldn't swing a cat without hitting three spectres, to the extent that he never needed question the validity of such manifestations. As to the explanations behind them?

At the age of twenty, his earnest search for spiritual truth led the young man to leave Catholicism and become heavily involved in Charismatic Evangelicalism. After serving as a part-time youth pastor while working in the corporate world, he eventually took voluntary redundancy to study at a Bible College in the USA. Missions in the Caribbean and sub-Saharan Africa followed, but a growing dissatisfaction with aspects of the theology and ministerial abuse by church leadership eventually caused him to break with organised religion and pursue a Post-Evangelical existence. One open to all manner of spiritual and human experiences his 'holy' life would never have allowed.

After church life, De'Ath served fifteen years with the police, lectured at colleges and universities, and acted as a consultant to public safety agencies both foreign and domestic.

A writer since he first learned the alphabet, Devon De'Ath has authored works in many genres under various names, from Children's literature to self-help books, through screenplays for video production and all manner of articles.

Printed in Great Britain
by Amazon